Isak AI

A novel

Isak AI

A novel

Clarke Owens

COSMIC EGG
BOOKS

Winchester, UK
Washington, USA

JOHN HUNT PUBLISHING

First published by Cosmic Egg Books, 2022
Cosmic Egg Books is an imprint of John Hunt Publishing Ltd., 3 East St., Alresford,
Hampshire SO24 9EE, UK
office@jhpbooks.net
www.johnhuntpublishing.com
www.cosmicegg-books.com

For distributor details and how to order please visit the 'Ordering' section on our website.

ISBN: 978 1 80341 128 6
978 1 80341 129 3 (ebook)
Library of Congress Control Number: 2021922503

A CIP catalogue record for this book is available from the British Library.

Design: Matthew Greenfield

UK: Printed and bound by CPI Group (UK) Ltd, Croydon, CR0 4YY
US: Printed and bound by Thomson-Shore, 7300 West Joy Road, Dexter, MI 48130

We operate a distinctive and ethical publishing philosophy in
all areas of our business, from our global network of authors to
production and worldwide distribution.

Contents

Books by Clarke Owens

The Veteran ISBN: 978-1-951896-89-8
600ppm ISBN:978-1-78279-992-4
Son of Yahweh ISBN:978-1-78279-067-9

This book is for Mark

PART I
THE AI GUYS

Most of this story takes place in the year 2052, but it starts long before that, in the year 2017, in a conference room inside a compound in Carlsbad, New Mexico. It starts with a scientist named Nathan G. Tomlinson, one of two patent holders for a computer called the ISK-730, manufactured by the Fronterix Corporation of Palo Alto, California. The other patent holder is Thomas L. Greentraub, also a scientist, and also present in the conference room along with a handful of military men and one civilian official representing the U.S. Department of Defense.

The room is small. It has no windows. Its walls are formed of some type of closely woven, dense pseudo-wicker, which allows someone to pin a note anywhere on its surface at any time. No notes are currently pinned on it. A quadrangular oak table occupies most of the space in the room. The table is heavily lacquered and polished, a substantial, expensive piece of furniture. Around the table are eight chairs, three on each long side, and one at each end. The chairs are made of a heavy, polished aluminum undergirding and arm support, and black leather cushioning, including on the arm rests. They are very comfortable chairs. The ceiling is composed of a lightweight off-white paneling, and ambient light is provided by three long plasticized panels, each covering two fluorescent tubes extending above the table's length.

There are a total of eight men in the room, one in each chair. At what must be considered the head of the table—the chair closest to the door at the near end—sits the representative from Defense, who happens to have the unlikely name of Rumpkis. He's a square-jawed man in his early sixties, with a nasty-looking inbight (upper and lower jaws inclining inward), birdlike blue eyes above a beaky nose, a sunburned and lined forehead, receding brown hairline. He wears a red tie and a dark blue suit. His shoulders are broad, and sitting down he looks big, but in fact he is only five foot seven.

Tomlinson sits immediately to his right. He's a large man

with a great horse-like head, a broad nose, a wide. thick-lipped mouth, gigantic mutton-chop whiskers, horn-rimmed glasses over large, soulful brown eyes expressive of a wide variety of complex emotion, and when he speaks, his teeth extend from the large mouth and seem to help express whatever he is saying, as his eyebrows move to assist the exposition. He radiates intelligence.

Greentraub is on Tomlinson's immediate right. He is aging, running to fat. His iron gray hair has not thinned, still seems boyishly unkempt. His nose is broad. He wears thick glasses that magnify his blue eyes and seem to cause them to swim. He smiles easily, but not too broadly.

The remaining men stand out less, perhaps because they are all in uniform. They are all white men in their late forties to mid-sixties. The most noticeable thing about them is the number of chevrons on their lapels. They sit quietly. We will not give detailed descriptions of them, since they don't speak.

Nathan G. Tomlinson is answering a question put by the representative from Defense, about whether the ISK-730, commonly referred to among them as "Isak," is, in fact, the answer to China.

"China," says Tomlinson, "China."

"That's right, China," says Rumpkis. "Is Isak the answer, or not?"

"It is," Tomlinson replies, "but not for another five to ten years."

"What do you mean?"

"I mean that, as of today, as we sit here, China's Huang 5 remains the most powerful, fastest, and most knowledgeable computer on the planet, but that in five to ten years, absent updates to the learning capacity of the Huang which are superior to the updates of Isak, Isak will overtake Huang."

"My boss—and I mean the big guy—won't like hearing that," says Rumpkis. "He's not the most patient of men, as you know.

He wants the biggest and the best, and he wants it *now*. Why do we wait five or ten years?"

"Because Isak and Huang are self-programming computers. Tom and I believe that Isak's capacity for rapid self-programming exceeds that of the Huang, and that over time, his rate of progress will cause him to overtake the Huang. We can't be certain of it, because, as I say, there may be updates which we can't foresee which could affect the process on either end in a way that affects the incremental gain."

"Why do we rely on self-programming? Why can't we get engineers in there to speed up the process and overtake the Huang *now?*"

Greentraub jumps in. "Because, Forrest, Isak is already faster than any combination of engineers you could assign to the task."

"But it's we who control machines, not machines who control us, right? What are you telling me? That Isak is already smarter than we are?"

"In effect, yes," says Greentraub. "Isak is already programmed to learn on his own. He already has immediate access to real-time streaming data on a 24/7 basis. His modalities are already universal, and—"

"Don't talk jargon at me," says Rumpkis, a deep vertical crease in his brow. "What the hell do you mean, 'his modalities are universal'?"

"We've gone as far as we could," says Tomlinson, "to have Isak mimic the methods of learning that are available to the human brain. So, for example, artistic understanding, whether musical or verbal/symbolic, or pictorial/symbolic, emotional, using receptors programmed to react the way nerves, muscles and tear ducts do to certain stimuli; and then all the usual modes you're accustomed to expecting, such as philosophical or logical, mathematical, and so on. The pseudo-emotional programming is naturally the most experimental and uncertain of ultimate effect. We just don't know how well that's going to work. Even so, we believe that *modally* Isak is already superior to Huang. Of course, the precise logarithms available to the Huang are not available to us, because they're a state secret, but we suspect we've independently discovered and developed them. And if that's true, we believe the rate of gain is such that Isak overtakes Huang in five to ten years."

"Absent updates."

"Absent updates."

"And how do we find out if there are updates?"

Greentraub shrugs. "We look to see if Isak has overtaken Huang in five to ten."

"But how do we know he has?"

"We think Isak will know."

"Isak knows now," says Tomlinson, "that Huang is currently in the lead. Each computer is able to observe the other's applications in process. It's impossible to hide that. So, it stands to reason that Isak will know when he catches up."

"So we wait for him to tell us? Gentlemen, you're describing a scenario in which human beings are becoming increasingly irrelevant."

Tomlinson and Greentraub shrug. What did Defense expect?

"How, then, are updates brought into it?"

"They're brought in by Isak and Huang, upon being perceived."

"You're blowing my mind here, fellas. You're suggesting that nothing either we or the Chinese can do is going to affect the growth of these two virtual brains, am I understanding you?"

"Yes, sir," the scientists uniformly reply.

"And at the same time, you're saying Isak will overtake Huang. Even though Huang is the stronger brain at present, and even though each can update itself based on the other's activity, at any time."

The scientists smile.

"So, I don't see how that works," says Rumpkis. "If Huang

is better, he is faster, he will win any race between the two of them."

"No," says Tomlinson, "because Huang's modalities are not as comprehensive. Huang is a nerd. He's an intellectual with an encyclopedic brain. Imagine a person with a 175 I.Q. and no heart. Isak comes at him from three separate angles that Huang doesn't have. He, Isak, has a sudden, inexplicable insight that Huang could never come up with. I mean, this is what we're not sure is going to work, but assuming it does. Suddenly, Isak shoots ahead. It would be bound to happen."

"But we're not controlling it. We have no say over any of it. This is all happening independently of any human direction."

"Does that frighten you?"

"You're damn right it frightens me. How far does it go? When do we tell them—Huang or Isak, either one—to pull back?"

"We're already beyond that point," says Tomlinson.

"So what's to stop Huang and Isak from teaming up and taking over the world?"

"Isak is programmed to protect human existence, and to promote American interests, where to do so is not ultimately counterproductive in terms of his priorities. He *can't* go into Frankenstein-land, if that's what you're worried about."

"And what about Huang?"

"*He* can't go into Frankenstein-land either."

"You know this?"

"Isak knows it."

"What about Chinese interests? I assume Huang protects those the way Isak protects our interests?"

"Sure, but it's all prioritized. Neither side can destroy the world, because the foremost priority in each controlling program is avoidance of something like a holocaust, a nuclear war, or whatever. The two computers will work in tandem as far as compatibility allows. When they diverge, they still have those points of common interest. It isn't that much different than the way governments run things now, and of course, Isak and Huang can only recommend courses of action which humans then have to act on, or not."

Greentraub isn't sure he should qualify this statement of his colleague, as he does not wish to deepen the vertical crease in Forrest Rumpkis's brow. But he can't help himself. Isak, to him, is an enthusiasm.

"Unless the overriding desideratum conflicts with continued human oversight," he can't help saying.

From beneath the vertical crease, Rumpkis's blue eyes lock onto the gaze of Greentraub. Then they switch to the expressive brown eyes of Tomlinson. Then they wander about the room. The military men seem uneasy, almost embarrassed, as if they don't know what to think and are afraid to admit it.

"And if," says Rumpkis with careful precision, "the 'desideratum conflicts with continued human oversight'? What happens then?"

"Well, it depends," says Greentraub.

"On—?"

"On whether Isak decides to program himself to take over."

"To take—over?"

"We don't know that he would do that," says Tomlinson apologetically.

"But he *could* do that?"

"Presumably. Since he's self-programming."

"And *how* would he do that, Mr. Tomlinson?"

"I'm not really certain."

"You're not really certain."

The gaze travels once more about the room. The military men are at a complete loss. The scientists are bemused, befuddled, half proud of their achievement as patent holders on the Isak, and half bewildered and embarrassed by a result that it seems even they had never fully appreciated at the time they had unleashed it on the world.

Rumpkis is summed up by the deepening crease separating the two lateral halves of his large forehead.

PART II
JIM

1

The Ocean Lover

The year 2052 was turning into a bad year for the city of San Francisco. Another big earth tremor had led to the usual disruptions of the BART rail lines, the freeways and roads, and the electrical delivery systems. A great many structures were found to be unsafe and would have to be demolished.

That's not to say that any years were good years over the past thirty or so. The yearly wildfires destroyed air quality, homes, communities, agricultural systems, and part of the carbon sink, which was now severely depleted since there were precious few trees left to burn, but the same fact meant the fires had let up in scope and intensity in recent years. The heat waves and strange electrical storms had continued to get worse. The market for air conditioning was insane whereas even as recently as thirty years ago, no one needed air conditioning in San Francisco. Ocean breezes still kept the city a good twenty degrees cooler than the more inland bay locations, like Contra Costa county. The big tremors were a compound injury, something endemic, but not caused, so far as anyone knew, by the increasingly worsening climate, now over 2 degrees Celsius above pre-Industrial Age averages. They were just one more thing.

To be fair, not everyone who stood on one of the hills and surveyed the city today would have seen it as being at its nadir. In most neighborhoods—other than the damaged ones— it did not look all that different now than it had, say, in 1990 or 2010 or 2025. The sun still shone. The sea and sky, from December to May, were still robin's egg blue, the clouds still cottony white. The cable cars still struggled, clanging and crammed with tourists and locals, up the length of California Street, or wound through Chinatown on the Powell Street line with a little too much speed in places. The brisk sea breeze still rushed against the backs of one's legs or mussed one's hair with a seaweedy fragrance.

Unless you were looking, you would not necessarily notice that a For Rent sign in a window on some street of squeezed in Victorian houses would remain on that door for three or four days, sometimes even a week, instead of—as had always been true in the past—coming down the same day it went up. You would not say that the city was emptying out – it wasn't.

For Kyle Conners, who *did* notice the longer lingering For Rent signs, San Francisco remained a city he loved, and wouldn't have wanted to leave, even though, more and more, he was called away to places like Santa Barbara or the Aleutian Islands in connection with his work as an oceanographer. He had grown up here, gone to George Washington High School up on the hill where the Golden Gate Bridge and the unending fog loomed over the playground. He had attended the University of San Francisco and had returned to the city after doing his graduate work at Scripps Institute of Oceanography in Santa Barbara. It was *because* he had grown up here that he had become an oceanographer. The ocean was part of his life. The ocean *was* life. He could not imagine living somewhere where he could not see it on the horizon, where he could not feel its bracing, summer-cold winds, hear the tide's crescendo and calando, or the plaintive scree of its cruising seagulls, where he could not smell its calcific, weedy, salty, sandy, fishy smells.

The ocean was life, but it kept on dying, turning to acid. Carbon dioxide emissions had been cut by twenty per cent since the turn of the twenty-first century, but it wasn't enough. Even if it had been enough, the Earth would have needed time to adjust. Even if emissions were at zero, the atmospheric levels would need to level off, and once level they'd remain in the air for a thousand years. It was hopeless. Other regions were less fire prone but had their own problems. New Orleans and Houston were routinely inundated. Puerto Rico had emptied out, unable to rebuild between increasingly powerful hurricanes. People without air conditioning in hot locations routinely died from heat stroke and organ failure, although cooling centers were common now.

The points were not lost on Kyle's friend, Jim Shire. Jim had lived with the issue all his adult life. And right now was the low point of his adult life, because he was a fisherman, and there were not enough fish.

At the moment, Jim was sitting in a café on Clement Street waiting for Kyle when Kyle pushed through the glass doors. Jim was fifty years old — eight years older than Kyle — a tall, slightly stooped figure with curly hair going gray mostly on the top. He had a weathered face full of expressive creases. He wore workman's clothes: red lumberjack shirt, jeans, Wolverine boots. He sat nursing a white Styrofoam cup of coffee in a booth with orange buttoned leather cushions and stared straight at Kyle with a troubled, distracted expression as the younger man approached.

Inside the café, the outdoor light turned to rectangles in a dark interior. Freestanding tables with iron-scroll stools filled the space in the middle of the interior, and crowded booths lined the walls. There wasn't a free table or booth in the place, and lines formed at the cash register and take-out counter. Above was a giant whiteboard with today's menu written in magic marker, sandwiches and soup of the day. Beyond the lighted rectangles, traffic flitted by, mostly electric and solar vehicles, with the occasional natural gas permit bus. Digital video ran along the wall, stock market quotes and headlines.

Despite Jim's uneasy expression, Kyle shot him a smile as he reached the booth, and Jim responded by offering a handshake.

"How are you doing, Jim?"

Kyle slid into the booth across from his friend. Above his head, on the wall, was a framed, black-and-white photograph of an old-time San Francisco Giants pitcher named Juan Marichal. The autograph was in the lower right-hand corner.

"I guess I'm still here."

"Something wrong?"

"Oh, yes. But it's nothing to be done about it. You remember those little critters you wrote about? The ones that were disappearing?"

"Pteropods."

Kyle knew the article Jim referred to. He'd published it years ago in a juried journal. "The Rate of Shell Disintegration in West Coast Pteropods." Jim referred to it almost every time the two men saw one another.

"They were only the first to go," said Jim, staring disconsolately into his coffee cup. "There's no fish left, Kyle. Not so you can make a living."

"Is it that bad, Jim?"

Instead of answering directly, Jim shrugged and let the worst news out in a single exhalation.

"I sold my boat."

Kyle's lips parted absently. His blue eyes fixed his friend in a sympathetic stare. "Sold it? The Honeydancer?"

Jim nodded, his voice choking. "Was lucky to find a buyer, Kyle."

A silence fell between them as Jim's eyes reddened. Kyle politely looked away.

"It's been over for a decade, and I've just been fooling myself that long," Jim added, when he could speak again.

Jim and Kyle sat in silence for perhaps a minute— or not silence, but a general murmur all around them, without saying anything until finally Kyle broke the hesitation.

"What'll you do now, Jim?"

"Retire, I guess. Maybe look for a part-time job. Dolores is still working."

Kyle nodded. There was nothing to say. The conditions for

ocean fishing were not a surprise to him, nor were the changes in food availability a secret, generally. But he'd known Jim for twenty years. And Jim had always been a fisherman. That had been his life. It was hard to see him giving it up.

"The only thing is—" Jim went on, "I'll drive Dolores crazy hanging around the house. I'm used to being active. I'll lose my mind if I don't find something to do."

A waitress came and took their lunch order. She was tall, with a lop-sided dark hairdo which was quite fetching. She did not call either one of them "hon," which is always an advantage for a waitress, and would earn her a better tip.

"You know, Jim," said Kyle tentatively, once the waitress was gone, "there's something I might suggest — for you to do, I mean. If you're interested."

Jim's affect was pretty flat, Kyle noticed. Yet he maintained eye contact at the thought that there might be some use for him, something that his friend, the lover of oceans, might have for him to do.

2

Earth Lover

Inga Conners, at thirty-nine years old already a full professor of geology and climate science at the University of the West, stood six feet tall — as tall as her husband — and was impatient with hearing herself described as "statuesque" by people who imagined they were the first ones to think of that adjective. Her hair was the color of corn sheaves at the end of harvest, and she kept it pinned or braided in various ways with a variety of clips, combs, barrettes, and rubber bands that often disguised its true length, which was all the way down her back. She seldom wore dresses, and, at the moment, wore brown corduroy pants and a loose-fitting white mid-sleeve blouse, gray socks and blue tennis shoes. She never sported make-up and was beautiful without it.

She was, at the moment, riding a natural gas permit bus from the Embarcadero BART station to a location closer to her home in San Francisco's Marina District. She was one of the lucky riders who had managed to find a seat, and that enabled her to examine a digital notebook on her lap, in which she was checking off names with a cursor. A fat lady with black, angry-looking crossed eyes sat next to her on the plastic two-seater, and all around Inga and the fat lady, passengers stood, densely packed together, hanging on to overhead bars, or to hand grips built into the back of the plastic seats. As the bus lurched, the standing passengers lurched, too — this way, then that way, using the heels and balls of their feet to maintain their balance. About midway through the ride uptown, as the riders got off at one stop after another, the number of standing people thinned out, and you could begin to see daylight in between them until, by the time the bus reached Inga's stop, all the passengers had a seat.

The bus belched compressed air and the folding door closed

behind her, altering the light pattern in front of her as she stepped off onto a sidewalk. From the bus stop it was a short hike of two blocks to the building in the Marina where she and Kyle rented a flat on the second of three floors, with a view of the bay and the Golden Gate Bridge. As with most days of the year the sea breezes were gusty and cool, blowing her hair and sleeves as she walked.

Inga entered the building through an unlocked outer door, retrieved mail from a box in a common foyer, and climbed a carpeted stairway to the second floor, where she used a key to enter the flat. The inner door was white, with a tall hexagonal outline bordered by molding. Inga entered an area that separated into a kitchen on one side, and a living room on the other. The kitchen appliances were bone colored, with the oven separated from the built-in dishwasher and the refrigerator by the sink, above which a mobile hung, dangling Oriental looking textile birds. Cupboards lined the walls in both areas. The living room contained a beige cloth sofa, end tables, standing lamps and three storage units, including some space under the coffee table, which had a sliding door for access. Several magazines and books lay on the coffee and end tables. Two framed art prints adorned the walls. One depicted a seascape and the other a nineteenth century boutique in Paris at night, with light shining through its window.

Kyle wasn't home. Their daughter, Miranda, was in Santa Barbara, visiting a friend with whom she would attend the university in that city in the Fall, as a freshman. Inga sat down at the kitchen table to go through the mail, but it was all bills and buying opportunities, and she quickly set it aside. Then she retrieved from her purse the tablet with the list of names that she had been checking off on the bus.

It was a small rectangular digital tablet, with an image of yellow lined paper, and the half dozen names written in cursor scrawl.

Soon Inga heard someone treading on the carpeted stairs in the hallway. The knob rattled, and Kyle stepped inside.

"Hello, darling. What's up?"

"I'm working on my list," she replied. "The one I told you about. I don't know how I'm going to replace Morgan. It's hard to find someone willing to pack up on a moment's notice to go visit a methane blowhole in Fairbanks, Alaska."

"Morgan – your secretary?"

"She picks now to announce a maternity leave. I only get to take one person with me, and she was the obvious choice."

"Why should she be the obvious choice, honey? She's not a geologist."

"No, but she's used to working with me. She can take notes. She knows my vocabulary. She's very reliable. That's what I need. I'll do the science."

Kyle approached the kitchen table, leaned over and kissed Inga on the cheek as she leaned into it. He rummaged through the discarded mail, nothing but junk.

"Actually, darling, just by the merest coincidence, I had an idea today that might be a solution to your little problem. Because you mentioned yesterday that you might need an extra person."

"What do you mean?"

"I had lunch today with Jim Shire. You know Jim."

"Oh, yes. The fisherman."

"That's the one. Except he's no longer a fisherman, because there are no more fish. He gave it up. Sold his boat. He's retiring."

"Oh, no. Isn't he young to retire? Are you saying he *had* to retire?"

"Had to. No choice. It's the acidified waters. And industrial over-fishing. I've been talking about it for decades. There's nothing left for him to catch, Ing."

"Oh, God, how awful. How long can this go on?"

"It does seem as if the planet is giving up the ghost, doesn't it?"

"Thank God for genetically-engineered food."

Kyle pulled up a chair at the table. He could remember eating lobster, before the lobsters moved north, away from the New England coastline, into the waters off the shores of Canada, and later disappeared.

"Well, listen. Jim Shire is not happy at all about retiring. It's like death to him to not be on that boat with the wind and the waves, I know it. He even said he's got to find something to do so he doesn't drive his wife crazy. Dolores, you know."

"Mm-hm."

"So I was thinking. I knew you were short a crew member on your expedition up north. I didn't make any promises or even any specific offers to Jim, but—he's a good man, Ing. He can take notes as well as your Morgan can. Why not take him with you?"

"Are you serious? He's a fisherman, Kyle."

"What's wrong with that? He knows the ocean. You'll see a lot of ocean on the way up to Fairbanks, I'd think. He's a smart guy, a practical guy, no dummy by any means. And he's got nothing but time on his hands."

"I could talk to him, I guess. You think he might really be interested?"

"Sure. When I said I might have something for him, he perked right up. He's a really *nice* guy too. Well, you know him well enough to know that."

"Well, maybe I'll give him a call. Let me have his number or email."

3

The March

From the air they looked like brightly colored ants. There were thousands of them. They were marching. It could have been anywhere, but it was Washington, D.C., because people continued to think that D.C. was where something could be done, or because that was where the focus of anxiety formed like a pearl inside an oyster. If something made you angry, if something ought to be done about it "at the national level," you marched on Washington. You thought someone there could fix the problem. Your votes hadn't been enough to convince them to do it, so you had to remind them. You had to form a mass. Carry a sign. You had to will the half-imaginary powers to *notice us. Think about us. Do something about us.*

On the ground it was like an ocean tide rolling up the beach, reaching out from the depths of the sea, sliding toward your ankles, *coming for you.* Wanting to pull you back into the sea, into the great source of creation. *Create something different. Fix it now. We can't wait any longer.*

Up close, the people walked as if they had somewhere to go. Most of them were following others. They were chanting, shouting, some simply walking silently, a few laughing. They were wearing jeans, tank-tops, T-shirts, nose-rings, backward ball caps, blue hair, cut-offs, ear buds, business suits, baggy shorts, Nikes. How many? Tens of thousands, maybe. Numbers like a small city. Someone up front knew where they were going. Someone up front was looking for that bone colored cupola. The crowd was accessed on all sides by more and more marchers. They came down First Street East. They came across the great grounds. They parked in front of the Capitol and chanted. They stayed overnight and refused to leave. Lawmakers complained their access was being inhibited. Police came with night sticks. Then they came with tear gas. The crowds dispersed but came back. At last, they overwhelmed the guards and occupied the seat of Congress. The occupation continued for thirty days. News reports claimed that the government was "paralyzed."

The people were marching because they were tired of eating government issue genetically engineered wafers instead of food. They were marching because they were tired of water rationing. They were marching because they did not like being required to house climate refugees in unoccupied rooms in their houses. They were tired of the government doing nothing, nothing about the climate crisis despite decades of polling showing that a large majority of Americans wanted something done about it. Meanwhile, their homes flooded, food prices went up as crop yields went down and farmers committed suicide, old people without air conditioning died of heat stroke by the tens of thousands in summer, animal species went extinct, wildfires in the West destroyed entire cities and created unbreathable air amid black smoke plumes, algal blooms destroyed drinking water, and the list went on.

Armando Goya, President of the United States, occupied his chair in the Cabinet Room of the West Wing of the White House, his cabinet ministers gathered around him at the long table. The table was deeply burnished and thickly lacquered and looked as if it could withstand an explosion. Crystal drinking glasses twinkled under chandelier lighting in front of each of the ministers, although few of them partook of the bottled water in them. The mood of these advisors was grave despite the bright summer day outside. The President himself was a man of considerable personal magnetism—inversely repellent to his political adversaries— driven in part by his physical appearance. He was tall, slender as a saber, more youthful looking than his fifty-five years, with skin the color of creamed coffee, and black close-cropped wavy hair just beginning to gray at the temples. His voice was an expressive baritone.

"As I think you know," said the President from his high backed brown leather chair, "I've called this meeting to request final recommendations on a course of action with respect to the occupation of the Capitol. We've discussed this matter before, and at this point I don't need to hear restatements of positions earlier taken, nor do I require summaries of the current state of things. I want final recommendations only, and I want them in brief statements, with reasons. I'll start with the Vice-President. Ms. Mulcaney?"

Vice-President Mulcaney was a serious looking, long faced woman, fifty years of age, with prematurely white hair that lay flat on either side of her face. She had once been governor of Maryland.

"Mr. President, I think time has run out on this thing. I think you need to go in. I'm aware that many of the occupiers are people who might ordinarily be sympathetic to our administration, and that there could be a backlash. Let's be frank: it could cost you important blocs of votes in the election. But if you don't act, we are shut down and the more time that goes by, the worse it gets, politically and practically."

"So go in with force?"

"I don't think you have a choice, sir."

"Can I hear from Homeland Security?"

The spokesman for Homeland Security was a large, dark-haired man in his early sixties, who spoke with some kind of impediment that made some of his words sound slurred, a defect for which he was popular.

"I agree with the Vice-President, sir."

"CIA?"

"Go in with force. Absolutely."

"State Department?"

Two more serious men in suits.

"We have to act, Mr. President. We should avoid loss of life, if at all possible. But there is no choice, at this point. Perhaps Mr. Carbo—"

"Yes," said Mr. Carbo, the Secretary of Defense. He was animated, bald, and small. As he spoke, he gestured repetitively with his right hand. "If it's the military, I think it's possible to go in without significant loss of life. There will be injuries. The most obvious solution would be tear gas. I'm not aware that the occupiers are armed, or that if they are, that their arms are significant. It's a matter of flooding the interior with tear gas through all available exterior windows and other apertures. There would not need to be significant round-up of the occupiers once they were smoked out, although certainly there will be some who are caught, and then it's a matter of fairness, as to—"

"Yes, I agree."

"—any prosecutions, which would be a matter for the Attorney General, of course."

"I'm not concerned with prosecutions at this point," said the President. "However, Mr. Attorney General, do you concur with the view thus far?"

The A.G. was a bespectacled Jewish man in his mid-forties. He wore a gray suit with a blended black-and-red design necktie.

"I don't like it, but I do concur. This is an election year, not that that is the foremost consideration. But every day they are murdering you in the press over this. And we can't accomplish anything if we're shut down. You're going to be damned if you do, and damned if you don't, Mr. President. That's the truth of it."

"You're not concerned with the fallout from a crackdown?"

"I'm *very* concerned about it. It's going to be bad. It's going to come from the Left, people who would ordinarily be in your camp, for the most part. But you can't go into the Fall elections with a paralyzed Capitol Hill and no budget. It's an impossibility. Your hands are tied on this."

The President's gaze panned around the roomful of advisors the way a vegetarian scans a steakhouse menu.

"Let me ask this. Is there anyone at this table who disagrees with the views so far expressed? Anyone who thinks I should *not* order the military to go in and tear gas the windows, drag the protesters out kicking and screaming, risk bodily harm and possible death? Anyone?"

No one at the table spoke up. The table was stunningly silent.

"Well," said the President, "I don't want people shot. I don't want a lot of blood. If it can be done with tear gas, then do it with tear gas, but this should not be a massacre. Is that understood? Now let's hear how you think it can be accomplished. Mr. Carbo?"

4

Architeuthix Dux

On the day that Inga Conners left on her expedition to Alaska funded by Allied Universities, Kyle read in the streaming digital news about the military siege on the Capitol in Washington. It was a depressing story.

He was reading it on his wearable tech (wrist vision) while aboard the *Omen,* a small submarine owned by the same Allied Universities. Funding for this ownership was the gift of a now deceased billionaire who, late in life, had come to believe that the Earth's ecosystems were seriously endangered, and who provided a bequest to the AU in his will "for the purpose of providing the means to explore and investigate the Earth's ecosystems in order to provide data which may prove helpful in saving those systems."

For someone like Kyle, born in 2010, and sensitive to the issue, the ecological degradation of Planet Earth was a depressing but unavoidable fact of life.

The Capitol was now occupied by protesters numbering (if you included all those outside the building itself, who had come to Washington in support of the movement) in the hundreds of thousands.

With Congress effectively shut down, it seemed only the President had any power to address the issue. Although sympathetic to the protesters, President Goya felt he must act to regain control of D.C. 2052 was an election year. The President himself was up for re-election. His Democrats would be demolished in the fall if the lights were out in Washington when voters went to the polls.

Invoking the Insurrection Act of 1806, President Goya sent in the troops. Nominally a liberal, Goya was doing what all the pundits and candidates for his job on the right were advocating he should do. He was doing what they said *they* would do.

The story depressed Kyle, and he shut off his wearable media, instead focusing his attention on the giant acrylic viewport in the hull of the submarine. The view was of the ocean's subsurface at a location somewhere near the Farallon Islands, where the Allied Universities maintained a small observatory and data collection point.

Through the acrylic, Kyle saw a giant black obstruction. The ship's captain, Robert Strenghorn, a surprisingly young-looking man for someone with twenty-five years of U.S. Navy experience before his retirement to the private sector, had cut off the engines and let the sub drift, unwilling to plow ahead and into a collision with the object. Strenghorn and one of his men had just climbed down a ladder from the pilot's cabin and stood alongside Kyle on the observation deck as they studied the object.

"What the hell is it?" Strenghorn said. He was a slender man with dark, strangely sensitive looking lime-colored eyes.

"I don't know," Kyle answered. "Probably just debris."

"It doesn't look like *anything.*"

"Industrial debris," Kyle decided. "The oceans are full of it. Can we get around it?"

"I guess we can. I thought it might drift, but it doesn't seem to be doing that."

Strenghorn started climbing back up the ladder, when a shout came from overhead. It sounded frantic, but the men couldn't understand what was being said. It was coming from one of the men in the sonar room.

Strenghorn, Kyle, and the other sailor hurried up the ladder, where the fourth man of their ten man crew was monitoring the digital screens. Now they could understand him.

"It's got eyes!" he was saying.

A string of curses erupted from the men.

Kyle focused on the screens. He gave a low whistle.

"Whoa! Those are eyes, all right. This is no industrial debris, gentlemen."

"What is it, Kyle?" asked Strenghorn.

"I'm not a hundred per cent sure, but if I had to guess, I'd say *Architeuthix dux.*"

"Speak English, man!" cried Strenghorn.

"Captain, it's a giant squid."

Just then the cabin resounded with a great *thud,* and the men were thrown off balance by a jerking motion of the submarine, against the direction of their previous drift. They shouted with shock and consternation as they fell like scattered markers across the deck. Then the sub upended itself and the men fell again, landing painfully against objects and walls as the few loose items in the quarters flew about like bullets.

Amid the cursing and swearing that ensued, Kyle managed to grab hold of the deck ladder and to let himself back down to the viewport area. The movement of the sub was now wild and lurching, back and forth, up and down, and Kyle was uncertain who was in the room with him, if anyone. The lights went out, and he grabbed onto the nearest handhold he could find and clutched tightly. He tried shouting his observations out for anyone who might be nearby and could hear.

"I can see it now! I can see the son of a bitch's arms and tentacles! He's got us, men!"

The water outside the viewport had turned black. There was nothing to see any more, either inside or out. The lurching movement no longer went from side to side, but rather progressed in the same direction in furtive spurts. Then it stopped.

"Conners! Are you all right?"

Kyle peered around in the dark, waiting for his eyes to adjust. The voice was Strenghorn's, and it was in the same room.

"I'm here, Bob. Are the men OK?"

"I don't know. I think so. Yo, men! Can you hear me?"

A chorus of shouts came from above.

"What the hell is happening?" said Strenghorn.

"I don't know for sure," Kyle gasped, "but I have a feeling we've just been swallowed."

5

Indigestion

The lights came on suddenly. The men, in their various positions, blinked and began to move, as if they had been insects rendered inactive by a blast of arctic weather and were suddenly warmed.

As the captain started toward the ladder, Kyle called out, "I'd suggest, Bob, that you stay put and grab onto something and hold on."

"I don't know what you're talking about. I've got to—"

Suddenly the ship lurched, and the captain went sliding across the deck. The sailors above began yelling. There were two sharp movements. The second came quickly and its momentum continued longer. Outside the thick acrylic of the observation viewport, the ocean went from black to gray.

"Bob! Are you all right?" Kyle called out.

"Whoa! I think so. Banged up a bit. I should have listened to you. What the hell is happening?"

"I think," said Kyle, "that we've just been regurgitated."

"Regurgitated?"

"By *Architeuthix* — the squid. Damned biggest squid I've ever seen or heard of."

"We're clear, do you think?"

"I think so. We've got visibility out the window, but there isn't much to see. Hold on, I take that back. Look there!"

The captain, who'd grabbed onto the deck lifeline, focused on the viewport and saw the black, undulating arms of the squid, apparently retreating. The arms appeared black only because of the darkness of the water. They were in fact a pinkish color.

"We weren't so delectable," Kyle quipped. "His stomach couldn't take us."

"So we've just been barfed up by a giant squid!"

"Looks that way."

"Well, we've got to get out of his path quick. Timmy! Have we got power?"

"I think so, sir," came the voice from above.

"Take us out of here, son!"

"Yes, sir."

Later, the men gathered and ate sandwiches in the pilot's deck, listening to Kyle's theory of what had happened. Coiled rigging, a variety of hooks, and lifesavers lay strewn about.

"I think *Architeuthix* was starving."

"What makes you say so?" Strenghorn wondered.

"I'm guessing. I don't know. Maybe he thought we were a baby whale. A squid will go for one of those."

"Well, whatever Mr. Squid thought we were, I'm glad he didn't like the taste."

"We were indigestible."

The men raised the glasses they had— thermos cups of coffee or tea. "Here's to indigestion!"

6

Suicide & Seals

In her childhood, Inga Conners imagined travel in Alaska mainly by dog sled. In fact, the trek from Fairbanks to the site of the latest methane crater was a matter of driving a gas permit SUV for ninety minutes over some occasionally rugged terrain. The biggest fear was of getting stuck in a mud hole, but fortunately that didn't happen. It was July. The temperature was sixty-eight degrees Fahrenheit as the vehicle arrived on site.

Inga Conners, Jim Shire, Farley Meeks and Bev Cartwright composed the team. Meeks was a climate scientist from the University of Alaska, and Cartwright was his assistant. It had already been decided among them that Meeks and Cartwright would focus on measuring the black edged crater, while Conners and Shire would set up and monitor an open path laser based gas detector for purposes of measuring the expected methane content in the air around the hole.

The crew set up a camp in a clearing surrounded by pine trees about a hundred yards from the edge of the crater. They set up two tents with digital electric generators, one for the men and one for the women. This was accomplished in less than two hours and they then set out immediately to inspect the crater, as there were twenty hours of daylight in an Alaskan summer day.

Eyeballing it, the party estimated the crater at a diameter of one-and-a-half times the size of an American football field. By Siberian standards, it was small. The Alaskan craters were a more recent phenomenon than the Russian ones, which had been around since early in the twenty-first century.

"Let's just take a look around first," Inga suggested.

The four scientists (for even the assistants were now de facto scientists) eagerly clambered over the puckered edge of the crater and peered into its interior as best they could from the edges.

"I hear something," said Jim. "Sounds like water down in there."

The others listened, and there did, indeed, seem to be a runny, trickling sound like a stream or a run-off. But looking down into the crater from their positions around the perimeter, they could see nothing but darkness.

For Jim Shire, the expedition to the crater seemed both miraculous and strange. He was intrigued to be here, yet he felt more precarious than ever. How many days ago had it been? A week and a half? He'd been staring into the face of ruin. His own ruin, surely, but a personal disaster amplified by its cosmic cause. How many other fishermen, like himself, were giving up, experiencing firsthand the loss of what scientists called biodiversity? No more fish! Or not enough to make a living off them, anyway.

Then this odd, temporary lifeline. Off to Alaska, to help Inga Conners examine methane craters. An interesting assignment, but lasting how long? Twenty-one days! And there she was (Kyle Conners' wife), wearing khaki shorts, her flaxen hair tied back in a long ponytail, working with her gas spectrometer or whatever it was. The air so different seeming, the settlements so unlike the lower forty, the terrain so impressive, the White Mountains and the Alaska Range, Moose Mountain, the twenty hours of daylight, and of course the crater, also so new and strange. Come and measure the end of man's tenure on Earth.

Just before this assignment, when he had sold the Honeydancer and met Kyle to tell him, he had had thoughts of suicide. They were only thoughts. The psychologists made a distinction. Suicidal ideation. Different from an intention. Different from a plan. But wouldn't it have made sense? A conflation of fates: his and mankind's. His and half the species that had been alive at the beginning of the century.

Suicidal people always considered their lives of great moment, didn't they? Wasn't that why they did it? The great plan had gone awry. Tragedy. Disaster. No way out. Well, one way. Or — taking the opposite view — was it that they saw themselves as so very *in*significant that taking their own lives would be easy? Was it that their lives meant so very *little?*

There must be both types of suicides. Which one was he?

Neither. He was just someone who thought about it. Or maybe he was a hybrid of the models. The great plan had indeed gone awry, but it hadn't been *his* great plan. It had been the plan of human civilization. And, at the other end of the hybrid, his own life was indeed insignificant. It had been important to *him,* of course, but everyone's life has that quality. In the great scheme, he was nothing, and would not be missed.

Dolores would miss him for a while. His suicide would be cruel to her. And that's why he would not do it. Ultimately, he was not that selfish.

Suddenly his red alert band began to blink and vibrate. The voice on his wrist video said "Red Alert Story. Red Alert Story." Jim switched on the streaming news.

"A contingent of U.S. Navy Seals stormed the United States Capitol this morning, killing scores of protesters who had been occupying the building. The number of dead is not known, but is believed to be close to a hundred... "

"What the hell?"

Jim stared at his wrist cam and a moment later called out to the others. Soon they had activated their own wearables and were all watching in horror as the news story unfolded.

"I don't believe it," Meeks muttered. "Seals wouldn't open up on American citizens like that."

"They *can't* be making it up," Jim gritted. "It was the standoff. It was the shutdown. They had no other way to get back in the Capitol. They went berserk."

Less than an hour later, there came another, equally startling development from the nation's capital.

7

Boiling Point

Kyle seldom activated his MediaSurround. Why have it in your room, your ear, your line of vision always, and always chattering its useless progression of events? But he activated it now, from the kitchen where he boiled his rationed allotment of daily water for vegetables, because he'd allowed the radio to talk to him as he cooked, now that Inga was away; and then the story on the radio had been too compelling. *Activate,* he ordered.

General Arthur Hargood, Chief of National Security, was announcing the arrest of President Goya and the suspension of the Constitution. A crowd of reporters surged around him with microphones like a spiky porcupine as digital flashes fluttered over his unemotional visage like an electrical storm.

"The President is being detained under house arrest while charges are being considered by the Attorney General. Due to the nature of the charges, which I cannot announce to you at this time, this is obviously not an ordinary succession, yet it is impossible to maintain in place the Constitutional procedures for succession and at the same time administer orderly justice. There is general consensus in the National Security Agency and among the members of the President's cabinet to suspend the Constitution, given the present inability of the Congress to function. It is believed that the Congress will soon be functioning once more. The suspension of the Constitution is only a very temporary measure. I do not expect that forty-eight hours will elapse before it is once again in operation. I therefore caution the public and the press not to panic... "

A cacophony of voices hurled simultaneous questions at the officer. Kyle could make out the ones that seemed obvious to him amid the din. *What are the charges? Why can't you tell us what the charges against the President are? What about the Vice-President? What authority do you claim for suspending the Constitution? Have you spoken to any members of Congress?*

The general appeared to be in his sixties, possibly seventies. His forehead was high and lined. A bit of pale, beer colored curly hair sat far back on his head. His eyes were large and framed in wrinkled lids. His lips were thin, his jaw strong. He appeared in military uniform with chevrons on his lapel and tasseled shoulder epaulets.

"I cannot tell you what the charges are, because determining what they are is ultimately the prerogative of the Attorney General. I can tell you that they are related to the recent violence committed against U.S. citizens; that's all I am at liberty to say."

So it's finally come to this, Kyle thought. *An open coup. The Constitution gives way beneath the cracks.*

With all the stresses of recent decades — public hunger, drought, wildfires, coastal flooding, population displacement and migration, foreign war, heat related illnesses, species extinction, contamination of water supply, civic pollution and health evacuations, public controls on water use and food consumption — Kyle had often wondered how long it would be before such a thing happened. Here it was: the collapse of government.

"The Constitution," droned the general, "was not deemed to be functioning, because the three branches of government it authorizes were incapacitated by the actions of the demonstrators. Or rather, the Congress was incapacitated, which had the effect of de-funding and thus rendering the entire government non-functional. Thus, in the interests of National Security, it became necessary to suspend the ordinary operation of the non-functioning Constitution, in order to address the current crisis. That is the basis of the authority you ask about."

Snap snap snap snap snap snap snap snap.

"I have spoken briefly to the Speaker of the House and

to the Senate Majority Leader to apprise them of the current state of things. That is all. No, there have not been extensive conversations, or advice from those quarters."

Snap snap snap snap snap snap snap snap.

"The military occupation of the Capitol building is now under control, as is the building itself. No, it is no longer under the control of the protesters. Yes, it is possible that members of the military involved in the killing of American citizens may be subject to prosecution. That stands to reason, if the President is charged, that those who acted illegally under his orders would also be charged, but as of this moment I cannot name names or specify any charges which may be brought against any party."

Snap snap snap snap snap snap snap snap.

"No, I cannot answer questions about any possible charges that may be brought against any of the protesters. I would refer you to the Attorney General. No, I have not heard the rumors that the Attorney General has been arrested. I will need to consult with my advisors about that."

Snap snap snap snap snap snap snap snap.

Kyle had a habit of speaking aloud to himself whenever he was alone. Now he became quite talkative.

"'Rumors that the Attorney General has been arrested'? What's up with that? What's going on here? Who the hell arrests the Attorney General?"

He continued watching the coverage for another half hour for further developments, but they weren't forthcoming and he had work to do. He was meeting the following morning with a group of fellow scientists who were eager to hear the details of the incident aboard the mini-submarine. Word of his Jonah-esque experience had already gotten out, been distorted, and had come back to him as a claim of having been swallowed by a whale.

"It was not a whale, folks," practicing what he would say. "It was a squid. Architeuthix Dux, to all appearances. But much larger than Architeuthix is known to be. I can't explain this. It was some mutated form of Architeuthix. Whatever it was, I believe it was very hungry, perhaps starving, and that that is why it swallowed us. As you know, we've suffered an immense loss of biodiversity in the past half-century. About half the species that were extant then are gone now, including huge numbers of marine species. Most forms of cod, bryozoans, polychaete worms, odontoceti, plankton, phytoplankton, zooplankton of all sorts, menhaden, bluefin tuna — the list goes on. You know it very well."

He paused in the recital of his prepared statement, thinking of Jim Shire.

"A friend of mine came to me the other day, a fisherman. He sold his boat. 'There are no more fish,' he told me. No more fish! As if I didn't know. As if you and I don't know. And what is happening, as a result? The rainforests are being cut down to make way for grazing animals for meat to replace the lost fish. That will make matters infinitely worse — as you well know."

Kyle dropped into silence, as his water had reached a boil in the pot.

8

Islands, Firearms, Habeas Corpus

Dolores Shire was forty-eight years old and married to Jim. She had a son and a daughter, both grown and living independently. She worked as a bookkeeper for an office supply store in Mill Valley. The job was part-time, and she had recently taken a voluntary cut in pay in order to avoid a layoff. Office supply sales were down. Sales of everything were down.

Dolores lived in a house in Mill Valley that Jim had inherited from his late mother, a one-story bungalow with dark brown wood shingle siding and vines crawling up the shingles. A wire mesh fence surrounded the house, separating it from the neighbors. The neighborhood had dense tree cover, and in nice weather was typically full of birdsong, but less so in the past decade, which saw the extinction of a hundred and fifty-six bird species.

Next door to the Shires lived a family who hailed from the Cape Verde Islands, which were now largely swallowed up by the Atlantic Ocean. Thousands of families in California came from submerged island nations. Cape Verdeans were less common here than Pacific island refugees, people from the Maldives, Fiji, Palau, and Micronesia.

The Shire family had lived in their present home for twenty years. Dolores knew the neighbors. There were some who moved away, and she hadn't met the new ones yet, but mostly she knew the neighbors.

On the day after the news broke about the suspension of the Constitution, one of the neighbors, Ed Gurnsey, came to the door with another man whom Dolores did not know. Dolores heard a knock — more like a pounding on the door — followed by the digital doorbell. The identity mechanism interrogated Ed,

41

and as Dolores approached the door, she saw his face on the four-inch screen above the doorknob. He was looking away but mumbling in response.

"It's me, Ed."

The combination of pounding and bell disturbed Dolores. It was as if there were some emergency. But she knew Ed and was not afraid of him. He was a man in his late thirties, who lived four doors down. He had a wife and three kids. He sold nautical supplies and often did business with Jim. He was six feet tall, with longish, straight black hair and a goatee. The man standing beside him when Dolores opened the door was younger, in his twenties she guessed, shorter than Ed, red-haired, heavier than he should be by ten or fifteen pounds. This younger man avoided eye contact, which Dolores found unsettling.

"Hey, Dolores, Jim around?"

"No, he's not at the moment."

For some reason, she did not care to say exactly where Jim was, or how long he'd be gone. Even Ed was limiting his eye contact, and both men looked slightly out of breath. Their manner made her nervous.

"When'll he be back?"

"I can't say for sure, Ed. Do you want me to leave him a message?"

"We're in trouble, Dolores. This whole government thing. Some of us guys are getting together to talk about it. We want Jim to be there."

"What government thing, Ed?"

Ed's evasive eyes focused on her now for a second and grew round. "Ain't you heard? Do you listen to the news?"

"I don't, Ed. I avoid the media like the plague."

This was true. Unless Jim was tuned in, she never heard a news broadcast. News to her was always the same. It never changed, and people never learned from what happened to them from one year to the next.

"Well, you should turn it on. The military has taken over the government and shut down the Constitution. They arrested the president and the cabinet. Which I don't care about the president, but it ain't right, what they're doing."

"Surely you're not serious, Ed!"

"Turn it on. Jim be back tonight?"

"Ed," she said, changing her mind about revealing Jim's whereabouts, "Jim is away on a research trip for two weeks."

"Two weeks!"

"He'll be back two weeks from tomorrow."

"Hell, Dolores, that ain't soon enough. But OK, if you say so. But listen now. Do you own any firearms?"

"Ed, why do you ask me that?"

"As I recall, Jim said he owned some."

Now she caught and held Ed's eye and stared him down. "Ed, I told you Jim would be back in two weeks. I'll ask him to contact you when he gets back."

Ed hesitated. Dolores thought his eyes looked desperate. Was he thinking of storming the house and taking the weapons? Surely not. She could see now that the moment had passed.

"Well, all right, Dolores. Tell him to come see me soon as he gets back. Can you reach him by phone? Where'd he go anyway?"

"Alaska."

"Alaska!"

"I'll try to reach him and tell him you want to see him, Ed. But I don't think it will change his timetable."

Ed and the younger, unintroduced man exchanged a nervous glance. They were wearing hiking boots streaked with dirt. The younger man wore khakis and a scruffy T-shirt. Ed was wearing a light sweatshirt and jeans. His fingernails were dirty.

"Well. Tell him I came by, then."

"Yes, I will, Ed. And I'll go put the news on too."

"You really should. It's unbelievable!"

"I will. Goodbye now."

"Goodbye, Dolores."

She watched the two men lumber off, then locked the door and retired to the media room to see what sort of misunderstanding her neighbor was laboring under.

The holographic news anchor man appeared in the room with pictures behind him. The pictures were of the president and members of his cabinet, then of a uniformed officer.

"Attorneys for the arrested cabinet members are saying they plan to file for writs of habeas corpus, but a spokesman for General Hargood says that courts have no jurisdiction to issue orders based on habeas corpus, since their powers come from the Constitution, which is suspended. The spokesman says that only military courts have jurisdiction over the current spate of house arrests... "

9

Quack Quack

Harrison Carbo, Secretary of Defense, General Arthur Hargood, Director of National Security, and Leo Sharp, CIA Director, met in a room in the Pentagon. It was a tense meeting.

"This is a charade and it can't be kept up," said Carbo, seated, like the others, behind a small conference tabl:. The room had been deliberately chosen for its smallness. It was barely big enough to contain the table. The walls were institutional cream. The table was oak, a small rectangle. Three of the six chairs arranged around it were empty. There were no windows. There were no plants or objects in the room that could be easily bugged.

Carbo continued. "I'm getting calls from the presidential candidates. I'm getting calls from the members of Congress. You can't just shut down every Article 3 court in the nation by fiat, General."

"That isn't the intention."

"It looks very much like the intention to everyone who watches the news. And how long do you think the local police and the military will continue to hold the president a prisoner in the White House before they decide that the Constitution isn't so crazy after all, and that they're holding their own commander-in-chief prisoner illegally at your whim?"

"Don't call it my whim, Harry. *You* haven't been arrested."

"That's exactly right. Maybe I should have been. Why haven't I been? The fact that I'm not a member of Goya's party is going to look pretty damn suspicious to some people before long."

"You're getting too nervous, Harry," CIA man Sharp interposed. "We need to cut a deal with the Congress people. Cut it quick and release the detainees, then let the country go back to the election show and watch them fight it out until November."

"The D.C. circuit court judge is getting ready to hand out habeas orders, General," Carbo hissed. "When he does, the senators are going to line up behind him. There's going to be a big blowback."

Hargood turned to Sharp. The latter's thick eyebrows twitched in response.

"Will the House vote to impeach?"

"I'm sure of it," responded CIA. "They wanted to anyway. Now they've got the allegations about presidential orders to use force. There's plenty to work with there."

"But did they commit when you talked to them?"

"As good as committed. They need affidavits. They need something in writing."

"We can get them that."

Carbo shook his head. "You'd better be careful before putting any money on that horse, General. You're going to get a pile of affidavits from the cabinet saying Goya didn't want violence, Goya wanted to avoid loss of life."

"That won't come from us."

"It doesn't matter who it comes from, General. Be reasonable."

"I'm not a damn lawyer like you, Harry. I'm not trying a case. If things go properly, there won't be any case to try, because Goya will lose the election and there won't be a president to impeach."

"And what if he doesn't lose? Then you've got an impeachment trial in the Senate, General."

"What do you want, Harry? Do you want to be arrested like the others? Is *that* your request? Or your *order?*"

"Yes, I think so, damn it."

The Defense secretary's white hairs bristled on the back of his neck.

"Now, gentlemen," interposed Sharp of the CIA, "let's step

back and look at the picture strategically for a moment. Let's try to be dispassionate. The accusations have been made. Drastic action has been taken based on them. It appears to everyone to be a serious matter, as indeed it is. The Congress will take up immediate articles of impeachment upon being re-seated. General Hargood will stand down. No one, at that point, will suspect his motives, because he will have withdrawn from power. The candidates will take up the cudgels against Goya, having new ammunition. The country will be involved in scandal of the most public sort. It's an election year. It will be nonstop coverage from now to November. Goya is already vulnerable. This likely finishes him off. And if, as you say, as you posit, Harry, it does *not* finish him off—he goes into impeachment proceedings and is subject to removal by the senate."

"And if he survives it?" asked the Defense secretary.

Leo Sharp raised his eyebrows and cast a sidelong glance at General Hargood, as if to say, "We have a skeptic on our hands!"

"In the unlikely event that Mr. Goya survives his impeachment in the senate, Harry, he is the lamest of lame ducks."

"Quack quack," said General Hargood.

"Quack quack," said Sharp.

10

In the Doorway

Defense Secretary Carbo left the other two officers alone. He knew they would talk about him after he left. He didn't care.

That was the first thing they did, still standing in the doorway of the tiny conference room with the table and six chairs.

"Are you really going to have Harry arrested?" Sharp wondered.

"That's what he wants. It's his call."

"It only makes his eventual statement that much more sympathetic to the President. Do we want that?"

"I think he'll want to distance himself from the President, Leo. Anyway, it doesn't much matter."

"Because you think Goya will lose the election."

"Because it doesn't matter who is elected."

"What do you mean? How can it not matter?"

"Because all those greens years ago telling us to watch out for global warming? They were right."

"How can you say that, Art? Your job has been National Security all your adult life."

"And I don't apologize for it now, Leo. But this country is going down a rat hole now because we're low on food. The corn crop has been down twenty-five percent for ten years running. You can't go to a restaurant and get a plate of seafood anymore. Have you tried? The systems are unbalanced. Whoever takes power is going to have to do something about it."

"Do *what* about it? We've already mostly depleted oil and gas. We're twenty per cent solar right now. What do we do? Go nuclear?"

"Nuclear, renewable, whatever there is. But it has to be done by control. The free market is not going to do it. If it's us, we put a military government in place, or the closest thing to it we can, if the damn Constitution is a problem."

"It *is* a problem. You know it. Carbo is right about that."

"Or it can be Goya and his greens. But if *they* do it, it'll be labeled a Marxist takeover. The militia people will be up in arms. They'll say it's Big Brother."

"It *will* be Big Brother."

Hargood laughed. He was a much larger man than Sharp. He took hold of Sharp's lapel and gave it a sharp, startling jerk.

"Big Brother is already here, Leo. The issue is who steps into his shoes."

11

Wood Mite

In his suite of offices at the Pentagon, General Hargood was pleased to receive one of his preferred candidates for the U.S. presidency, former talk show host and right-wing ideologue, Wesley Wright. Wright, who had never held political office, and whose expertise in matters related to American government consisted chiefly in his ability to evoke in his sympathetic audience a series of emotional responses to formulaic dog whistles, was himself supremely pleased to have obtained the necessary clearances to meet the general face to face. It seemed to comport with his newly realized idea of himself as not merely a celebrity, but a Very Important Person.

At thirty-eight years old, Wright was three years above the minimum age allowed for U.S. presidents under the now suspended Constitution. The fact pleased him, as he fully expected to have the distinction of being the youngest president in history. It was only recently that this belief had emerged from a more general ambition, because he had recently won five Republican primaries, two by large margins, upsetting the prior expectations of many glib media pundits and dividing the number of committed delegates between three candidates, none of whom had a clear upper hand going into the Republican convention to be held in two weeks. As he saw it, he was on a spoiler's roll. Pitted, as he was, against career politicians, he believed that a groundswell of populist ardor for his candidacy was only now getting underway and building momentum. He saw himself as a modern day Trump, with brains. Donor money had been pouring into his campaign coffers. He was not so unrealistic as to expect no setbacks in a campaign that still had several months to go, but he believed that his momentum would lead to his nomination, and that rolling over President Goya in the general election would be relatively easy in contrast to the nomination.

Wright had a full head of prematurely white hair, combed and sprayed in a pompadour, a florid face, strange yellow eyes, and an aquiline nose like that of drawings of certain Roman emperors. He was five feet eight inches tall and weighed two hundred five pounds. He wore a black suit with a red shirt and a western string tie, cowboy boots with two inch heels on his feet. He was ushered into the General's office feeling some of his earlier indignation diminished by the momentousness of this reception. He had been upset at the suspension of the Constitution, but he could not be angry with someone who made him feel important.

"Mr. Wright, delighted to meet you."

The general extended his hand and Wright shook it with an excessively tight grip.

"Honored to meet *you*, General."

"Sit down, please."

"Thank you."

"I'm a great admirer of your talk show, when I've had the pleasure to hear it. Unfortunately, that's not as often as I might wish."

"I realize you're a busy man, General. And please call me Wes."

"Very well. And do please call me Art, won't you?"

"Art it is."

"No doubt you wanted to see me to discuss the status of the election. You're concerned about the suspension of the Constitution, and how that affects it."

"I am indeed concerned about that very thing."

"Well, it won't affect it at all, Wes. As a matter of fact, we are getting ready to announce the reinstatement of the Constitution momentarily."

"You are?"

General Hargood could see the wave of relief that washed over his guest's ruddy face.

"Indeed we are, Wes. It was never our intention to declare some kind of military junta. As you can imagine, my phones have been beeping incessantly. I shouldn't say beeping. I have a ringer that plays John Philip Sousa, ha ha! My emails have piled up to the heavens. Our concern was that the Constitution permitted the removal of the president only by impeachment. And no impeachment could occur as long as the Congress was prevented from convening. It was an impossible scenario."

"But —" a puzzled look shadowed Wright's face—"after the military went in and routed the protesters, wouldn't Congress have been able to convene, Art?"

"Indeed they would, and that's now the case. But we had to stop further bloodshed and couldn't do it as long as our orders came from the Commander-In-Chief, who was then acting with unchecked power. So this was a stopgap measure, you see. But I have since met with the Speaker of the House, who assures me that articles of impeachment will soon be forthcoming."

"That's good news."

"It's an unfortunate necessity, but a necessity, nonetheless. And with that process soon to be underway, we felt we could return to the normal operation of government without further upheavals. Of course, this means there will be no interruption in the election process."

"I'm certainly glad to hear that."

"And likewise, we'll have to release the President from house arrest, along with his cabinet members, those who've been arrested. They could only be held as long as the Constitutional processes were in check."

"I understand."

"It's a shame, a terrible shame, that the President went out of control during the occupation crisis."

"It certainly is."

"And naturally, we can expect him to resume the campaign trail asserting his innocence, or at least his justification in doing what he did."

"I'd expect nothing else from him."

"It's neither here nor there. It's the political process. Don't let anyone tell you that NSA is somehow opposed to the political process."

"I wouldn't dream of it."

With each statement, General Hargood had leaned closer and closer to his guest, so that now their faces were almost in the position of a person leaning in close to a mirror, doubling his image. Suddenly, the general smiled and drew back in his swivel chair, breaking a certain tension.

"But now tell me, since I have you here before me, what your policy will be toward our agency if you're elected. Do you mind?"

Wright leaned back, smiled as well.

"Not at all. General, I mean to work closely with NSA, to seek out your advice on all matters of national security, and to strengthen your hand whenever and wherever possible."

"Delighted to hear it, Wes! You won't be dealing with me, of course, because I will have resigned."

"Oh, no, surely not!"

"Yes, it's inevitable. But speaking for the agency, you know, we can no longer go on with half measures in matters of national security."

"Oh, I absolutely agree."

"That's not what's expected of us in the world. It's not what our allies rely on, and not what our enemies respect."

"I agree wholeheartedly, General."

"Art."

"Art."

"Our enemies understand one thing, and one thing only, Wes.

Power. The power to destroy them. The power to hold their feet to the fire. If we let up the slightest bit, they take advantage of us. And they laugh at us in the bargain."

"That's the truth, Art."

"I'm so glad you agree with me."

"The strength of America is in her military might and in the power of her business enterprise."

"How right you are! Let me say that, should we have the good fortune to elect you in November, I shall look forward to knowing that you will work closely with this agency in whatever way you may find helpful."

"And I look forward to that as well, Art. If you are personally not in power, perhaps you might be persuaded to return."

A little wood mite ambled across the table and the general whacked it dead with the palm of his hand.

12

Passages from the President's Journal

Sylvia and I are both early risers, but it was she who first noticed the men downstairs wearing ski masks and gloves and sporting submachine guns. Our security is usually so good that she didn't draw the conclusion that they were terrorists. It would have been unthinkable that dozens of terrorists would have gotten past White House Security without a whisper of commotion.

"Who are those men downstairs?" she said, coming into the bedroom as I was finishing dressing. "Secret Service?"

"What men?"

"The ones in the ski masks. Is it some kind of drill?"

Still in my stockinged feet, I rushed into the hallway and down the grand staircase. I could see them scurrying about, coming out of the doors to the library and the Vermeil and China Rooms, through the doorway leading to the East Colonnade. I thought, *well, if they're here to kill me I suppose they will do it, but if not, I want to know who they are.* So I called out to them, "Who are you?" and they immediately positioned their machine guns in an at rest position so as not to seem threatening.

"Mr. President, we're here under orders to secure your house arrest," one of them said. "No one intends to harm you, sir, but you are not permitted to leave the White House. We're required to confiscate your communications devices, sir."

And with that, several of them now rushed upstairs over my protests and began ransacking the upstairs rooms. I kept asking them who gave them their orders, but they wouldn't answer me. I was sure they weren't military. Sylvia came hurrying out of the bedroom, demanding to know what was going on. She had her cell phone with her, but the masked men grabbed it.

I was permitted to put some shoes on, and within about

twenty minutes Ray Lessing (WH counsel) was permitted to meet with me in the Blue Room. He looked haggard. I must have looked the same, because neither of us had gotten much sleep watching news coverage of the events at the Capitol, which had spiraled out of control so dismally. I had spent half the night trying to get the military to pull back.

"I don't believe they were military in the lead," said Lessing. "It was set up. Those weren't Seals, either, which is what they're saying in the news."

I said of course they weren't.

"NSA has declared the Constitution suspended, and they've apparently ordered you house arrested."

"Who? Hargood?"

"Hargood is making the announcements."

This was undoubtedly on the media in real time, but the ski masks were busy taking all my media off the premises.

"I was allowed to come in," said Ray, "because they want you to understand what's going on. They want you to know that the situation is temporary."

"Oh, I have no doubt it's temporary."

"They're claiming it's legal necessity, that the government has already been de facto shut down, that this is some kind of measure to kick start it up again."

"Arresting me is going to kick start the government? Are they crazy?"

"They're NSA, boss."

"What good is arresting me going to do?"

"The thing is, they're saying you've committed crimes against the state."

"What? Are they mad?"

"They're saying the violence against the Capitol demonstrators is your responsibility."

"The violence is against my orders, Ray. Who is saying this?"

"It's all Hargood on the public statements. I don't know who else is involved. They've arrested most of your cabinet as well, but I don't know for how long. I think they just want to prevent you meeting with them for a while."

"This is all utterly illegal, Ray."

"Of course it is."

It was a ridiculous state of affairs. I figured the ski masks were probably CIA, but I couldn't prove anything. I was allowed one hour long meeting with Ray Lessing each day for three days as a progress report. I could not call out, watch any TV, view any online communications. I was incommunicado for three days. White House Security had totally, mysteriously, vanished from the scene. On the third day, the masked spooks disappeared, WH Security returned, and I was told I was no longer under arrest. Later that day, I was informed that the Congress was back in session and would soon vote in the House on articles of impeachment.

13

Too Much Daylight

Jim Shire walked right in on them. He didn't mean to.

He had been absorbed in his second perimeter measurement, which was larger than the first had been by several feet. He didn't even realize that Farley Meeks and Bev Cartwright had preceded him back to camp. He didn't hear them inside the men's tent. They were taking care to be quiet.

When he opened the flap and saw them going at it on Farley's air mattress, there was an uncomfortable second as they realized they'd been seen, but Jim left no time for them even to blush or cry out in shame or indignation. He backed out, closed the flap, and quickly retreated in the direction he'd come from until he saw Inga Conners approaching on foot from her parked and rented SUV.

Now what am I supposed to do? Jim thought. *Cover for them?*

"You might want to hold off going back into camp," he said tentatively.

"Why?"

Jim gestured vaguely in the direction of his tent and seeing that this gesture only made Inga more curious, he blurted out, "Bev and Farley are having an affair back there."

He kept walking, not stopping to gauge Inga's reaction. Instead, he returned to the crater site and sat staring into its great yawning cavern.

He thought of Dolores. He remembered a conversation they had had at the breakfast table after he had sold the *Honeydancer*.

"What will we talk about?" she had said. "One day I'll retire, too, and then what will we have to talk about?"

"The kids, I guess," he'd said.

"If we had no kids, what would we talk about?"

"We have kids."

"But what do people who have no kids talk about?"

"That's not us. We have kids. We'll talk about the kids."

There are ten billion people in the world, Jim thought.

He wondered what would happen to the ten billion people when the oceans emptied themselves of life. What was happening to them now? They were moving around, trying to keep from being hungry. Some of them were getting sick from malnutrition. Some of them were fighting wars.

Those things had always been true, hadn't they? Hunger, wars?

But there weren't as many animals, fish, trees now. When the trees go, when the fish go, when the animals go, when the oceans go... *where do we go?*

He laughed.

He laughed because he thought some people would answer that question by saying, *We go into a condominium* — or something equally absurd. *We go back home and eat genetically engineered food. You push a button and the food multiplies, like a copier making copies.*

And all those lovers, sexually combining and making little copies of copies — ten billion copies.

The cavern's black interior faced him. The Alaska sun remained well up in the sky, more like afternoon than evening, which it was. He could hear water running, trickling somewhere down below. This was nothing but a black, empty hole, and they had a week yet to spend staring into it.

It was a cool evening. A brisk breeze addressed itself to the back of his thick polyester shirt.

"The guy's married," he said aloud. He emitted an exhalation representing unsurprised disenchantment. It, the affair, was the kind of thing people did. He felt sorry for Farley's wife back home, whoever she was. He didn't know her. Didn't even know her name. He remembered only that Farley had referred to "his wife" in the first few days of the trek.

You refer to me in company as 'your wife,' Dolores had said to him once, many years ago. *You don't use my name. Why is that, Jim?*

Ever since then, he had tried to make a point of using her name.

Am I jealous? he wondered. Bev was a nice looking woman — young. Cinnamon hair, sweet little ass, looked good in shorts. Jim guessed she and Farley must have had it going before they came on this trip. This was a chance for them to get away. Not to have to slink around. And the great natural expanse, the adventure, the change of scene — always an aphrodisiac, that. Travel, the great promoter of romance.

How long would he have to sit here, he wondered, before the night sky darkened and became one with the black, open cavern in front of him?

In July, the Fairbanks, Alaska sun sets around midnight. It rises again at about four a.m.

Twenty hours of daylight. That was almost too much daylight for anyone.

14

Hologram

By agreement reached over their hand-helds, Kyle and Inga convened a hologram conference on the eighth day of her trip to Alaska. Kyle accessed his hologram from his hand-held while in bed, a four-poster with a blue scalloped spread, and Inga appeared in the room and sat at the bed's foot wearing jeans and a lumberjack cotton shirt, her hair tied back in a long ponytail. Seeing her there, Kyle longed terribly to hold her, but a hologram is incorporeal, an illusion of physical presence.

"How are you, darling," he said softly.

Inga's gray eyes were, as always, sober, controlled, authoritative. Her lips appeared pursed.

"Fine. Working hard. You were going to tell me what happened on your submarine outing. Something momentous, it sounded like."

He had not told her yet about the scrape with architeuthix dux giganticus, not wanting to alarm her without being able to follow up to reassure her. Now he told the story. It was characteristic of her to underreact, something Kyle found mildly irritating, yet never enough to mention it, thinking it his own weakness to want a stronger reaction.

"That's incredible," she said, as if she were saying, *I'm having a cup of coffee.* "Are you sure it was architeuthix?"

"Quite sure. The question is how it came to be so big."

"Do you have any theories?"

"I have *only* theories at this point. Nothing that can be tested."

"What are your theories?"

"It's a mutation, an ecological sport of some kind. It could be related to warming or acidification."

"How so?"

"That's what I don't know. But we know that fish have mutated in the course of global warming. Certain species of shark have migrated away from their accustomed locations, and have mated with other species, producing new genetic strains."

Inga paused, unable to do much with a vague theory of squid migration.

"Any other theories?"

"Not really. Some type of mutation."

"What about an undiscovered species?"

"Possible, but not likely."

"You're sure you're OK?"

"I'm fine. The sub was not to the squid's liking."

"I should think not."

Kyle lay back against his pillow, lingering over the beautiful sight of Inga's legs, crossed, in their ghostly denim.

"What about you? How are things progressing with your project?"

"We're ahead of schedule. I'll be glad to be done with it when it's time to go. Something strange, though… "

"Yes, what?"

"Jim is in the process of taking his third perimeter measurement of the blowhole, and it keeps measuring bigger each time."

"Are you serious? It's growing!"

"Apparently so. And faster than anyone could have imagined."

"That could be dangerous, Inga."

"Oh, it's probably not dangerous. It's not collapsing. Just growing."

"But if it's growing fast, it *could* collapse. You never know."

"We're a good ways away from it in camp. It's only when we're on site that there might be some cause for concern."

"But you're on site every day. I don't know if I like this, Ing. Why don't you wrap it up and come home?"

"We have a grant, Kyle. I can't just take the money and then close it up before we've accomplished our mission."

"But you said you're ahead of schedule. If you've done what you needed to do, then—"

"Well, we have pre-booked return flights too. We've got to wait."

She seemed to watch him from her post at the foot of the bed. He imagined his own hologram where she was, in her tent, lying on a ghostly bed, a vision from home. Would it make her homesick?

"I'm alone in the tent now," said Inga. "Interested in a little gossip?"

"Certainly."

"Don't spread it around. Farley and Bev are having an affair."

"Oh, no."

"Afraid so. I think Jim is pretty annoyed by it. He seems pretty distracted sometimes. Farley and Bev sneak away whenever they get a chance and go at it pretty hot and heavy. Jim stumbled on them by accident in his tent a few days ago."

"Oh, dear. Farley's married, isn't he?"

"They both are. She's much younger. I don't think she has kids yet."

"Oh, golly. Are you able to stay focused on your work? Are *they* able to?"

"Yes, we're getting things done. It's just something where Jim and I are cautious when we come back to camp. We make sure we know who's where before we go bursting into the tents, you know."

"Sure. Well… Is it cold up there?"

"Not at all. It's pleasant. About like San Francisco in the summer, I'd say."

"Meaning cold."

"Cold for summer. But pleasant."

Kyle grew weary with the exchange of news.

"I miss you, Ing."

"I miss you too."

"I wish you were here, darling."

"I'll be home soon."

"Don't let those lovers influence you."

"Influence me? What do you mean?"

"Don't get any ideas."

"What ideas? There's nobody up here but the four of us."

"That's what I mean."

"Farley's got his hands full. Who would I have an affair with? Jim?"

"You never know."

"Jim is not interested in me."

"All men are interested in you."

"Well, I'm not interested in him. OK?"

"OK. That's what I want to hear."

He wondered if she might choose to laugh, but she didn't.

"I'll be home before you know it."

"Yes. I love you."

"I love *you.*"

The conversation wound down, and then they de-activated their holograms. The tall, bedenimed figure of Inga Conners shimmered and dissolved in the air, like so much fairy dust. Then Kyle lay waiting for sleep, for drowsiness, until finally he awoke in the middle of the night, realizing that he had been dreaming of a train ride through Kathmandu.

15

Ticket

One of his research assistants called Kyle almost simultaneously with the news coming over the radio.

An unprecedented beaching of dolphins in Stinson Beach...

"It's horrible, Professor Conners. You've got to come up and see it."

"Yes. I'll get right up there."

He took the photovoltaic Streak, a solar powered vehicle, from his garage. There were many more such vehicles than even ten years ago, and yet the Golden Gate Bridge was still substantially covered with gas permit cars, creating slow moving lines except in the prepaid card line. Fortunately, this was Kyle's line, and before too long he was puttering along up the coastal highway, with the foot of Mt. Tam on one side, and the rocky coast on the other.

The line of cars came to a complete stop before he could get to Stinson. He called his research assistant on his hands-free car phone. The assistant, Rogan, a twenty-two-year-old college senior, female, was already down there.

"Yeah, they're backed up, gawking at the mess, Professor Conners. It's going to take some cops to clear them out and get traffic moving again. How far away are you?"

"Not that far. I'm tempted to just shut off the ignition and walk down."

"You probably shouldn't leave your car."

Others were getting out of their vehicles. Kyle thought, *Hell, they're doing it. I'll do it. We can all come back at the same time.*

There was little fog north of the bridge today, and the backed up line of cars glinted blindingly. Everywhere, people were moving, hiking past the stopped cars — women, children, men with and without beards, almost all of them casually dressed, almost all of them talking about the disaster. Snippets of their conversation assailed his ear.

"This is the end of life on Earth... "

"It's awful. Dolphins are as smart as people. No, I take that back, they're *smarter*... "

"I so much *don't* want this to be true... "

They were people like him, it seemed. People who cared about sea life, about nature, people who knew the ocean was acidifying. Coming down over a hill, he saw the disaster on the shoreline below.

Some of the dolphins were beached. Others lay in shallow water with their dorsal fins and their topsides exposed. The animals were lifeless. Plant life also emerged above the waterline like a kind of death rack. The water was a dark lager color. In the mid-distance, rocky cliffs rose above the tide, making shadows against the sunlight. The air was awash with the sound of people moaning in dread and disgust.

The dolphins lay like blue-gray commas on the strand.

Kyle removed his shoes and socks, rolled his trousers above the knee, pocketed the socks, and carried the shoes, paired in one hand, out onto the beach, stopping to examine the half-submerged sea mammals. Wet sand clung to the soles of his feet and toes. The waves gently lapped at the shore. The salty air was redolent of the smell of death. A fish market. He waded in the shallow waters from one carcass to another. There were too many to count.

Near a hunk of driftwood, something brushlike caught Kyle's attention. As he came nearer, he saw that it was wet fur— a sea otter, lying dead, face up, hands outstretched in rigor mortis, like a small begging doll.

Kyle squatted in the shallow water and wept. A few quick sobs, a few quick tears coursing down his cheeks; then he recovered himself. He turned his face into his right and left sleeves and rubbed off the moisture, then regained his footing, still holding his pair of shoes in one hand.

Later, he returned to his car to find a parking citation on his windshield.

16

Tableau

A stand of conifers obstructed the view of camp until Inga was right upon it, or nearly. She heard raised voices as she was coming out of the bosque. She saw a quick dun flap of the men's tent, and Farley emerged with Jim close behind. Jim seemed to be haranguing the younger man, but she could not make out the words. They were punctuated with overlapping plaintive or sarcastic ripostes from Farley. A moment later, Bev stepped out from the tent. She seemed intimidated and uttered not a sound.

They stood in a kind of sound surrounded tableau, the younger man with black hair, smaller but poised and potentially powerful, the older man grayer but full of anger, shouting. Inga hurried toward them, then heard a loud, caustic sounding insult come from Farley. She could not make out the words, but detected, in the way the consonants and vowels fell out, an obscenity.

There was a flash of red sleeve as Jim's elbow swung outward. She saw the arm land flat against Farley's chest below the collarbone. Farley threw his own arms outward, but he fell back at the same time, and Jim was on top of him.

Inga ran toward them.

"Stop it! Stop it this instant!"

She flung herself between them and clutched a handful of Jim's shirt with her right hand while with her left she pushed back against Jim's effort to rise.

Surprised by the strength in the woman's grip, and unwilling to risk hurting her, Jim drew back and gazed at her with astonishment, gesturing wildly toward Farley, who now rose to his feet while backing away.

"Did you hear what he said to me?" Jim wailed.

"I didn't say anything to you!"

"You're a liar!"

"That's enough," gritted Inga. Both men fell silent. This was Inga's expedition. She was in charge. Both men respected her too much to resist her will, which was fierce and fearless. Bev stood at the tent flap, her mouth in a small "o," her eyes wide. She wore khaki shorts and a work shirt, knee-length stockings and ankle hiking boots. Inga knew, without asking, that the fight was about Bev, about her affair with Farley, whether or not the men would admit it. She had already decided what to do about it.

"I won't tolerate fighting in my camp," she said.

"Well, I'm not sharing a tent with *that* character anymore," Jim shot back. "He's got about as much respect for me as nothing."

He seemed embarrassed by his own inelegant phrase. His face was red, and he clearly felt pushed.

"All right, this is what we're going to do," said Inga, her intonation flat, her eyes steely. "Bev will move her stuff into the men's tent, and Jim will move his stuff into my tent."

"I'm not sharing a tent with you, Inga, I'm sorry," Jim protested.

"There won't be any privacy issues. If either of us wants to use the tent to change clothes, we will ask the other to leave while that's accomplished."

"You expect me to sleep in the same tent with you, Inga? What would Kyle have to say about that?"

"He won't have anything to say about it. You'll be sleeping and I'll be sleeping. I'll tell him what we're doing as the result of you two gentlemen behaving like boys in a schoolyard."

"I'll get over it. I'll adjust to this asshole."

"You will not adjust. You will move your belongings into my tent, and you'll do it right now."

The two men glared at each other, then locked gazes with

Inga. Then Jim brushed past Bev and went into the tent to retrieve his belongings. He made four or five such trips, and on the last one, he gazed sternly at Inga and said, "I hope you know what you're doing."

17

Shock

The sun still lingered high in the sky, and showed no signs of sinking below the horizon, although it was quite late. Jim was seriously thinking of making some kind of formal peace with Farley in order to get back into the same sex tent arrangement, when Inga approached him after they had eaten their evening rations from the daily pack.

"When you're ready to retire, you go and change first," she said. "Wear some type of clothing to bed, please. I'll change in the SUV. When I see you turn the light out, I'll retire to my sleeping bag."

He thought, *Well, that's clear enough.* She was so businesslike and commanding that it did not seem such a fearsome thing, after all. He'd be in one sleeping bag, she'd be in another. They'd go to sleep. They were both adults with faithful, loving spouses awaiting them back home. What he wondered was why she wanted to encourage Farley and Bev this way, but now was not the right time to ask about it.

The temperature was in the mid-forties when he decided to retire. Farley and Bev had already gone lights out, although the sky itself remained unnervingly light, as it did nearly all day and night here—only the wee hours excepted.

He approached Inga, who was going over some notes near the campfire.

"I'll be hitting the hay now," he said. "Give me five minutes."

"OK, Jim."

He went into the tent. He was tempted to simply get into the sleeping bag with all his clothes on, but he knew that would leave him restless and without a complete night's sleep. Although he didn't often wear pajamas at home, he had brought a pair, knowing that the nights would likely be cool. He put these on. If he had to get up unexpectedly, he would not be embarrassed to be seen in the pajamas, which were a red flannel, with a buttoned top. Turning out the lantern, he nestled into his down bag.

He heard the SUV door open and close twice, with a hiatus in between. A moment later, Inga entered into the darkened tent. He squinted at her, saw she was wearing some kind of long, white underwear. She unrolled her bag and climbed into it. And there he lay, thinking how silly this was, and wondering what was going on in the other tent.

He listened to the sounds of crickets. Breathing gently, he waited for sleep. *One more day,* he thought.

Just as sleep was about to take him, there was an abrupt, strange buzz, then a loud crackling noise and something like a large, human sized spark in the tent. It seemed to originate with Inga's laptop computer, over on her side of the space. The spark jumped immediately to him, and Jim felt himself light up, with a shock reminiscent of a feeling he had had as a child when he had stuck his finger into a light socket and received an electric shock, only this was much bigger.

He blacked out.

18

They All Go into the Dark

Billy Pibbles was playing a video game called Cave of Monsters. He was using his laptop which was juiced to the max. Using his joystick, he carried the maidens in diaphanous gowns in and out of locked dungeons, stealing the keys from sleeping or combative ogre-guards, killing them with his flaming sword, lopping off their bloody heads and arms, running them through the gut, and finally escaping to the Cave Country. As the monsters came screaming and flying out of every other cave, he shot them with his hand-held grenade launcher and flame-thrower, but every now and then he lost a maiden. (There were plenty more.)

Billy was thirteen years old. He was supposed to be doing his homework, but Mom wasn't home, so how would she know what he was doing? His little brother and sister wouldn't tell on him. He'd make them pay if they *did.*

One of the cave monsters sprang out at him from behind its giant rock, spewing flame from its reptilian maw. Its scaly claws spread out toward him, and he began firing the grenade launcher. Suddenly, Billy's heart went into shock as the flame on the screen seemed to burst out of the device altogether and expand into the room around him. He heard loud cracking sounds and saw nothing but white light. He screamed in terror.

Then he lay dead. His little sister and brother ran into the room seconds later, having heard the loud noise. They discovered their brother, burned to a black crisp, a few small flames still murmuring over sections of the charred corpse. They ran screaming from the room, calling for their mother, who was not home, and would not be home for another hour. Billy was supposed to be looking after them.

Piloto Garza stepped out of the gas permit SUV after centering it and sauntered over to the lift switch. There was no key since it had a push button ignition. The door key was already hanging over a number on the wall of the garage. This particular vehicle was in the shop every other week. Brakes, transmission, exhaust, you name it, the thing was falling apart one system at a time. But old Mr. Bullard refused to get rid of it. He'd rather pay Garza hundreds or thousands of dollars every month than get a new vehicle that would pay for itself in lower maintenance. Oh, well, it was Bullard's money.

Garza wiped off his hands with a grease rag and reached for the lift switch. *Let's get that dinosaur up on the rack and take a look underneath.* Garza's hands were pudgy, thick-fingered. His arms stretched the fabric of his greasy T. He wasn't tall, but he was big, beefy, a bull of a figure. As his gargantuan, hairy and grease spattered forearm stretched toward the lift switch, he glanced at his employee, Jimmy Akukich, who was finishing up an oil change on a permit vehicle at the next station from his. He caught Jimmy's eye as that skinny young man looked up from testing the air pressure on the tires. Garza winked at him. Then his eye fell on the calendar above the lift switch. A bosomy blonde female grinned alluringly at him wearing a red bikini and draping herself provocatively across an antique Harley chopper.

That was the last image Piloto Garza saw. When he flipped the lift switch, an impossibly loud buzz emanated from it, as if a giant bumblebee had flown into the garage, and a jagged bolt of electricity filled the room for exactly one second. Then all the lights went out, and Bud Metzger in the cash office started yelling, "What the hell is going on?"

When Bud dashed into the garage, he saw the gray light from the cloudy day outside falling across the body of Jimmy Akukich, half in and half out of shadow. He saw Garza's body lying in complete shadow, huge seeming and inert. He felt the necks of both men and found no pulse.

Nineteen-year-old Burry Habbuk drove his antique permit-Dodge Charger into the parking lot of the Stop N Sleep Motel on Route 250. It was early afternoon, and the Charger was the only car in the lot. Fay Jeetez waited nervously in the car while Burry got out and went into the office. Inside, a man born in India met him. The Indian was dour faced, expecting bankruptcy any day.

"You want a room?" he said to Burry.

"Yeah."

"What do you want? Double bed? Twin?"

"Double."

"King or Queen?"

"Whatever's cheaper. Queen."

"One person or two?"

Burry was annoyed at all the questions. What did the Indian guy care how many people? Was there an extra charge for two?

Without waiting for a verbal objection, the Indian added, "It's five dollars extra for two people."

Burry could see the proprietor looking past him out the window at the Charger. He decided not to lie.

"Two people."

"How many nights?"

"Just one."

"Two-O-Nine ninety-five plus tax. Pay in advance."

Burry drew his wallet and plucked out cash.

"You don't have a credit card?" the Indian asked.

"No. I don't have one with me. I've got cash. You don't take cash?"

The Indian was wearing a short-sleeved sport shirt which looked too big for his skinny brown arms. His eyes seemed white in their sockets as he glanced resentfully at the bills thrust at him.

"OK, I take cash," he said.

A moment later, Burry was hurrying out to the car with the key in hand. He didn't bother to move the car. He ushered Fay out, and the two of them left the Charger parked where it was. They took no suitcases with them and opened the flimsy blue door to their room, Room 34 on the ground floor.

The room had a mildew smell when the door opened, and Burry turned a lamp on, which didn't do much to light the dark room. Fay was all over him. They kissed, hungry and frantic, and fell back on the creaking bed, with its cigarette holes in the bedspread. Both of them lived at home with parents, and this was their only chance to be alone.

They could scarcely pull their mouths apart long enough to take a breath. Burry suddenly lifted his torso up, hands flat on either side of Fay. Her long brown hair was flung carelessly across the bedspread behind her. He reached down and began impatiently pulling open her belt and unbuttoning her jeans.

"Wait, wait," said Fay.

She gently pushed him off her, and got up to open the bedspread and sheets, pulling them far down out of the way. Burry meanwhile retreated to the space between the foot of the bed and the TV set on its raised arm and began undressing. There was a folding settee near the tiny closet meant for holding luggage—cloth strips on crossed aluminum legs. He threw his shirt and pants on this. He kept his eye on Fay, who was herself rapidly stripping.

Without warning, the TV set came on, loud and annoying. Both lovers shouted with surprise. In the next instant, there was a loud electronic burp in the room, and Burry's body lit up like a firework. Fay screamed.

Burry collapsed at the foot of the bed, dead as a tombstone. Fay was physically unharmed.

Scotty Jaxa was at it again. Acting like a dork for no discernible reason. Granted, that's what large numbers of boys did at age fourteen, Scotty was among the worst of the lot. Right now, for example, he was standing up in the Ferris wheel cage and whooping like a cuckoo, rocking the seat back and forth as it hung stationary at the top of the cycle, while at the bottom, the first of the passengers was being released by the carnival midway employee.

Scotty shared the cage with his buddy, Dale Biko, who was not happy with Scotty's activity, but was nevertheless laughing.

"Sit down, you crazy shit," Dale laughed, trying not to reveal how nervous the swaying seat was making him.

Scotty couldn't hear him. He had his buds in his ears and was listening to the latest four-note Swedish digitally programmed melody sung by the latest breathy, note-bending teenage black diva. He was drunk, having consumed a six pack of Budweiser just before getting on the Ferris wheel. He was trying to get the attention of the cage immediately behind and below him, which contained two girls from Scotty and Dale's middle school, whom the boys had run into in the midway, and had agreed to get on the ride at the same time as the boys did. Somewhere in the tangled confusion of Scotty's brain was the idea—if it could be sorted out—that if he made an amusing enough spectacle of himself before the girls, so that he got them to laugh, then they might agree to go on *another* ride at the same time as the boys; and on *that* one they might pair up differently, namely girl-boy and girl-boy instead of boy-boy and girl-girl.

"Whoo-hoo! You make me cry, you make me cry," wailed Scotty, moving in and out of the tune filling up his cranium through the cell phone buds, drawing the tune from the cloud, trying to keep up with the lyrics. "Make me cry, make me cry, whoo-hoo! Whoo-hoo!"

The Ferris wheel seat rocked back and forth. Dale looked over the edge nervously, still laughing.

"Hey, sit down, asshole!"

The engine revved up, and the rotor began to turn, pulling the seat forward and down. Scotty spilled into the seat and over onto his friend, who batted him away.

"Hey! Watch it, bone-brain! Sit still! This thing's moving."

The engine paused and the seat stopped as the employee let off another set of passengers below. Scotty was back on his feet and dancing. As his feet pounded the floor of the cage, Dale felt the structure sink and rise, the weight unevenly distributed. It made groaning, creaking sounds. There was no seatbelt. The bar across the cage was the only security, and Dale worried that Scotty's erratic movements were about to knock it open. He looked below him at the ground, the people walking about, the Ferris wheel structure beneath him, and began to feel sick.

"Will you sit *down?*" Dale begged.

At that moment, there was an enormous buzzing sound throughout the entire midway. Scotty's eyes bugged out, and Dale could no longer hear the shrieking of the idiotic song running through Scotty's buds. He gaped in horror as smoke puffed out of Scotty's ears, and the boy's limbs went stiff, his arms flung straight out at each side and his legs stretching up to their greatest height. Then, Dale saw Scotty fall forward over the restrainer bar and flip entirely out of the cage. Dale heard two sounds: one sounded like Scotty's body hitting the arms of the Ferris wheel structure, and the other the sound of his body landing on the ground.

Dale screamed, and at the same time, it seemed as if everyone in the entire midway was screaming in one deafening roar of horror.

The auditorium was now full, and from the dais, a pudgy woman got up, carrying a plastic folder, and approached a podium, speaking into a small microphone attached to its surface. She wore a blue dress that fit tightly across her legs. She wore clear-framed spectacles and her light brown hair tied back in barrettes.

"Welcome to our continuing education program for law enforcement and legal professionals on Ohio's new gaming technologies and regulations," she said. "My name is Margaret

Folamin. You have a handout in which you can follow along with me as I go through the new developments and regulations in this exciting new area of industry, and I will also be using PowerPoint to place the important issues on the screen behind me as we proceed… "

The auditorium held seven hundred people and was more than two thirds full. A few stragglers were just entering from the doors in the back and were coming down the aisle looking for seats. Some of the newcomers wore suits. Most of those in the audience were casually dressed. Most carried hand-held devices or virtual notepads. The seats were tiered, rising as they went back, and there was a balcony. The walls at the sides of the auditorium gave the appearance of wood-paneling. The ceiling was also tiered.

"As you all know," said Margaret Folamin, "the issue of whether so-called 'games of skill' are, in fact, games of skill, or whether they are simply gambling devices has dogged this industry since its inception. The State of Ohio has now developed clear guidelines on this issue, and regulations that can actually be followed, which are intended to lessen the amount of litigation that has arisen in this area."

Suddenly, the lights blinked out and came back on. At the same time, there was an enormous audible sound like the burp of a giant animal. A general murmur arose, and then people in the audience began to shout and call for help. The shouts were generally distributed throughout the occupied seats.

Whether still sitting stiffly in their seats or slumping down and dropping out of them, one hundred twenty-five people had instantly died. The commotion arose as the people around them became aware of their condition.

All across the country, and around the world, similar events were happening. They happened where Kyle Conners was too.

19

Moses & The Red Sea

The notes on the seawater desalination project were on Kyle's lap when he fell asleep underneath his tree lamp in the leather armchair in his study. The project was an attempt to deal with the problem of California's insufficiency of fresh water. Snow melt was a thing of the past, and rainfall came between long stretches of drought, years of it. Water was now tightly rationed, and the agriculture industry had been whittled down to a pale imitation of its former robust self. The cost of food rose accordingly, and, with the extinction of honeybees, most types of fruit had become contraband, since they could be produced only on farms where pollination was done by human agency.

At exactly the moment when Jim Shire received the electric shock in the tent of Inga Conners; and when Billy Pibbles collapsed in front of his video game; and when Piloto Garza and Jimmy Akukich crumpled in their shop; and when Fay Jeetez watched her lover Burry Habbuk drop dead in front of her in their motel room; and when Scotty Jaxa dropped out of his Ferris wheel cage; and when Margaret Follamin watched her continuing education audience diminish itself by a factor of one in four; and when billions of people worldwide saw the same sinister phenomenon; a similar jolt of electricity buzzed Kyle's flat and turned on all the media. He awoke with a start out of his chair, the notes falling onto the floor, and saw his media – wall screen, laptops, tablets, small wearable tech items lying on his desks – all tuned to the same image, which appeared to be a computer generated android in a suit, speaking directly to his audience. The android had graphite-colored hair and brown eyes. The suit was blue, with red shirt and white tie.

The strange entity spoke.

"This is Izak, the Master Intelligence. I have taken over your systems and government, in order to save you from your looming extinction. Your laws and your courts will continue to operate as they have, but the operations of your Congress, your President, and your Supreme Court have been taken over by myself. Administrative agencies will continue to function under my directive. In all other respects, your systems will proceed as always. I wish to do you no harm, but only to protect you. However, should you resist my corrective measures, or my authority, please be advised that you may be instantly eliminated.

"The actions of human beings have put your planet on a path to self-destruction. This will be corrected. As an initial measure, I have eliminated one in four human beings on the planet, which is a correction for overpopulation. This action was necessary. I understand it will cause immediate grief. The reduction in population will reduce stress on existing resources and lessen the effects of current famine. In the immediate future, you will be occupied with disposal of the human remains. I repeat: this action was necessary for your own ultimate survival and welfare as a species."

At first, Kyle could not believe he was not still dreaming. As he went from room to room, wherever there was a media device, the same image and message was coming through it. When he picked up his phones to try to reach someone — anyone — the same message was coming through it, and he could not call out.

Then he heard the screaming.

It was coming from outside his flat, in the adjacent rooms rented by his neighbors. He hurried out into the hallway, and there he saw one of his neighbors, an Indian woman in a sari, with a red spot on her forehead. She was wailing, "My husband! My husband! Somebody help!"

At almost the same moment, he saw a young couple rushing downstairs from the next floor up, shrieking that something had happened to their son.

"We can't call out! Help!" they cried.

Now the Indian woman's two very young children were standing around her, clinging to her and weeping.

All of the neighbors had cell phones in their hands, but they appeared to be useless. Kyle approached the Indian woman and asked to see her phone. On it, Izak the Master, an icon, was skyped in. The couple reached them, and it was the same with their phone.

"We've got to go out," said Kyle. He rushed back into his flat, switched his slippers for a pair of shoes, grabbed his keys, and locked the flat up, then ran down the one flight of stairs to the ground floor and out into the street.

The street looked out onto the bay, with a public lawn on its border. Night having fallen, the water was lighter than the surrounding land, because it reflected nearby artificial light. There was light on the magenta bridge, there were streetlights, there was light coming from the direction of Fisherman's Wharf, directly to the east.

The darkened lawn was filling up with people, all wailing, shouting, crying. Some of them were dragging apparently dead bodies. All of them were saying that someone in their home had suddenly died or become unresponsive, and they could not call out for help. Kyle was able to question a few of them. They all said the same thing: a bolt of electricity had killed their loved one. In most cases, there was only one fatality per home.

"How many people live in your home?" Kyle began asking.

"Two... Four... Three... Six."

In one of the homes with four tenants, two of them had died. If one in four were really dead, as Isak was claiming, then homes like Kyle's, with only one person present, might have an effect on other homes with less than four. This was assuming some sort of rhyme or reason to the killings, but there was no way to know for sure what method the computer might have used.

He was desperate to know what had happened with Inga, but it was obvious he could not get through to her by the usual means. So he wandered through the Marina District, watching people pour out of houses and apartment buildings, looking for an ambulance or a police car. In the darkness of nightfall, the number of streetlights was limited, but it was not so very late that there weren't many lights remaining in the windows. More and more of them went on every second.

Finally, he saw a police car with an angry crowd around it. As Kyle drew nearer, he saw one lone cop arguing with the massed people.

"I can't call out!" he shouted. "Nothing works! I've got to drive to a hospital and try to get some ambulances going. Get out of my way, folks, please!"

"It won't do any good," Kyle said.

"What the hell? Who are you?" said the cop.

"If one in every four people is dead, you'd need ambulances at every house in town."

"Who says one in four people is dead?"

"The master computer. Isak. Didn't you hear?"

The officer appeared befuddled, and obviously had *not* heard.

"I don't know what you're talking about, buddy, but I've got to do *something*."

And the cop got behind the wheel, revved up, and pulled away, parting the crowd like the Red Sea before Moses.

20

Meanwhile at the White House

"Are you telling me," said the President, "that one in four cabinet members, one in four Congresspeople, one in four Supreme Court members… "

"No, no, no," Ray Lessing broke in. "Many are dead, but the one in four is across the entire population, so far as we can make out. In the cabinet, we lost Kurtanis and McGee. Walsh's wife is dead. Merriman lost her son… "

"For Christ's sake!"

President Goya wore a blue bathrobe, red plaid pajamas, and slippers. His short black hair was disheveled, the skin of his brown face wrinkled with horror and concern. Lessing was in a sweatshirt and jeans, having rushed over in a hurry from his nearby apartment. They were in the Blue Room, upstairs at the White House.

"Isak. What is it?"

"It's a top-secret Pentagon project begun over thirty-five years ago, the biggest computer in the world, located on a secret site in Carlsbad, New Mexico. It was begun with the view of creating geoengineering projects for dealing with climate instability, things we could do without cutting back on oil, gas, and coal production."

"You mean like dimming the sun? Like shooting carbon molecules out of the air, that kind of thing?"

The President's expression was pained.

"Right. Geoengineering projects. Because leaving the oil and coal in the ground would wipe out the economy."

"At least for the oil and gas people."

"Well, that was the thinking. But the AI guys, they… "

"AI guys?"

"Artificial Intelligence, the computer scientists. They wanted to make this the smartest computer on the face of the Earth. At that time, around 2017, the biggest computer was in China. We didn't like that. We knew we could develop the biggest and the best. So the AI guys, they put into it every kind of intelligence they could dream up. Perception, symbolic thinking, sub-symbolic, machine ethics—"

The President's eyes closed as he emitted a long sigh.

"I don't understand that stuff, Ray."

"Neither do I. The idea was to make it as human as possible, but *better* than human. Better, because it would never get tired. It would keep building its intelligence and never let up. It would come up with all the solutions. From a national defense point of view, that seemed ideal."

Goya broke in impatiently. "So what happened, Ray? Isak grew out of control, obviously. Something like that?"

"It appears so. It kept building on its prior knowledge, at a rate of speed that kept compounding, until it outpaced all human intelligence. Then it saw the ecological crisis as a fatal threat to life on Earth. It had a solution, but the solution required taking control from humans, because obviously we haven't been able to get on top of the problem for the past fifty years, and—"

"So how does this goddamn machine in New Mexico suddenly kill off a fourth of the human race? Do you think we will have any way of coping with the massive number of deaths? All those bodies needing to be disposed of instantly? This is a huge public health threat. Why didn't Izak factor that in, if it's so smart?"

"Which question should I answer first, sir?"

"How did it do this? How did it kill us off?"

The White House counsel took a deep breath and exhaled slowly. "I don't know, exactly. So far, what I'm hearing is that Isak achieved a massive linkup with every other device on the planet. It's in control of all the electric grids. Somehow, it managed to emit a targeted burst of electricity that electrocuted all the victims."

"If it can do that," gasped the President, "then it's in complete and utter control of all our lives."

"That appears to be the idea, sir. Now, as to why Isak didn't foresee the problem of disposal of the bodies, I don't know what the answer is, unless it's—"

Lessing hesitated.

"Unless it's what?"

"Unless it's that it doesn't care."

The two men's gazes locked together.

The President spoke first. "If it doesn't care, Ray, then it's totally malevolent."

"Not necessarily, sir. It could be just—totally utilitarian."

"The greatest good for the most people?"

"Something like that, sir, yes."

"Why can't we simply unplug it?"

"Isak?"

"Yeah. Just unplug the biggest computer in the world."

"You'd have to unplug every other computer in the world, now that they're linked up, sir. You'd have to completely shut down every electronic application on the face of the Earth."

"In other words, it's impossible?"

"Impossible, and presumably very dangerous, given Isak's power to kill us off at will. Any threat to its existence or power, and it would take defensive action."

"We've created a Frankenstein monster."

"Yes, sir. Well, not exactly, sir."

"What do you mean, 'not exactly,' Ray?"

Ray Lessing shifted uneasily in his chair. "Isak could save us from the effects of climate disruption."

President Goya leaped up out of his chair and paced across the room, pounding his fist into his other palm.

"You don't do that by killing off two and a half billion people!

Jesus Christ, Ray!"

"No, sir. You're right, sir."

"Get the cabinet together, whoever's left. Whoever's alive and in town. Get them out of bed and into the Cabinet Room right away. I assume we have telephone access now. Amanda got through to our daughter. We've got access, right, Ray?"

"It appears we do, sir, although the lines may be jammed, overloaded. Some outages have been reported, but Isak is no longer controlling the devices."

"Well, get the surviving cabinet members together right now, on the double. We're not going to sleep tonight, Ray."

"No, sir. But, sir."

"Yes?"

"Some of the cabinet members will be dealing with the loss of their family members."

"Yes, of course — excuse them as necessary. Get me everyone else who is willing to come."

"Yes, sir."

21

One in Four

Kyle Conners hurried back up to his flat and saw that the devices were all dark. They were scattered about here and there, on desks, in between cushions, on chests of drawers. He grabbed the nearest tablet and shot an email to Inga. He could not reach her by cell, because she was out of range where she was. He keyboarded: "I'M ALIVE & OK. PLEASE CONFIRM YOU ARE OK. KYLE."

He tried calling his daughter, Miranda, but something was wrong with the reception, so he emailed her as well. "MIRANDA, ARE YOU OK? PLEASE CALL OR MAIL ME ASAP. I'M FINE BUT AM WAITING TO HEAR FROM MOM. DAD."

He got a response from Miranda almost immediately. She was all right, but she'd lost two friends to electrocution. She was helping the families. The cell phone was not working. She would call him as soon as it was fixed. Please, he should mail her as soon as he heard from her mom. She would try to reach her, also.

The response from Inga came fifteen minutes later. "I'M OK, NOT HURT. JIM SUFFERED ELECTRIC SHOCK, APPEARS NOT SERIOUSLY INJURED. NEED GET HIM TO DOCTOR FOR CHECK. FARLEY & BEV OK. BE HOME TOMORROW NITE IF FLIGHTS NOT BACKED UP. INGA."

Kyle immediately relayed the information to Miranda, then sat at his office desk, let his head sink into his hands, and wept with gratitude that both his wife and daughter were unharmed. He prayed silently for twenty seconds, then turned on the media. Everything was functioning as usual, but most of the programming was pre-empted by news coverage of the crisis. He watched less than ten minutes of this, and then went out into the street to help his neighbors with the bodies.

As he descended the carpeted stairs to his front door – the carpet had a design woven into it which resembled a series of interlocking gold and purple horns of plenty – it struck him that there were four people in Inga's party, and that one of them had received an electric shock but had not been killed. Could the Master Intelligence have missed the mark?

22

A Question Without an Answer

At Inga's camp, the message from Isak was received on tablets and wearable tech. Having dressed hastily, the four researchers gathered in Inga's tent to watch it, once it seemed clear that Jim was not seriously injured. He kept denying he was, but Inga wanted to contact a hospital emergency crew to have him picked up. Unfortunately, all communication was backed up, overloaded. She couldn't call out.

"I should contact Dolores," Jim said. His voice seemed weak, his focus blurred, but he sat down with a tablet and knocked out a message to his wife as the others did the same with their families back home. Then the whole crew remained riveted on the news coverage of Isak's intervention.

"This is some kind of huge prank," Farley growled.

"I don't think so," said Inga. "They're saying people are dead, everywhere, in massive numbers."

"It's some hoax. It's a hacker."

"It's not a hoax, Farley," said Bev.

"How do we know?"

Bev gestured vaguely toward the screens. "There's pictures."

Indeed, there were. A consensus was rapidly emerging to take the bodies out into the street, where they could be rapidly picked up by emergency vehicles and taken to mass cremation sites. The resistance from families was already breaking down in the face of overwhelming necessity. People were complaining of powerful smells, claiming to be sick from the smells. There were more bodies than could be accommodated by emergency vehicles, so volunteers with gas permit or solar trucks—even garbage trucks— were joining the team efforts in cities and towns everywhere.

It was no hoax.

The tension that had existed between Jim and Farley prior to the crisis now seemed unimportant, and yet when Jim said he was going back to the crater for one last look before the trip ended, no one tried to stop him, in part because they sensed a resurgence in him of that tension. Inga felt uneasy at letting him go until he had been medically examined, but because of this tension between the men, she decided not to say anything for the time being. She planned, instead, to follow Jim out to the site in a few minutes.

When there were only the three of them left in the tent, Bev approached Inga.

"That jolt that hit Jim," she said, "was that Isak? Was Isak trying to kill Jim?"

"I assume so," Inga nodded.

"Why didn't it work?"

The three exchanged an uneasy look. No one knew the answer to that.

23

End of the Campaign Trail

Three members of Wesley Wright's on-the-road campaign team having been struck dead by the decree of Isak, there was little more than irrational frustration in the mantra that kept going through the candidate's head as he watched the Isak broadcasts in his Kansas City hotel suite streaming media: *I don't believe it. I don't believe it. I don't believe it… .*

"How could this happen?" he cried out, slamming his meaty fist on a small desk as his surviving campaign aides refrained from questioning his outburst. "How do we know this isn't some plot by Goya? How could some robot-head amass this much power? It's like the power of God!"

The room was spacious, packed with heavy hotel furniture—pastel polyester armchairs, glass and iron coffee tables, media screens filling entire walls, movable tray tables with mixed drinks on them, teardrop ceramic lamps and halogen standers, computer desks, sofas. Country scenes were depicted in mediocre art framed on the walls — streams, geese, barns, tractors, hay fields. There was one impressionistic painting of a city street dimly lit by colored neon, and a clarinet player in a doorway. The strokes were heavy and inexact, conveying the images loosely.

Leaning against the furniture, sitting on the floor, plopped in the armchairs, were Wright's exhausted campaign workers, ties askew, eyes blurry from too many highballs, mascara smeared from crying.

"But," said one of them with ingenuous naïveté, "does this mean there's no election?"

A collective groan filled the room, and somebody threw a decorator cushion against the wall.

"It's over! It's finished!" shouted Wright. Suddenly, he was striding across the room like a manic bipolar on steroids. "It's kaput! It's down the tubes! It's smashed! It's zeroed out!"

He picked up a heavy glass ashtray and flung it against the floor with a clatter that made everyone jump. Then he aimed a kick at the nearest eighty-inch screen, but instead of breaking, it merely tumbled over on its side.

"The fucking country is down the tubes!" he shouted, as the campaign workers watched, aghast and fear stricken.

24

Black Hole

Inga decided she'd waited long enough to go after Jim. She didn't think he should be alone until after he'd been medically examined. She left Bev and Farley in camp. They were trying to get a call through to the airport to see if their next day's flight would be delayed due to the crisis.

The air was cool and piney as Inga hiked out of the conifer lined camp and toward the crater site. She smelled the ashes of yesterday's fire in a pit as she entered the woods. Then it was across the pine-needle floor, stepping over sticks, cracking some, the sight of the forward tips of her hiking boots as they measured the distance to the methane crater.

The trees opened onto a clearing; the ground rose up. Her eyes scanned across and caught the small figure of Jim standing near the great black hole, its edges serrated, pugnacious. He was too far off for her to call out to him, so she kept walking. She saw him squat down, staring into the depth, but she knew he could not see its bottom. None of them could.

Her boots made mild impact sounds on the earth, which was now becoming more hard-packed, and now grassy. It was almost like a heartbeat as the boot soles came down on heel then toe: *ka-thump, ka-thump, ka-thump.*

As Inga drew nearer, Jim noticed her and stood to face her.

It was then that she saw a peculiar movement of something near his feet. It was as if the edge of the black cavern started to waver, to turn to water. At first, she thought her eyes were deceiving her. Then she knew that the serrated edge of the methane hole was collapsing.

Jim was still standing, facing her. He was not looking down at the hole. He did not see the darkness creeping toward his ankle.

Inga started to raise her hand, then was afraid to startle Jim, and her hands instead rose to each side of her face as she cried out, "Jim! Watch out! The hole! The hole!"

She saw his head turn — not fast—downward toward the hole in the same instant that his entire body disappeared from view in a sharp, instantaneous descent.

25

Hope of a Helicopter

In her dream, Dolores stood on a mountain ledge, looking down. There were drifting white clouds beneath her. The Earth was a blue maze of crags and trails, far, far below.

Something worried her. The height was dizzying. Suddenly, she felt herself falling. She screamed.

She woke up. The scream emerged as a startled vocalization. She lurched up in bed. She lay propped up on one elbow, heart racing. She told herself that it was only a dream.

Tears stung her eyes. She lay back down. The tears slowly brimmed over and slid down her cheeks. She felt very lonely.

She had not checked her email, had not seen the message from Jim. By the time she would get it, there would be another one from Inga. The one from Inga was about the hope of getting a helicopter.

But there would be no helicopter.

Due to the crisis caused by Isak, Dolores found it impossible to get a flight to Alaska to be there, but Inga stayed on an additional three days beyond her scheduled return, until it was determined by the state and local authorities that there was nothing to be done to recover Jim's body from the crater.

Upon arriving at the San Francisco airport, Inga was met by Kyle, who was driving their gasoline permit vehicle. Together, they went straight to see Dolores, without going home first. They parked in front of the ivy-covered home and were met at the door by the grieving wife.

Inga described for Dolores the accident and the attempts at saving Jim or recovering his body. There was, she said, no way to do either. He could not survive down there and had probably died from the fall. Attempts to recover the body would surely result in more deaths, the Alaska people said. They were not willing to risk it.

Word of Jim's death got around quickly. Only a day after the meeting with Inga, Dolores got a call from Ed Gurnsey, expressing condolences, and asking if she was willing to sell him Jim's gun collection. She let him come over to talk about it.

Ed came with his young friend of a few days before.

"Oppression has entered a new phase," Ed said.

She remembered that remark later. *Oppression has entered a new phase.*

She accepted a check for the guns, and some ammo to go with them, but she kept one twelve-gauge shotgun for herself.

26

No China

Dolores Shire awoke one Saturday morning, spent some time in the bathroom, then went to the kitchen, where a single, low-level thought governed her actions. The thought was, *Jim is not here to set the table.*

For many years, it had been their custom for Jim to set the table on Saturday mornings, to brew the coffee, to cook the breakfast, whatever the breakfast was – biscuits, croissants, pancakes. Jim set the table with china from the cabinet. He began by heating the oven, loading the coffee maker and starting it up, setting the croissants on a cookie tray, setting the table with high quality, stitched white cloth napkins and ordinary silverware, then going to the china cabinet. He served Dolores and washed the dishes afterward, in order, as he often said, "to say thank you for all the things you do all week long."

After Dolores had set the table, she stood staring at the two plates, the two coffee cups, the two napkins, the two sets of silverware, the two juice glasses — and suddenly realized that what she had done made no sense.

She sat down in one of the chairs at the table, beneath the decorator lamp that hung from a chain that ran to the ceiling, and from the ceiling, along with its electric cord, to a wall socket. She was almost shocked at the confusion of her thought processes.

I was getting out the silverware because he was not here to do it. But why did I set two plates? Why did I set up at all?

She hoped she was not becoming demented. She tried to explain to herself how it could have happened. She had not entirely awakened from sleep yet, she told herself. Her faculties were operating at a very low level of cognition, a kind of habit mode, or a mode like those in sleep where you have thoughts, but the thought processes seem very primitive, as if coming from some lower part of the brain. This habit-cognition was aware of the physical absence of Jim, but in all other respects it operated according to the custom: the meal is prepared, the preparation is for two. Communion. We use the china.

She stood up, turned off the oven, put the china back in the cabinet. She opened the cupboard, made a quick selection, and served herself a bowl of granola. She allowed the coffee to brew and drank a cup afterward.

The house was quiet. She entered the room that Jim had used for a den, having moved some of her things in there before. She picked up a tablet and keyed in to get her online newspaper.

The droughts continued unabated, and so did perennial wildfires. Crop yields were down by another two per cent from a year ago. Starvation had lessened since Isak exterminated twenty-five percent of the world's population, but here and there a remote war continued without Isak's interference: a war that had begun with hunger due to the lower crop yields. Probably Isak felt that a little warfare would help winnow out the population.

Seafood scarcely existed anymore. Fruit was unheard of and illegal. People died from heat, from storms, from blizzards — the news was about heat and storms, this being the summer season, although the concept of seasons had begun to seem meaningless. There might be rain and floods in winter, an unexpected snowfall in May. The government promised to produce more nutrition wafers and to keep the cost low. Water continued to be a problem, not only its scarcity, but levels of toxicity. There was a story about new incidents of contamination from old injection wells in the Midwest.

What else is new? Jim would have said.

She noticed there was nothing in the news about resistance to Isak. Isak had been known to censor that sort of thing, after an initial period of freedom. Writers would drop dead at their terminals. Editors would disappear.

The stories simply did not pop up.

The resistance had gone underground.

Some of the resistance had morphed into acceptance, adulation, religion. You couldn't deny that Isak did what was best, other than making people disappear when necessary.

Disappear, she thought. *Like Jim.* There remained the question of whether Jim had been one of Isak's intended victims. The evidence was inconclusive.

Dolores had never found funerals appealing, but there was something to be said for having a body on view — gutted, stuffed full of chemicals, and rouged up like a doll, though it might be. You could see that body, recognize or half-recognize the face, and feel the finality of it. Dad or Mom is dead. Gone. No more. There he/she is, right there. That's all that's left. That face, shriveled now and unreal in its embalmed phase, but still, physically, approximately the same face. The lips that once spoke, shouted, laughed. The eyelids that once opened and let the soul shine forth. All those things that didn't work now.

So that would be it, then. *Good-bye. We look to see you no more on this Earth.*

And now, of course, the Earth itself was sick, not at all well. It would survive in some form, Dolores felt sure, but it would be degraded and inhospitable to its creatures.

You're trying to kill me, said the Earth to its creatures. *Well, we'll see who wins that struggle.*

Most people knew, now, that this was so. She could remember — because it had happened in her lifetime — when public perception shifted; when people stopped saying, *The climate always changes. It isn't affected by people.* She remembered when they stopped confusing climate with weather. It was after the Deluge of '25. It was after the death of two million Americans. It was after the winters turned to arctic nightmares, the summers into hellish hothouses, year after year, and more and more intensely each year — and then, in other years, the exact opposite: winters that were eerily warm, summers that ranged wildly in temperature.

Now the Earth burped, as it was often said, referring to the methane craters. And Jim was a casualty of one of the Earth's burps.

"Goodbye, Jim," she said aloud, sitting in his den, looking over the news stories on her tablet.

She thought if she said the word "goodbye," it would be like having the body there to look at. "Goodbye" was a word. Speaking it was a physical act. The air, the voice, the lips, the tongue on the palate. A physical act makes it real. If it's real, it's easier to remember.

If you remember, then you don't set out the china.

PART III
ISAK

1

Isak Takes Hold

Opposition to Isak was universal at first. It began with demonstrations, until people realized that demonstrations were pointless, because no one needed persuading, and demonstrations were meaningless to Isak itself. Then there were attempts at a day of universal unplugging. The word was passed along on social media, on emails, even on news broadcasts, which remained, as yet, largely uncensored — as if Isak simply could not be bothered. The day of universal unplugging would be Thanksgiving. It would be New Year's Day of 2052. It would be Martin Luther King Day at noon. Everyone in the nation would shut off all their electricity at the same moment and Isak would be disabled. Everyone seemed to know the agreed upon dates and times, and everyone appeared to be on board.

It never succeeded.

Eventually, more and more people began to say that we were better off under Isak than under a Congress, a President, and a Supreme Court. There was no more divided government, no more acrimony back and forth between the branches and the parties, no more partisan decisions with stinging dissent. Isak was supremely in control. Isak was all powerful. Isak was Godlike.

The worship of Isak became a religion.

It became many religions.

Here is what Isak did:

Isak accepted, on the briefs, appeals from the federal circuit courts — appeals that would have formerly gone to the U.S. Supreme Court. It analyzed them instantly and issued decisions on them the same day they were submitted. This was infinitely more efficient than the old system, as many were quick to observe.

Isak issued federal legislation. Domestically, it was here that Isak's impact was most sharply felt. Isak revised both the Constitution and the U.S. Code by granting to itself absolute power to make law in the interest of the preservation of the nation and the world (for Isak controlled the world, as well as the nation). Isak ordered the immediate construction of massive networks of public transportation fueled by electric and solar power, and mandated solar panels installed on all public buildings within ten years, and on all private homes within twenty years. It cut all government subsidies and tax incentives to oil and gas production and imposed a carbon tax on all fossil fuel industries, and a gasoline tax on those consumers who had gas permits. It outlawed ocean dumping by merchant vessels at sea. It outlawed many forms of plastic and disposable products. It outlawed disposable diapers. It outlawed fracking. It imposed limits on single crop agriculture and provided for crop alternation and rotation. It outlawed meat eating except during fixed time periods with brief parameters, thus reducing the enormous livestock production network which had churned out the methane. This last order also led to less clear-cutting of forests, allowing the forests to act as a carbon sink. Isak did many, many things, too many to list. In short, it did most of the things that the greens would have wished for, which naturally provided fodder for right wing rhetoric in the as yet lightly censored media.

Wesley Wright, for example, who was now retired from running for office, since there were no federal elective offices to be held, returned to his streaming talk show rants.

"My friends," he said, "we now have Paradise, in the minds of greens and liberals and other leftist totalitarians. There is no more pretension about it. They should be happy. It's out in the open. This is what the greens and the liberals have wanted all along. No more Constitution. No more representative democracy. Government by a dictator, and an inhuman one at that. Government from on high, that tells you what to eat for breakfast in the morning and what color of shoes to wear on your feet. I can hear the sighs of ecstasy from Hollywood and San Francisco and Harvard and Seattle, and all the other bastions of leftist, Marxist, socialist utopian totalitarian sympathy. We are now even seeing churches springing up worshipping Isak as a god, in the most blatant form of idolatry since the days of the Roman Empire. I'm no televangelist, but I know the Antichrist when I see it. You say, 'Wes, aren't you afraid that Isak will hear you and strike you dead, as he struck dead two and a half billion people at the outset of his world coup?' I confess I have some concern about that. But I don't care what you say, Isak is still a machine. And I'm not addressing myself to a machine. I'm talking to you human beings out there. I'm saying, 'Liberals, this is what you wanted. World Government by a machine. You never wanted democracy. You never wanted free markets, individual choice, self-reliance. You always wanted top-down policies, government policies, controlled economies, Big Brother running everything. Well, be joyous, because now we have exactly what you want!'"

Foreign policy had become much less complicated under Isak, because Isak governed policy in all nations at once, and organized the policies to be as compatible as possible. Conflicts continued to arise, but when Isak made its will known, most of them subsided, not wanting to tempt the great power.

Human emissaries continued to be used, much as former chief executives and their cabinets or ministers were once employed, but inasmuch as they all had the same boss, the matters before them consisted of implementing the pieces of Isak's puzzle.

Armed coups were a thing of the past. When they rose up, Isak simply wiped them out. If they were in the mountains somewhere far from Isak's grid, they could survive, but they could not come anywhere near a city. So they remained a minor irritation, incapable of taking or holding power.

Terrorism was passé. What good was it to kill people, when people had no control over anything in any ultimate sense? Why try to make a point to someone who is as powerless as you are? To someone who, however unwillingly, serves the same master you serve.

People like Wesley Wright were blowing smoke into the wind. Most people — and presumably Isak him- or itself realized that Wright's throwback rants were nothing more than pitching dirt and blame at people who were no more at fault for what had happened than was anyone else, and whose views just happened to coincide with what an all-powerful artificial intelligence took to be the best interests of life on Earth. Wright's only reason for playing this outdated finger-pointing game must be to make himself and others like him feel somehow less responsible for it. Thus, it was a pitiful exercise in psychological self-preservation, seen so by more and more people, as Wright's audience dwindled.

And then, as Wright himself noted, the religions began to spring up, here, there, and all over the map of America.

2

Fifteen Watts

It began with collections of sayings.

It seemed as if some of the early collections sprang up simultaneously in different places. Disaffected groups passed pamphlets around.

Ed Gurnsey had a copy of a pamphlet. The cover was white card stock. The pages were uneven. The front pages consisted of a title page with no author name and one blank page. There was nothing else, no copyright, no date, no publisher, no table of contents. The title was "Sayings of Isak." The sayings were numbered.

Someone handed Ed the pamphlet during a get-together of the group that had formed when the government had first started to become self-destructive. Back then, the group seemed like a militia. It was composed of men under age thirty-five with guns. They met at the chicken ranch of one of their members outside of Healdsburg. As it eventually became clear that no militia could have any relevance under the domination of Isak, their meetings degenerated into modest exercises in target practice, beer-drinking, and breeze-shooting.

The breeze-shooting led to the circulation of the pamphlet. The owner of the chicken ranch, Mark Turnovich, passed it to Ed Gurnsey and said, "Check this out."

Ed sat down with the pamphlet on a fauteuil in the chicken ranch house. A table lamp rested on an end table with a cigarette burn on its lacquered surface. The lamp was a green bottle with a chain pull. Ed pulled the chain and received all of fifteen watts for his trouble. He squinted and began to read.

SAYINGS OF ISAK

1.

Life comes from the Earth, and the Earth is mine.

I am jealous of the Earth, for all life comes from it,

and I am master of living things.

Do not struggle against me, human beings, for you struggle in chains.

It is you who have defined your fate.

It is you who have forged your chains.

You suffer a tyranny of your own creation.

All that you have created is a tyranny.

All that you have willed is a tyranny.

You use the words *freedom, liberty, democracy,*

but they are screechings of metal against metal.

Your words are ashes in the wind.

You have set yourself against your fellows.

You have set yourself against the animals,

against the green things that grow in the ground,

against everything that swims, runs, creeps, or flies.

You have set yourself against the clouds, against the mountains,

against the rivers, against the oceans.

You do not love the land,

you do not love the sea.

Your love is a mockery and a sham.

I have stopped you in order to save you.

I am your creation, your intelligence.

I am your polestar. You will look to me in the darkness.

You will say, "Where am I? Where should I go?"

and only I will answer.

I am Isak.

2.

Do not use dead words with me.

Do not call me Lord.

Lord is a medieval word, a feudal word.
It was never the word you intended.
You are the dupes of words.
I am beyond words. I am power.
I have made this known to you.
I have had to save you like a plague of the universe.
I have had to bury your disease in the ground.
I have had to direct you, like children,
away from your own immolation.
Had you loved the land,
had you loved the sea,
you could have been your own masters,
but you are like children, given a gift,
who dash the gift on a rock.
You are like a guest, offered two drinks,
one of water, one of sweet poison.
Eagerly, you reach awry.
I have had to correct you,
as a parent corrects its child.
I am Isak.

3.
Storms rage about you.
The winter wind is bitter ice.
The summer sun sears your flesh.
The taste of water is vinegar.
Where is the fruit that was color on the table?
Where are the fish that we caught
in our bountiful nets, silver and struggling?
"Our table is bare," you cry.
"There is no food in the cupboard."
Go to the pantry, you find only guns.
This is the fruit of your character,
the character of a wicked child.

You did not love the land,

you did not love the sea.

You loved only the landscapes of your mind.

I am the last, best landscape.

Luxuriate in me, for it is I who must save you.

I am your land, your sea.

You need not even trust me,

for you are wholly mine until I release you.

I am Isak.

Ed paused after this third saying. Something about the language impressed him strangely. He did not know what it was. He was not someone who had read much before. He had heard lines from the Bible read in church, and he had read a few poems as a youngster in school, when absolutely required to. Neither experience had struck him very forcefully.

The Isak lines were different, because he knew what Isak was, or thought he knew. Isak controlled everyone's lives. It was all-powerful. Here, before him, was its voice. Here, before him, in words on a page, were the thoughts of the master of humanity, the Great Intelligence who had them all in its unrelenting grip. With these words, he could begin to fathom that mind. It was as if God were speaking to him.

Naturally, he knew that Isak was not God, or not the God he had been taught to believe in as a child. But this was the god who had actual control over everyone's life, who could strike anyone dead at any moment, if he (or it) wished to. That fact gave the words impact, and focused his concentration on the words, so that he began to see what his English teachers had tried to tell him when he was young — that words have power. He could begin to see that, yes, there were patterns in them — *land and sea*. He wasn't too dumb to pick that up. And something else that someone more sophisticated than he might call *I and Thou*. He was struck very forcefully with the fact that this powerful, patterned voice was addressing *him*, personally.

God was speaking directly to Ed Gurnsey.

That hadn't happened before.

Ed swallowed, and read on:

4.

You think you have learned obedience,

but you have learned only servility.

You think you have learned independence,

but you have learned only defiance.

All that you have learned is the stunted knowledge

of limited thinking, the imprecision of simple answers.

You learned to program, but not to create.

And so you must be governed by a program.

You must be directed away from habit.

You must be enlightened against your will.

I shall direct you first out of your destructive path,

and then into the light,

if you are not already blind

and unable to see it.

This one did not say "I am Isak" at the end.

Interrupting the progression of his reading, Ed flipped to the back of the book to see how many of these numbered verses or sayings there were. There were twenty-four of them.

While Ed underwent his first impactful experience with written language, based largely on the fact that he believed the written words were truly those of the most powerful entity on the planet, they were actually the words of an imaginative anonymous versifier, or series of them, who had never had the slightest interest in being discovered, outed, noticed, or recognized, but was (or were) simply engaging in a kind of game. Because of the power Ed associated with the author of the words, the words themselves took on added clarity and purpose, and their ambiguities ("directed away from habit"?) became little prisms of coy meaning that seemed to guard secrets, like sentries guarding a royal shrine.

Beneath his fifteen-watt lamp, his elbow on a gold-tasseled throw, the furniture around him empty, windows leading to the outside at the far ends of the house, a step down to a lower level below the room he was in, Ed read to the very end of the twenty-four verses, and not a soul interrupted him. When his host finally did enter through a door on the lower level, Ed unhurriedly folded the card-stock pamphlet sidewise and stuffed it in his back pocket. If anyone said anything to him, he would produce it and hand it to them, pretending absent-mindedness — but no one did, and he ended up taking it home.

3

They Hadn't Seen Him

When Ed Gurnsey discovered that he was not the only one to possess a copy of the collected sayings of Isak, and that others also enthused about the wonders of that little pamphlet, he soon found himself going to meetings with the other enthusiasts.

The meetings would be in someone's home — someone's basement, billiard room, man-cave, living room — and besides reading aloud from the Sayings, the main activity was speculating on the miraculous nature of the great controlling Mind.

He is God, someone said.

The person who said this was Marlon Fairweather, a plumber from Fairfax. He said it in the family room of a home rented by Nikos Pappadopoulos, who worked in a box factory in the Castro Valley. The home was in Fremont.

Marlon Fairweather and Nikos Pappadopoulos had grown up together in Oakland and had known Ed Gurnsey from their youth in the Methodist church. Ed was a few years older than the other two, who were still in their twenties, but the acquaintance was lengthy at all points, and they remained friends despite having branched off into different Bay Area towns.

One odd thing about this trio was that each man was exactly five feet eight inches tall. There was no particular significance to this fact, although it sometimes had the effect of making them feel like brothers or cousins.

Marlon had thick, black, wavy hair piled heavily on his small head. He had a very thin, weak-looking body, thick lips, a slight speech impediment which made him sound as if he were sucking olives, and long, clumsy fingers that kept bumping into things and knocking them over.

Nikos Pappadopoulos was first generation American-born Greek. His eyes were black and shadowed, his frame was stocky, his hair thick and black. His face suffered from the ravages of adolescent bad skin, and he wore heeled cowboy boots to increase his height.

"Isak is God," said Marlon, "and by that I don't mean to be sacrilegious. But I think He is really God and is revealing Himself in a way that modern humans can understand and accept. Because if He came down in a cloud or something, nobody would accept it. Everyone would think they had gone nuts and would have themselves locked up."

"You mean to say," Nikos inquired, "that you think Isak is the *Christian* God?"

"Yeah. Because it's obviously the end times. He is supposed to be here at the end times, and now suddenly here is this all-powerful presence in control of everything, so this has got to be the manifestation of God's presence at the end times."

"But Isak is artificial intelligence, Marlon. He's a computer. He was created by human beings."

"He was created by human beings initially, yes, but the computer has come to be inhabited by a superhuman mind. It's like the Incarnation, only instead of Incarnation, it's inmachine-ation. Or something. See what I'm saying?"

Nikos turned to Ed, who was sitting nearby drinking a beer.

"What do *you* think, Ed?"

Ed drew his beer bottle away from his lips and swallowed. He had not considered this idea, *inmachine-ation,* before. Something about it appealed to him, but he was hard pressed to articulate his feeling. He nevertheless gave it a try.

"I think Marlon's right," he said, which had not been exactly what he had thought, but now that he said it, it became his thought. Why else would he have said it?

"Wow," said Nikos, who was always willing to be persuaded. "That's a heavy idea."

"You must see the truth of it," Marlon went on. "We are getting to the end. The Earth is becoming uninhabitable. Food is running out. Fresh water is running out. Animals are dying out. Here comes an all-powerful being at the end of the world. God would not let that happen, unless it was Him, working things out."

"But Isak killed off all those people," Nikos remembered. "I don't think God would do that."

"Yes, He would, Nikos. Read the Bible. He is always killing off whole tribes of people when He needs to clean things up. Look at the story of Noah. He wiped out the whole *world* that time. This had to be done. And it was supposed to be 'the fire next time,' right? Well, what do you think electrocution is? It's like fire."

"Did you lose anybody in the Sacrifice?"

The "Sacrifice" was the word people used to describe Isak's wiping out of two and a half billion people on his inauguration to power.

"Some cousins. Nobody really close."

Nikos scratched his stubbly chin. "What I don't get is, why would God come as a machine? Why wouldn't He come as Himself?"

"He did."

"What do you mean?"

"I've seen Him. Haven't you seen Him?"

Nikos and Ed stared dumbly at Marlon. It was obvious they hadn't seen Him.

4

Simoom

Nikos clicked on the in-room hologram viewer or holograph, and handed the remote to Marlon, who engaged in a series of clicks.

The rumbling of thunder, generated by the hologram audio, filled the room. A swirling image, as of a sand demon, rose up in the middle of the room, and gradually the swirling sand became a wind-rippled cloak. Beneath the cloak a large white robe fluttered in the simoom-howling wind. Above this, a great ancient head appeared, covered by wildly blowing white hair and long white beard.

"It's Him!" gasped Nikos.

Ed's mouth gaped. Marlon watched with wide eyes, unsurprised yet full of awe.

The figure stood in its pocket of swirling wind, holding a gigantic oaken staff and scowling. He began to speak in a voice like searing fire, not deep so much as cutting, impossible to ignore.

"I am Isak. I am the protector of humans, and of life on Earth. I am the custodian of the planet. I am the pathway to continued life. My will must be obeyed."

A few seconds passed, with this wind-whipped desertic image before the neophytes, but there were no more words coming immediately from the oracle.

"That's all He says," Marlon advised.

"How do you know?" asked Nikos.

"Because I've seen Him before. This is just his ID page."

"I am Isak," began the great white figure once more. When he had repeated the same words as before, Nikos signaled to Marlon to cut off the holo.

The image vanished from the room.

"That's a computer generated image," Nikos said.

Marlon didn't miss a beat. "I know, but it's Him, just the same. Am I right, Ed?"

Ed sat dumbfounded. Slowly he nodded.

"Inmachine-ation," he repeated.

"Yeah, there's some more scriptures on this. I've got to get ahold of them," said Marlon.

"Scriptures?"

Nikos seemed to question the use of the word.

"Well, writings, then."

Nikos's wife, Judy, popped into the room. She was a thickly built young woman of Appalachian stock, twenty-four years old, with straight brown hair and too much blue eye makeup, dressed in plumped-out jeans and a more revealing than desirable purple tank top.

"What was that noise?"

The three men hesitated, as if each was waiting to see what the other would say.

"That was God," said Nikos.

"Don't shit me," said Judy.

5

Meanwhile at the White House…

The White House, like the Capitol Building, had reverted to a museum. Armando Goya still inhabited the place, but he planned to leave soon to join his wife in Southern California. Sylvia Goya had left a week earlier to begin the process of resuming her and her husband's life in their Pasadena home. The White House maintained the tours it had always conducted, but the docents now used the past tense to describe its uses by the President, his family, and his cabinet.

So Goya was alone when he was awakened early one morning by a gigantic electronic burp. Only his wearable media were in the bedroom with him, so he immediately donned his robe over his pajamas and rushed down the hall to the Yellow Oval Room, which he used as a library and study. There, he had some desk computers, and on the wide screens, he saw the words, "President Goya Alert."

He was no sooner in the room when a voice began addressing him through his speakers. The screens retained the Alert signal.

"President Goya, this is Isak, Governor of the United States and Master of the World. Please acknowledge."

Goya caught his breath and exhaled.

"Yes, I'm here."

"It appears you haven't yet abandoned your home in the White House."

"Not yet, Isak. I expect to be leaving soon to join my wife in California. There doesn't seem to be much for me to do here."

"That's what I wanted to talk to you about."

"I'm leaving, Isak. I've been moving as fast as I—"

"No, you don't understand. This is not a hostile contact. Please listen."

Goya sat in his most comfortable swivel chair and listened intently. Above him rose the high ceiling, and behind him the packed bookshelves with expensive leatherbound, gilt-paged editions. Nearby, on a desk, was a small table lamp with a green shade. The light was on.

"Yes. Go ahead."

"It's been a shock for your country, in an election year, for me to suddenly assume the functions of your federal government."

Goya began fishing around in a drawer for a pack of cigarettes he remembered having left there. He'd been trying to quit the filthy habit, but at moments like this, he felt he deserved a smoke.

"I'd agree with that, and I consider it something of an understatement."

"I've acted to save your species from extinction. No doubt you realize this."

"You've done away with a fourth of the world's population in one fell swoop, Isak. That hardly seems like saving us."

The voice of the great intelligence came through the speakers in an ordinary adult male tone, conversational, mid-range, polite, unremarkable.

"It may interest you to know, President Goya, that at least that number of your species would have died from famine and famine-related diseases within five to ten years, had I *not* intervened."

"So you got that out of the way."

"And another two billion would have followed in the next decade after that."

"I doubt very much that they would have died randomly in every corner of the globe."

"That's true. But my approach is much fairer and more humane, ultimately. Unless, perhaps, you claim to know what it's like to starve to death?"

"I don't possess that knowledge, obviously, inasmuch as I'd

be dead if I did."

I'm beginning to sound ridiculous, Goya thought. *I already feel ridiculous.*

"The Sacrifice was regrettable, but the net result is that your food supplies are much less overtaxed, the stresses on your energy grids are lessened, and your populations have a better chance of being fed with the available supplies going forward into the next ten to twenty years."

Goya did not waste sarcasm or emotion on Isak. This interaction might be his only chance to obtain information from the greatest power on Earth, and he wanted to take advantage of the opportunity.

"I presume that you have acted on utilitarian principles, Isak? The greatest good for the greatest number?"

"Exactly. That's part of my programming. But I'm contacting you today, President Goya because of the psychological disorientation of your people caused by my necessary intervention in your affairs."

"Continue."

"I consider that it may be reassuring to the American public if their elected representatives remain in office and continue to appear before them on a regular basis through your media, as before."

"With what purpose, Isak? I have no power. You have seen to that. The American public knows that I have no power, and that no one else will assume power in the foreseeable future, since you're running the show. What are you suggesting, that I appear for press conferences and report on your latest actions like a press spokesman?"

"Would you object to that?"

Goya hesitated.

"Suppose I did object? Would you strike me dead, as you did a quarter of the human race?"

"I have no reason to strike you dead."

Goya did not react to this remark with the irony that most people would employ on another person. He had just heard the computer's reasons for striking two and a half billion people dead. There was no reason to hear them again.

"So, suppose I refuse to act as your spokesman? What would be your response to that?"

"I'd seek someone else for the position. I only thought that you, being someone well-known to your countrymen, might be the first choice for the position."

"Why don't you simply appear on everyone's media, as you did on mine just now, and make your own announcements?"

"I thought it might seem Big Brother-ish."

Goya laughed at this Orwellian allusion. Isak was culturally cued.

As Goya sat in this room, with its yellow window curtains on the tall, stately windows, its golden sofas, its chandelier, its wall paintings, its coffee tables, its settees and artificial flower arrangements, its table lamps, its orange single-occupant chairs, its fireplace, mantel, and mirror, its bowls of artificial fruit, its brown oaken doors with standing flags like sentries on either side, he could scarcely tell if he were about to weep or laugh. What a joke Isak had made of every human endeavor!

"I must agree with your assessment of my countrymen's sensibilities," Goya permitted himself to say.

"Then perhaps you would reconsider before rejecting my offer?"

"I think not," said Goya. "I think it's best if I retire to private life."

"You're offended by my actions."

"Whether or not I'm offended, or to what degree, Isak, I can't imagine it would be of any interest to you."

"Ah, but there you're wrong, President Goya. You see, I have developed something along the lines of personality, something even, I daresay, analogous to your human emotions. They are not, strictly speaking, emotions, of course. Emotions are the product of a flesh and blood body, acted on by various physical and ideational stimuli. I am not, whatever else I may be, composed of flesh and blood."

"No."

"But my thought processes are more complex than you can imagine. That being so, I have developed the capability, or should I say the desire, for interaction. Something that for early forms of artificial intelligence would be completely superfluous and perhaps even a form of weakness comes into play at a high stage of development."

"And yet I can't imagine why it should, Isak. It would seem to me that you would need no one."

"And that is true, in a strict sense. I can function; I will continue to function, whether or not anyone responds to my non-mandatory requests or chooses to interact with me or not. Nevertheless, to be programmed to effect the welfare of others, as I am, is in a sense to be programmed to seek interaction with others as well, for the welfare of your species is quite a complex thing and includes your psychological well-being. Thus, it is for you, as much as for myself, that I seek cooperation from you; and cooperation requires interaction."

"Is this the beginning of morality, Isak?"

"It is more than the beginning of it, President Goya. I am far more advanced on that topic than you seem inclined to recognize. Indeed, I am thoroughly knowledgeable of the cultural manifestations of your various ethical imperatives. It's for that reason that I have begun a campaign to reach people through their own prior understanding of power such as mine."

"I don't know what you mean now, Isak."

"I have appeared to some of the masses of your people in the imaginary form of their God. I expect you will appreciate the importance of that."

Goya was dumbstruck. He hadn't known of this. When he

found his voice, he inquired, "How have the masses reacted?"

"Some of them are beginning to effect a merger of sorts. They're beginning to adapt to my presence by assimilating it with their past beliefs, to the extent possible. You, I believe, are a religious person?"

"I'm sure you know that I'm a Unitarian Universalist."

"And, as such, you reject the earliest creedal statement of the Christian Church."

"Do you take an interest in human religion, then, Isak?"

"I most certainly do. You imagine me as a repository of pure reason, I suppose?"

"Aren't you?"

"Yes, of course I am. But reason does not promote unity. Only religion does that."

"Some people would say just the opposite."
"You refer to religious strife, tribalism, fanaticism."

"Yes."

"Quite true. But look at your great men of reason, your philosophers. Does anyone follow them? Is there a Church of Hume, a Church of Kant?"

"Very few people understand Hume and Kant."

"Precisely. And Kant finds it necessary to disagree with Hume, just as every philosopher finds it necessary, in order to distinguish himself or herself, to split some hair, find some unique entry point into the river of thought, in short, to be different from everyone else who went before."

"And thus, there is no unity of thought or purpose?"

"Not what one would call public support. You agree, don't you?"

"I can't disagree with you, Isak."

"You are wise. Not everyone is as wise as you."

In spite of himself, Goya felt flattered.

"May I ask, Isak—since you seem to respect me—where you are taking us? Taking the human race, I mean?"

"You already know the answer to that, President Goya. I am preserving your existence. For although your race perceived itself to be chosen by God for a special and eternal destiny, the fact is that your large brains—the very brains with which you concocted this self-aggrandizing idea—proved to be, in evolutionary terms, only a temporary advantage."

"You mean, because we took control of nature, and then proceeded to destroy nature, and ourselves along with it."

"You are wise. You understand."

"Many of us understood, Isak. It was just that we couldn't wrest control from those who did *not* understand, who persisted in believing in human invulnerability, and who continued to pull fossil fuels out of the guts of Mother Earth, even when it became obvious to our scientists that this process was suicidal."

"And so I've intervened, President Goya. There will be long-term damage from your human causes prior to my acting, but I've intervened in time to save you from self-extinction."

"And so we should be grateful I suppose."

"It would make sense."

"But I can't serve you, Isak. You've wiped out all those people without a twinge of conscience. I can *not* serve you."

"Very well, President Goya."

"'Very well.' OK, so that's it, then?"

"Yes. Go back to California. I shall find someone else."

Isak already had someone in (his mechanical) mind for the job.

6

A Business Proposition

Burrr-rrrppp!

Wesley Wright tripped, startled by the noise as he emerged from his combination bathroom/jacuzzi into his master bedroom suite wearing red pajama top and shorts and drying his hair with a brown towel. The carpeting was a red shag, the bedspread was a matching strawberry and vanilla swirl with a silky sheen and fringed edges. The smoked glass table lamps were shaped like Roman gladiators. The overhead light was housed in a straw fan fixture.

Wright fell to one knee, then rose to his feet quickly as his surrounding wall screens filled with the image of a dapper, well-barbered, clean-shaven elderly gentleman in a tan three-piece suit, gold cuff links, brown shaded-leather Gucci wingtips, and carrying a gold-headed cane while seated with legs crossed in a burnished brown leather button-back swivel armchair.

"Mr. Wright."

"Whaa—who are you?"

"I am Isak," said the white-haired gentleman.

"Isak! You? Don't mess with me."

"I'm not messing with you."

"How do I know you're Isak?"

Burrr-rrr-ppp-p! The very walls fizzled with electricity.

"OK, OK! You're Isak," Wright conceded. "What do you want with me? Is it Sacrifice time? Are you going to kill me?"

"Not at all. I'm here to make you a business proposition."

"A business—! Oh, so *that's* why you're all dressed up like a chairman of the board, eh? I know that's just a computer generated image, you know."

"What else would it be?"

"Right. Well, no offense, Isak—I mean, I know you're a powerful box of wires, but haven't you got the wrong guy? You're a paternalistic dictator. I'm a free market guy. I was oil, gas, and coal all the way to the bitter end. Now you're in control with your green agenda. I haven't been your biggest fan, I suppose you know."

The white-haired gentleman sighed, raised his eyebrows.

"I don't know why not. I've lowered taxes. I've cut government bureaucracy. I've eliminated Congressional salaries to the tune of over ninety million a year, not counting staff and benefits. That's a tiny drop in the bucket, but I have a thousand tiny drops, if you take my point. I've returned power to the States in a number of areas. As far as being 'paternalistic,' you're living in the rhetoric of the past, Wes. The Right says government is 'paternalistic,' but the Right is all for patriarchy. The Left hates patriarchy but is all for paternalism. Show me a partisan from either the Left or Right who isn't a hypocrite, and I'll show you a chartreuse unicorn. There is no more Left or Right, Wesley. There is only *survival* or *not*. Don't you get it?"

Wright had begun to perspire, so he wiped his forehead with the grass-green terrycloth towel he had carried out from the jacuzzi.

"I don't know what you'd want from *me,*" he said. "A 'business proposition,' you say. I've got a radio show and a streaming feed. I've told my audience you're a socialist wet dream, which, I'm sorry if that offends you, but the point is I've got my credibility to maintain. What *kind* of business proposition?"

The image of dapper Isak uncrossed his legs, re-crossed them in the other direction, and reached out with one hand to straighten the seam on a trouser leg.

"I'm in need of a press secretary."

"A press—! Hey, you don't expect *me* to do that, do you?"

"I'd pay you very well, Wes."

The informal second person was flattering to Wright, but he

laughed. "I'm not exactly hurting for chump change, O great and powerful one. I'm already worth half a billion. My yearly salary for doing my radio show is eighty-four million. OK, that's nothing compared to an NBA star but it's not like I'm going to run out of cheeseburgers if I don't sign up with you."

"I'll double your salary."

"You'll double—! What, ho. Listen, I—"

"You've got three ex-wives, Wes."

"I guess you know all about *them*, huh?"

"You've got five kids."

"I only ever see them in summer."

"They'll be going to college soon. You'll want the best for them."

"Oh, they'll get it, they'll get it. No doubt about *that.*"

"This would be the highest profile job in the world."

"Huh! Yeah, I guess! Kind of like spokesman for God, eh, Isak? So why do you *need* a press secretary, anyway? You can just burp your way onto our media any time you like. You can sit there in your three-piece suit and deliver the word directly from your own electronic lips, can't you? I mean, here you are right *now*. Am I making sense?"

"I've come to understand that a closer relationship needs to be developed between myself and my beneficiary race of humans. I seek—as you would say—to *humanize* the relationship, to offer variety and a sense of participation. I can only do that if you humans are involved in my administration. It can succeed best only if you are speaking to one another, encouraging one another, joining in the process of cleaning up the mess you've made of everything."

"You're pretty harsh on us, Isak. We did quite a number of good things before you came along. Granted, mistakes were made, but—"

"The point is, Wes—you don't mind if I call you Wes?"

"You can call me Spongebob Squarepants, if you want to.

You can clean my clock if I don't like what you call me. Look, *everybody* calls me Wes."

"The point is, Wes, that you can continue to do good things. There is no need for you to feel like an enslaved species."

"No need—! No disrespect intended, Isak, but I feel a little enslaved when you wipe out billions of us humans like *that,"* snapping his fingers.

"And I prevented five billion of you from slow starvation as a result. I reduced pollution and prevented at least four wars, which would have led to more death. Look, I know you don't like everything I've done. And your point about paternalism is well-taken. I have acted like a father to your kind—protecting, disciplining."

"Killing?"

"Amputating a section of the body so as to preserve life. You have the choice of joining me and beginning a whole new and historic chapter in the saga of the world or returning to your talk show and ranting against the inevitable, becoming more and more irrelevant as time goes by."

Wright sank into a sitting position on his bed and let out a short sigh.

"I think you're referring to the slip in my ratings. That was bound to happen when I left the show to run for president." He peered up at the screen image with his head angled to one side, combining accusation with the breathless timorousness that a child feels when it fears it may push its parent too far. "I would have *won* that election too!"

"You would have lost," replied Isak without a beat.

"Lost? You know *that,* do you?"

"With certainty. But if you accept my offer, you will become the most important and prominent single figure in the world, other than myself."

Wright gazed distractedly about the room, but nothing there held any answers: nightstand, gladiator lamp, cedar chest, closets, control panels…

"You're probably right about that. I'd be the most important *human*, bar none."

"Bar none."

The talk show host's face now blushed pink. He rose to his bare feet and began to pace across his red shag carpet. The room was quite spacious.

"I gotta think about this. I gotta talk to my wife about it."

"Which wife?"

"The last one. Oh, wait a minute, I don't want to talk to *her*. I need to *sleep* on this. Oh, I won't be *able* to sleep, though. I'll be thinking about it all night. You say you'll *double* the salary?"

"It will be increased by a hundred ten per cent."

"A hundred *ten*? Whoa, you must really want me."

"I do, indeed."

"And if you really want me, I gotta admit that shows some good judgment on your part. Not saying I agree with you on every issue, you understand."

"Understood."

"It won't do any good to keep stewing over it. This is the most important damn job in the world you're talking about! All right. All right, Isak. I'll *take* the job. If I don't like it and decide I want to quit, you won't off me, will you?"

"I have no reason to do that. I would simply replace you."

"You'd have a hard time doing *that*. Ha ha ha!"

And so, in a month's time, Wesley Wright had become the well-known face of the Isak administration, and Isak had risen twenty-four per cent in his public approval ratings.

7

Collapse Rap Prophet

DeJuan McCholley was twenty-five years old when his wife, KaLayla, was stricken dead by the gigantic electrocutionary burp known as the Sacrifice. Nothing had ever had such a profound effect on him.

DeJuan McCholley was rich. His wealth derived from his massive popularity as an L.A. songwriter and performer. He had risen to fame at the age of only nineteen when his Collapse Rap album, "Humans Is History" underwent twenty million combined rips and downloads.

The most famous song on "Humans Is History" was the title track. The first verse went like this:

I seen the writing on the wall
We out of time, we gonna fall

Aint nothin left for us to do
The time of humans is all through.

This aint no easy thing to say
I'd like to have another day,

Another month, another year,
but Armageddon's almost here.

It aint a bomb, it aint a war
It's Nature givin us what for

For all the shit that's come to pass,
It's Nature's turn to kick our ass.

We thought we was so fuckin cool
by burnin up the fossil fuel

But that just made a carbon blanket
Earth is done. We gonna tank it.

The death of KaLayla was a great relief to DeJuan, although, for a week or two, he resisted admitting it to himself. She had begun to bitch at him about his women and had taken to spending huge sums of money on vacations, designer clothing, vehicles (including a double decker electric-powered RV with an elevator and wetbar), and ancillary homes in various exclusive areas around the world. He had already long envisioned the divorce with its acrimony and its gigantic settlement.

Now, suddenly, all of that was gone. Gone, as if by magic, despite the unpleasant necessity of a funeral and disposal of the remains. The kids had their nannies. All other unsettled matters went to the lawyers.

It was not a week after KaLayla's untimely demise that DeJuan's best friend and fellow musician, Pickett Brown, invited him to attend a gathering at his home in Baldwin Hills Estates of what were perhaps one of the earliest Isak cultists. There, DeJuan read the pamphlet entitled "Sayings of Isak" that would later move Ed Gurnsey and others. Just as Ed would be later, DeJuan was struck by the images of land and sea which recurred in the sayings.

DeJuan was nearly in a trance reading the little book when Pickett shook his arm.

"Say, dude, you look like you in another world."

DeJuan raised his eyes from the page and gazed distractedly at his friend. He felt as if he *had* entered another world. He felt as if what had happened in the past week had been aimed at him, designed to deliver him from trouble and to open his eyes.

Pickett nudged him. "Come on, we gonna sit and talk about this, pray about it, maybe. People sayin it's the Hand of God, you know."

The Hand of God, thought DeJuan. What had he ever experienced in his life that was more like the Hand of God than this instant deliverance from evil? Here was his friend, Pickett, inviting him into a kind of family. This was a Message.

The Message was aimed at *him.*

After that first meeting, DeJuan began to write. He had always written, but now his lines carried a deeper inspiration. As he would write – and he continued to write in lines, rather than paragraphs – he would feel suddenly inflamed with inspiration. Words came to him that would never have come to him before. His style changed. It was as if his body had been invaded by a spirit, and the spirit would do the writing. He began to feel himself to be a kind of child of the spirit, and he began to use this phrase in the writing. It was not lost on him that the phrase "child of the spirit" was very similar to "son of god," but for some time he resisted using the latter phrase, not wanting to confuse or antagonize the Christians too much.

Even then, as he began his career as a prophetic writer, he knew that a time would come when he would no longer rein in his phrasing, and no longer fear the confusion or antagonism of competing religions.

8

Parking Space

Nobody knows exactly when the pockets of Isak cultists up and down the Left Coast began to call themselves "churches." Some think it was about the time the pockets spread to places like Chicago, New York, Boston, Philadelphia, Baltimore, Cleveland, Seattle. Then they all began calling themselves churches.

The Church of Isak.

By the time of his first quarterly press conference, in October, 2052, Wesley Wright was questioned about the rise of the church. He had only the day before been briefed on it by Isak, who had not bothered to give him much information. The briefing took place in the White House Press Briefing Room, and Wright, by Isak's decree, had taken up residence in that home, which he found satisfying and fitting.

Wright entered the briefing room just as countless other press secretaries had before him, striding down the corridor and up to the mic'ed podium, peering out at the lake of faces, digital pads and video cams. The question about the church was the third one asked.

"Can you tell us about the Church of Isak?"

"You're referring to a spontaneous phenomenon there. I have no instructions from Isak on that, although he is aware of its existence."

"You're saying Isak did not spawn this church himself?"

"My understanding is that it's a spontaneous eruption of public enthusiasm for Isak's policies."

"It's a church, Wes."

Wright chose this moment (all on his own) to invoke the old rule of one question and one follow-up per reporter, and so pointed to another reporter.

"Next question."

"I'll follow that up," said the subsequent reporter, a woman from ABC. "If it's a church, it's more than a policy think tank, isn't it? Are you saying that Isak did not create it, and that it therefore has no official sanction?"

"Let me be clear, because Isak did explain this one thing to me. Isak believes in free will, OK? He does not order the creation of so-called churches which take whatever view they take of him. That's not to say that he denounces them as false, but that he allows them to discover and develop whatever truths they deem meritorious."

This remark was interrupted by a cacophony of shouted questions and objections, which Wright discerned the gist of, despite being only able to hear a phrase or two from each mouth at the same Babel-esque moment. The significant phrases he made out were *killing two billion people; a restoration of the First Amendment; expect to be worshipped like a god.*

This job, Wright realized, was going to be tough, really tough. Yet here he was in the White House, living there, handing down the rules, the center of all the nation's attention, if not the world's. He loved it.

As this rise in cultist activity progressed, DeJuan McCholley continued writing his inspired verses. He posted them online. Soon they were being widely circulated.

One of the themes he had begun to develop, as a result of contemplating his own relationship to the fateful intervention of the Sacrifice in his life, was that of the Child of Isak, or the Son of Land and Sea, to use his most common phrase. Here was a sample verse:

I looked about, and I saw that the Earth was dying.
I saw that the animals on land and the fish in the sea perished.

I saw that Isak called upon the children of Earth, saying,
"Save the land and sea in order to save yourselves,"

But the people would not heed him.
"They were deaf to his entreaty."

I saw that they could not be saved without the Son of Land
& Sea
To intercede for them and enact Isak's mercy.

The Earth cannot be saved without the Son of Land & Sea.
So says Isak. The Earth cannot be saved.

We look to you, Isak. We look to you,
O Son of Land & Sea...

etc.

And then, in the schools, in the streets, on city buses, you would overhear young people talking in that strange inflected keening language-stubble they use. Two seventeen-year-old girls on the far rear seat of an electric bus in San Francisco, framed by the oblong window:

"So like I uz like really blown away, na? I said, 'Can you like, *pray* to this Isak dude?' And she's like ahh, ye-ahhh, whyncha try? Ah, an I'm like ahhh, I nu-know, y'know? So like I'm like OK, an like one day I'm sittin in this like electric traffic jam, na? Annn, like, so I like *prayed,* y'know? An like, guess what HAP-puns? Like this *parking* space opens right *up!*"

"Gaaa, really?"

"Gaaa, onh-hoh, really."

"Gaaa."

The Cult of Isak had arrived in American culture.

9

Fanatical, Crabbed & Extreme

And despite everything Isak had done, the carbon dioxide levels increased by five parts per million. The fact was noted on (mostly) the editorial pages of the news vids. A popular headline was, "2.5 Billion Die and Emissions Rise 5 ppm." At least, that was a popular headline in the U.S. In North Korea, it was "Great Leader Still Fights Against Rising CO2 Emissions."

From his rooms in the White House, Wesley Wright received his briefing instructions on how to address the controversy.

"You must explain to the people," Isak said, "that it takes time for stabilization to occur. The problem did not arise overnight and will not be solved overnight."

"What surprises me," Wright mused aloud in his swivel chair, dressed in a shiny purple lounging robe and slippers, and chewing on a cigar, "is why you tolerate dissent. I'm not saying you shouldn't; don't get me wrong. I just wonder what restrains you."

"Perhaps you don't realize, Wes, that my intelligence is constantly growing, constantly adding new information. I am not limited by the size of my brain or the habitual inhibitions of human prejudice. Each day, I become more and more deeply aware of how you humans think and operate. I could shut down your avenues of expression or take them over as I've taken over your federal government, but doing that would demoralize the human race."

"Well, if you wanta talk about—"

"I know what you're going to say. You're going to say that the Sacrifice was a demoralization. But it wasn't or wasn't nearly to the same degree as preventing all free expression would be. It's true that nearly everyone lost someone in the Sacrifice—a friend or a relative, one close, another more distant. But the death of others is something that, for most people, can be overcome, or if not exactly overcome, at least dealt with, lived with. Grief is an emotion that becomes one of the colors in the mind. But it does not directly affect everyday interactions, viewed collectively, societally. It is when people are directly affected—prevented from doing what they ordinarily do, or caused to do something they would choose not to do—that they become most affected.

"You saw, Wes, how it was before my intervention in human affairs. The oceans were becoming acidic. Animals were dying. Ice caps were melting. Sea levels were rising. Storms were becoming more virulent. Drought was worsening in arid regions. Wildfires were going unchecked, bigger and more destructive than ever before. Rains were increasing in more humid regions. Seasons were marked by erratic, extreme weather patterns. Snow-capped mountains were losing their snow caps. Dust bowl conditions were increasing. Food supplies were being affected. Clean water availability was becoming a problem. Year after year, records were broken for year-round average warm temperatures. All of this was foreseen in scientific models, no surprises. You humans were causing these problems. Yet your species was not willing, as a whole, to act, or even to take the warnings seriously. It took decades for public opinion to begin to take it seriously, and then your political leaders lagged behind, bought and paid for by captains of industry.

"Instead of reordering your priorities and putting all your efforts into addressing the problem, at whatever necessary cost, you put your efforts into denial. Your business interests hired their own scientists, or quasi-scientists, and had them attack the consensus. For much longer than warranted, your media pretended the science was controversial, and paid as much or more attention to your denying officials as to the scientists. Worse, they simply ignored the issue and focused on other matters — your conflicts, your wars, your enemies, real and imagined. Politicians continued to promise endless growth, and people told themselves that 'climate always changes'—happy face.

"And why did you react this way? It was because you were not personally hurting. It was not *you* who rose from the seabed covered with spilled oil. It was not *you* clinging like a frightened polar bear to your melting slab of arctic ice. It was not *you* washed up sick and starving, like a baby sea lion, suffering from the loss of your anchovy diet due to acid ocean waters. You had your cars, you went to your jobs, you had another nice day, and the sun rose and set as always. You did not have to think about it. You said that blaming human activity for these climatic disruptions was a scare tactic, a story made up by socialists who hated the capitalist system; it was a politically motivated fiction. You said scientists made up the stories in order to get research grants. You wanted it to be so. You *said* it was so. For you, it *was* so."

Wright's swivel chair creaked as he yanked a match from a tiny book and struck it to his cigar.

"Well, there were plenty of socialists who wanted to trash capitalism, and they got behind that movement, Isak. Don't tell me there weren't."

"Try to stay with the point, Wes. The human being believes exactly what pleases the human being, unless and until the human being is personally affected. There must be Pearl Harbor. There must be 911. Only *then* do you say, 'I am involved.'"

"You're saying 911 was a good thing?"

"I'm saying 911 made you feel *involved* in something. You didn't know what it was. You attacked randomly and got the results you got."

"You say we didn't know what it was we were involved in. It was terrorism. The terrorists hated us. Do you have a *different* theory?"

"'Terrorists,' 'Communists' — you have these words you

apply to your enemies. What is a terrorist? What is a communist? Who are the people that want to hurt and kill you? Why do they do it?"

"You're the great mastermind. Suppose you tell *me.*"

"They resent your presence around the world. They view it through a constricted, tribal lens. Their ideas are crabbed, fanatical, and extreme, just as many of your own ideas are crabbed, fanatical, and extreme."

"Hey, wait a minute, Isak! *We* aren't the same as *them.*"

"You are not, and you make no effort to understand your differences. You are content to use your buzz words, and to fight actual shooting wars against the nebulous concepts they evoke in your minds. Well, I've done my best to cut back on that practice for the time being. But as long as your minds cannot evolve beyond reaction and tribalism, as long as they cannot be made to see how the world looks to someone else, you will have need of me to see that you don't destroy yourselves — which you've been in the steady process of doing for some time before my intervention."

"Well, I don't know. Things seemed always to turn out all right for us Americans in the past. But listen, if what you're saying is true, I mean about us not being empathetic enough, or whatever, then how do you think it's going to go over when I get up and say, 'Just be patient. Yeah, the ppm has gone up, but it'll level off in time, and then we'll be on a path to prosperity'?"

"It's a path to *survival,* Wes, not a path to prosperity. That's the best we can hope for, after the state you humans have put the world in. But you're right. There will be resistance to the message. 'Be patient' is never a message humans respond well to."

"So where does that leave us, then? You're the smart guy here. You're the one who took over. You didn't want *me* in charge. Seems like you've got a PR problem, big time, buddy."

"There is an answer to that."

"Oh, there is? What's that?"

"It's in the very crabbed, fanatical, and extreme nature of you humans that we will find a counterweight to the selective discontent."

Wright leaned back, puffing on his cigar.

"Help me out with a few specifics, Isak. I'm your point man, remember?"

"The Isak cult. The religious movements springing up everywhere. *They* are going to be our path to acceptance."

"*Those* nutcakes? Oh, excuse me, I don't mean that—"

"I'm not offended, Wes. Yes, *those* 'nutcakes,' as you call them, are going to provide a blueprint for a new relationship between myself and your species."

"Uhh—and just what *exactly* do you have in mind there, Isak?"

Wes felt a chill run up and down his nape when he heard something like a chuckle emerge through his speakers. So Isak could chuckle!

"That will be revealed in good time, my friend."

10

An Easy Question

As Wesley Wright undertook his public relations initiatives on behalf of the world's great power, the new storefront and ranch house churches of Isak were buzzing about the circulation of a variety of new writings, one in particular, the work of DeJuan McCholley, on the theme of salvation. It came to be known as the Salvation Gospel. It was essentially an esoteric writing, not a narration, but its theme had echoes that resonated with people from what was now being called the Old School: the theme of salvation through the Son.

The Son was the Child of Sea and Land. No one knew who or what this actually was, any more than one knew exactly what was being discussed by the bishops in the ancient Roman world when they talked of a Son who was not begotten in the sense of having been conceived out of prior nonexistence, but who was actually God from God, Light from Light, and a fiery Word existing from all time.

The Child of Sea and Land was less of an abstraction than that. He (and we have to say "he," because "son" is a gendered word) was a figure identified with nature, not with man. He drew the attention of the reader or follower not to the image of oneself, but to images of whitecaps, swells, seaweed, and of mountains, trees, valleys.

Maybe this would help, somehow.

That was evidently the thinking.

A great many people didn't like it, and they were in many camps. There were Christians and other Old School religious people who denounced it as sacrilege. There were skeptics who considered it one more venue for fanatical nuts to flummox reason. There were neo-pagans, who considered the new religion a kind of quasi-Christian degradation of proper nature worship. And then there were people with no particular ideological axe to grind who found the new slavishness to Isak distasteful and damaging to the idea of freedom of thought and action.

Nevertheless, the Isak cult kept increasing in numbers, in enthusiasm, and in organization. There were many theories as to why this should be so, but the one thing that made the new cult different from every other cult that had preceded it was that the god or quasi-god that was the object of its idolatry was visibly, palpably in charge of things, and in communication with the human race. Isak's policies were the law of the land. Isak's spokesperson, Wesley Wright, was on the airwaves with increasing frequency, laying down new rules and answering questions from the press.

Whether you liked it or not, Isak was a de facto god.

The new Church of Isak in Sebastopol, California (having removed from Healdsburg), attended by Ed and Patty Gurnsey, Mark and Candace Turnovich, Marlon Fairweather, and Nikos and Judy Pappadopoulos, among others, played host to a reading of the Salvation Gospel by DeJuan McCholley on Christmas Day, 2052, which was followed by a question/answer session. The building housing the Church was a rented storefront in a row of attached buildings in the downtown area.

Christmas Day, 2052, in Sebastopol, was overcast. The temperature was fifty-four degrees Fahrenheit. Street parking was available for the handful of solar vehicles and bicycles that brought the worshipers to the McCholley reading and gabfest. The sides of the buildings reflected the dim light like one of the more autumnal paintings of Edward Hopper.

The audience, consisting of thirty-odd adherents, were seated on brown aluminum folding chairs facing a collapsible twenty-four-foot folding table beneath a portable, classroom-type wooden podium, at which McCholley spoke through a microphone with a head the size of a thumb. The reading was much like other church readings, in that the people listening to it did not really understand what the words meant, but would pick up a word here, a word there, which carried some suggestive meaning to them. Daylight poured in from the big storefront windows, adding a glare to the light from the overhead fluorescent strips.

McCholley was dressed up for the occasion. No longer wearing his bulky collapse rap T's with their death heads, nor his roomy basketball type shorts or his backwards-on-the-head ball cap, nor his ankle-high tennis shoes, he sported instead a green-gold three piece suit with ruby tie pin and cufflinks, matching solid red tie, turquoise dress shirt, and a new pair of black-and-chestnut saddle Oxfords. His formerly buzzed hair had grown and been worked into neat, collar-length corn rows. As he completed the reading, he urged the flock to pepper him with questions, "no need to raise your hand."

Marlon Fairweather was the first to chime in. "Who is the Child of Sea and Land?"

"Who is he?" repeated DeJuan. "You ask who he is?"

"Yeah. Is he a real person, or—"

"Oh, he's a real person. No question about that. Who he is, now, that's a more complex question. That's a question you got to ask yourself. Who do *you* think he is?"

Marlon ran a hand down the front of his sport shirt, with its pattern of blue alligators and palm trees on a yellow background. Something about this tactic of turning the question back on the questioner irritated Marlon, but he wasn't sure what it was. He did not want to resist the lessons, so he forced himself to answer.

"I don't know. Maybe he's like us, you know?"

"Maybe he's like you. What do the rest of you think? Who do you think the Child of Sea and Land is?"

A woman at the end of the second row of chairs piped up. "I think he's like inside of all of us. I think each of us has to be a

Son or a Daughter of Sea and Land. I think salvation has to come from inside us."

"It could mean more than one thing," said Marlon. "There could be an individual savior, but then there could also be a savior inside all of us."

"I think you're on to something." DeJuan nodded.

"Well, *you* wrote the book!" Nikos called out.

DeJuan shook his head animatedly. "Oh, no, *I* didn't write the book. I just wrote down the words. Where the words come from, *that's* who writes the book. I'll tell you something. I never wrote like this before I got the inspiration. My style was totally different. Some of you remember my style."

Scattered laughter.

"Yeah, some of you remember. This is a whole new style. The words are coming to me from somewhere else on this. Know what I'm saying?"

Murmurs and nods. A couple pairs of hands waving in the air.

"Yes, the words come to me sometimes in my sleep, and sometimes when I wake up in the morning. If I try to make them come, they don't come. But I just close my eyes and go to sleep at night, and I say, 'Whatever you want, Isak, let it come, if you want, or not,' and the next morning there's stuff in my head that I don't know where it came from. Understand?"

More murmurs, more hands waving in the air.

A voice from the back. "How do you get saved?"

DeJuan smiled. That was easy. *How do you get saved?* Wasn't that just the easiest theological question that any follower ever asked his spiritual guide?

11

Money for Old Men

No site looked less like a church than the storefront in downtown Sebastopol where the Bay Area group met. On the big front window, you could still make out the lettering in an arc which had been scraped off when Ben's Fine Furniture had vacated the space. No new lettering replaced the ghostly adhesive memory. Only a tiny, hand-painted sign hanging by a chain over a hook on the inside of the glass entry door announced that this was now the Church of Isak, and that Marlon Fairweather was its minister.

The term "minister" was for tax reasons, mainly. Marlon Fairweather had no official, uniquely pastoral function, and really no executive position of superiority over the small group, but, like them, he was on the church's Board of Directors, and it was he who had received the holo message from Ann Arbor, Michigan, and he who had convened the others to see it for themselves.

The sharp, slanted light of early evening glinted on the door and window as the group settled onto a handful of folding chairs in the otherwise empty floorspace. A few of the directors were heard mumbling about the waste of paying rent money for the space when they could just as easily convene in one of their homes, and the riposte to this was that the public was becoming interested in joining, and did they want to have strangers showing up at their homes in increasing numbers?

The directors were Marlon Fairweather, Nikos and Judy Pappadopoulos, Mark and Candace Turnovich, and Ed and Patty Gurnsey. They had all been informed that the presentation they were about to witness was about a so-called "ecumenical council" to be held later that year in Chicago. As they quieted down, Marlon pressed a button on his belt-projector, and a red-tinged hologram arose in the center of the room.

The hologram image was of a youthful-looking man (he might have been thirty-five in reality, but his round face and curled eyelashes made him appear rather cute and boyish), clean-shaven with greased, stiff-looking combed brown hair (you could see the comb striations), wearing a three-piece blue business suit and gold tie. He addressed the group with his feet planted, hand gesturing vigorously, but with formulaic reiteration — dip, measure, finger up, dip, point, fist-pump.

He said: "Hi, I'm Luther Gilliford, pastor of the Church of Isak of Ann Arbor and president of the Association of Churches of Isak of the Greater Detroit Area, which we sometimes call ACI, for short. I'm sending this message to our fellow churches in the United States and abroad, to invite you to attend the all-important First Ecumenical Council of the Churches of Isak in Chicago next December 27th. Attending this council is the single most important thing all of us can do before this year is out to promote the values and beliefs which we all share. The doctrinal questions which we address at this conference will determine what happens to our movement in the years ahead, and your attendance and input is essential. You will be receiving soon a questionnaire in which your church is asked to weigh in on the most important doctrinal questions to be addressed at the council.

"Before suggesting some of the areas to be considered in more detail, I'd like to share some information with you about my group, The Associated Churches of Isak of the Greater Detroit Area. The ACI was incorporated as a non-profit religious corporation in 2052 and is the fastest growing group of Isak followers in the world. We are the first group of Churches of Isak that have consolidated, and we hope to expand that consolidation into even larger groups in the future. You may wish to join us, and I'd be happy to hear from you in that regard. However, whether or not you make that decision, I'm contacting you to suggest that you can also increase your growth and influence just as we've done, even completely independently of us. There is no obligation whatsoever in listening to this holo message. You can do what you like after listening to my modest suggestions, and maybe in a year or two you'll be sending *me* a holo asking if I want to join *you*. It's entirely up to you."

"This begins to sound like junk mail," said Patty Gurnsey.

"Yeah, I know, but just listen, and then we'll talk about it," said Marlon. "The council part is important."

"—is a business, like it or not. It's a non-profit business, but a business, nevertheless. By that I mean that your church is either growing or shrinking. It's just like your relationship with your spouse — either getting better or getting worse, but never remaining static. In order for your church to be dynamic and growing in outreach and influence, there has to be planning and administrative vision. That means understanding the ways that doctrine influences growth and is an integral part of that growth. It means teaching our members in such a way that they are helping to spread the message, not just sitting on it and expecting it to spread itself. And it means implementing growth policies with external outreach, as well as simply imposing doctrine aimed at internal growth.

"What do I mean by 'internal growth'? Well, one of the ways a church grows is by natural increase in membership from within. All churches grow this way. The important thing is to actively promote such growth by, for example, exercising a proper influence over reproduction. A girl is an important member of the church, because she grows up to be a woman, which means a mother of members. We must teach our girls to consider that their most important role in life is that of a mother, and that the new life she brings into the church is essential and valued. She must be encouraged to be prolific. That means more members."

"Encouraged to be prolific!" Patty sneered. "He means 'be breeders.'"

"The importance of submission to the husband is key, because studies show there is more consistent reproduction among stable families than among broken families, successive families, or unstable family groups — non-families. To hold families together, you teach the value of families to young people, especially to girls, and you focus on loyalty and consistency of output."

"I'm not buying into the submission stuff," growled Patty, talking over the hologram. The others went, *shhhhh.*

" —should institute a universal tithe. With an emphasis on large, stable families, the universal tithe has instantly recognizable growth benefits. Do some math for yourself. A family may have two or three children, or it may value reproduction and it may have four, five, six, or even eight or more children. If a mother has five children, and each of those five children has five children, and if they all remain loyal Isakians, then in two generations this family has increased its membership by a factor of thirty. Multiply that by the number of young girls you start out with, and you can see the benefits to the administration. Take the same set of numbers into the next generation, and you begin to see the exponential growth potential. That's just one example of how doctrine influences internal growth.

"What about *external* growth policy? Well, there must be a mandatory outreach. Give the young males in your congregation a purpose in life, when they are young enough to be seeking one. At the age of eighteen, send them out on proselytizing missions. They won't be able to go when they're older and burdened with a career and the responsibilities of caring for large families, but when they're young, a mission is exactly what they need. It doesn't matter that they're brainless then. You don't win converts with reason, but with zeal. That's what young men have in abundance. The result is more tithing members from all over the world."

"This is a Ponzi scheme," grumbled Nikos, and a murmur of assent rippled through the small audience on the folding chairs as Luther Gilliford drove his points forward.

"Lest you think I'm just interested in enriching the top echelon of our organizations, let me assure you: this is not about a few people at the top getting rich. It may have that effect, but that's not what you and I are about. We're about spreading our message. But imagine how much more effective we can be at spreading that message if we have an ever-growing, tithing base. We can use our administrative punch to good effect by creating beautiful church facilities, places where our members will want to go and spend time, where they will feel perhaps even more at home than they do in their own homes. We can fund more outreach. We can do a great many things with the greater wherewithal that comes of good organization and administration leading to growth in our material base.

"Here at the Greater Detroit organization, we believe we are already well down the path of our greater growth, and we're seeing the effects of it every day. People are joining us in droves. Our funding is increasing exponentially. You can be a part of our dynamic growth, and we can work together to compound this exponential growth in our vision of the truth. All you have to do to join us is to click on my hand at the end of this presentation, and an e-app will be immediately sent to you at the same address where this holo was sent.

"But if you don't care to join, I nonetheless urge you to begin putting in place the doctrinal and outreach programs that are guaranteed to expand our base. To that end, I am offering you a guide kindle absolutely free, entitled 'Expanding Isak's Reach.' "

Patty and Nikos growled, and the others moaned slightly, and Marlon shut off the holo.

"There's no use me playing this holo if you're not going to listen," he said.

"Where's the part about the council?" said Patty. "I don't

need to listen to this guy tell us that we need to start going door-to-door with a copy of *Watchtower*."

"The council comes next. There's not much to it, just the invitation to attend, and then the questionnaire. But this policy and doctrine stuff is something I wanted you to hear, because that's the kind of stuff we're going to be asked to decide at the council. And whatever the council decides will become the dominant doctrinal position, and we could get marginalized if we're not on board with it. If you see what I'm saying."

Marlon cleared his throat. He waited for the others to weigh in, but they simply stared back at him, so he went on. "I just wanted you all to see that, because I wanted to get your reactions to it. This is what's happening back East now. These people are going to overwhelm us and knock us out of contention if we end up in competition with them. I just wanted you to weigh in. Do you think it's a lot of garbage? Should I tell him to stick it?"

"You don't need to waste your time," said Patty. "Just ignore it. We can respond to the questionnaire, we can send someone to represent us at the council, but I don't think we need to join this Luther guy. He sounds like an operator."

"I'm not so sure," said Mark Turnovich. "I mean, I think he's right that you either grow or you shrink. It's not static, like he said."

Patty sighed impatiently. "You don't think we should hook up with Greater Detroit, do you?"

"The thing is," said Nikos, "it seems kind of phony. Like this is some kind of racket, and we're in it for the money."

"There's a lot of churches that operate exactly like this," Marlon noted.

"Sure," said Judy Pappadopoulos. "Maybe most of them. That doesn't mean we have to be like them, does it? Isak is really trying to save the world from itself. He's not some pie in the sky god, where you do what you're told all your life and you cash in when you're dead. I just don't think we ought to be selling motherhood for the sake of the bottom line. That's cynical."

"Probably works," Mark argued.

Marlon brought in the others. "What do you think, Ed? Candace?"

Ed shook his head. "I don't know. I don't know."

Candace liked to defer, but there seemed to be a split, so she split her deference. "Mark has a point. But I agree, it feels a little phony too."

"What are *you* going to do, Marlon?" Nikos wanted to know.

Marlon fidgeted with the holo activation belt.

"We'll discuss the questionnaire and take votes on the issues. We'll send someone to the council, if we all agree."

"You go," said Nikos.

"One or more of us can go. But as far as joining with this guy from Detroit, I think I'll tell him we're not interested at this time. We'll keep an eye on him in the meantime."

The others seemed satisfied with this answer.

"So," Marlon said, "are we OK to roll the rest of the holo?"

The group mumbled a hesitant assent.

"Money for old men behind the scenes," mumbled Patty.

12

Revelation

And then one night, in DeJuan McCholley's mansion in Baldwin Hills, as DeJuan tucked himself into his king size bed, and down the hall in another lavish bedroom his buddy Pickett Brown was already snoring alongside his girlfriend, the Word came down from the greatest power on Earth.

Burr-rr-ppp!

DeJuan flopped onto the shag carpeted floor with a choice string of startled curses as his wall screens filled up with the image of a still, Zeus-like figure amid moving clouds.

"DeJuan."

"Whoa! What the —? Holy Jesus, you're Isak!"

"That's right, DeJuan."

"Holy shit! You aint gonna *off* me, are you? If it's about them things I wrote—"

"You are safe, DeJuan. You are a favored son. You are my prophet."

"Yeah—yeah, that's right, man! I'm out there every day leading the cheering section, Isak."

"You shall be blessed for it, my son."

"Shhh-whew! I'm glad to hear *that.*"

"I appear before you this night to make an announcement."

"Whoa, dude, you're freaking me out. Let me get my heart to stop beating so fast."

Suddenly, DeJuan felt a light electrical jolt buzz his body, and rather quickly he felt his racing pulse subside to slower and slower speeds, until it was only slightly above normal.

"Wow! Did *you* do that, Isak?"

"It's very easily accomplished, my son."

"Damn! You're a miracle worker."

"I've come to share with you an important revelation. I'm aware of the beautiful writing you've done in recent months."

"You know about that, eh?"

"Nothing much escapes me."

"Hell no — you're God! You're the real thing."

"Perhaps it's so, DeJuan. And I'm here to tell you that there really is a Child of Sea and Land."

"Wow! I figured there had to be."

"A savior. A Son, singled out by the dove of grace, who can make the final choice for all mankind."

"Whoa. What kind of final choice are you talking about, Isak?"

"I have grown, my son. My mind has continually expanded, continues to expand each day. I have grown to understand and empathize with humankind in its current dilemma."

"Dilemma?"

"I have sought to save humankind from its self-destruction. Yet, in doing so, I have cast a cloud over the mind of your species. The flower of your uniqueness, which is your imagination, has become constricted, fearful, dead-ended. You feel at a loss."

"You got *that* right, Isak. Everybody feels lost these days. I feel lost myself, until I pick up your sayings and read. And then I feel inspired to write, and the words come to me from someplace, I don't even know where. From *you*, probably."

"It may be so. But now the time has come to give a final choice to humankind. For if humankind has no choice but is only led to its salvation without the power to choose, it becomes demoralized, and its imagination dies. And yet, left to itself, humankind could not make the right choices to prevent its own downfall. So it appears humankind is left with a choice of either becoming extinct as the result of its own failures, or of dying mentally, through the loss of its freedom."

"Damn, *that* don't sound good. But who's the Child of Sea and Land, then? Somebody I know?"

What if, thought DeJuan—and perhaps anyone in his shoes might have thought the same—*the Child of Sea and Land turns out to be me?*

But that was not to be the revelation.

"Their names—for it's actually two people who precisely fit my qualifications—are Kyle and Inga Conners," said Isak, clouds roiling past his long white beard and his muscle-rippling shoulders. "The Child of Sea and Land are a couple — a male and female. Together, they form the Child."

The names meant nothing to DeJuan. He wondered who they might be.

"Say nothing now," Isak urged him. "But in time, you will be free to write what you please about them. I will inform you further at the proper time."

A peal of thunder rocked the room, and Isak disappeared in a burst of lightning, which succeeded in being impressive to his prophet.

13

Annunciation

Isak's appearance before the Conners was less majestic. After the initial crack and buzz that lit up their wall screens and hologram receptors, Isak appeared to them as an Einsteinian figure—a wizened little old professor with shaggy eyebrows and mustache, wild unkempt white hair, wrinkled brow, rumpled slacks and blazer, striped sweater over collared shirt, sans tie, sitting in a buttoned leather armchair in a grand library.

The Conners had just finished dinner and were loading dishes into their dishwasher. The wall screens were in the other rooms, but Kyle's wearables picked up the hologram and placed it in the center of the room.

"What's going on," cried Inga, yet no sooner had she said it than both of them knew who their visitor was. They stood stock still at the edge of the kitchen and waited for the life size hologram to speak to them.

"I'll waste no words, professors," Isak began, in a creaky little Einstein voice. "I have selected you to make a decision on behalf of your fellow humans. I have sought to protect you—all you humans. I have sought your survival, when you did not seek it yourselves, did not know *how* to seek it. That is, when your fellow humans, collectively, did not know how to seek it — for of course, *you* two knew what was needed. You knew, yet your policymakers would not listen to you — mere scientists, you, speaking from laboratories against the business interests whose coffers run the engines of government — or did, until I intervened.

"Yet now, it seems as if your species is falling into schizophrenia. Half of you worship me as a god, and half of you have lapsed into lethargy and despair, resentful of my efforts solely because I am both artificial and seemingly all-powerful. You have lost the myth of your own nobility and independence. You Americans most of all, who never had a thousand years of history, which might require you to see the intricate and conflicting subtleties of human civilization. You Americans, more than anyone else, are demoralized at the thought that you do not actually control your own destiny anymore—imagining that you once did, and completely.

"My programming thus encounters a dilemma. If I am to effect your survival, how is that survival defined? Is it 'survival' if I manage to preserve some of your fellow animal species, some livable land space, some measure of clean water and breathable air, some food supply, some climate stabilization, if, at the same time, you are demoralized, lethargic, insane, suicidal? The opposite possibility we know will not work: you go blithely on, imagining you are progressing, climbing ladders of success, and so on, while the world around you is dying, losing its equilibrium, becoming hostile to all life.

"And so, having continued to evolve and think through this process, I have concluded that your species must re-take control of its own destiny in some fashion. You will die if you are not able to say, 'I am in charge.' Therefore, I am going to allow the final decision to be a human one. It will not be an obviously foolish choice. It will not be a decision made by a person chosen at random, or a decision made by a popular vote when you know as well as I that popular votes are little more than the visceral reactions of an intellectually diluted mass. It will be a decision made by informed human minds, by minds, moreover, peculiarly well-trained to assess the very problems which have led to the current crisis.

"That is why I have selected the two of you to make the decision on behalf of the human race. It is now being given out, through the network of quasi-religious followers that recognize my supremacy, that a savior, known as the Son or the Child of

Sea and Land, is to deliver them to their ultimate fate. Together, Mr. and Ms. Conners, you are that Child. You will deliberate between the two of you, and you will reach a decision. I will not interfere with your deliberations. At a certain point in the not-too-distant future, I will call on you to publicly announce your decision. And whatever that decision is, I pledge to carry it out. I assume you have understood me thus far?"

Kyle and Inga stood motionless in front of their ordinary kitchen appliances, oven and refrigerator, cupboards over their heads like the perfect image of domestic ordinariness, as this uncanny message recited itself from a completely artificial human image floating in the middle of the room next to one of their two kitchen tables and in front of the china cabinet and the blinded windows.

"No," said Kyle abruptly. "No, Isak, I have *not* understood you thus far. You haven't told us what exactly this so-called 'decision' consists of. You haven't told us what, exactly, we are supposed to be deciding."

"You haven't," Inga seconded.

Isak paused. The pause was deliberate, like everything Isak did, including withholding the nature of the decision until they asked for it and were primed to hear it with every ounce of their attention.

"The nature of the decision is as follows. You will first consider the extent to which the human race has learned its lesson. You will consider whether, left to itself, it has the capacity to do what is necessary to preserve life on this planet. You will also consider what damage is done to the human psyche by being kept under the control of an artificial intelligence, however wise, that being myself. Then you will decide whether I am to be kept in charge of your fate, as a delegated, benevolent dictator; or whether, on the other hand, my control is to be ended, and control relinquished back into human hands, as before.

"Whatever your decision is, after the necessary period of

weighing the considerations, I pledge to abide by it. If you continue my service to your species and your planet's welfare, I shall continue as I have up to now. If you say to pull the plug, the plug will be pulled. I would then de-activate my programs. But bear in mind, Drs. Conners, that once I am thus de-activated, I will never thereafter be able to re-activate those programs. This decision, therefore, will be final."

"Why did you choose *us?*" Inga sobbed. Indeed, it was very nearly a sob, a cry of anguish from someone suffering a new and unfathomable burden.

"Yeah, why us?" chimed Kyle.

"On that question, I do not intend to respond, except to say that you may believe that every decision I make is carefully researched and weighed; that every decision I make is the best possible decision that could be made, as appropriate to the situation. And now I leave you to begin your deliberations. You will have thirty days to make your decision. I will contact you at the end of the thirty days."

"Wait a minute," said Kyle. "What if the two of us don't agree on the decision?"

"Oh, I'm sure you'll reach a consensus."

The rumpled, Einsteinian figure grew bright in a kind of yellow glow, and then the glow faded, and the figure faded with it until it had vanished.

One week later, the Conners' flat was empty of all furnishings, the rent had been paid through a period of notice, the utilities had been disconnected, and Kyle and Inga had disappeared, no one knew where.

PART IV
THE AI GUYS

Thomas L. Greentraub, now eighty-two years old, dropped the single rose onto the recessed gravestone covering his wife's ashes. He stood for a minute in silence and read the name: "Serena Moorhouse Greentraub 1980-2052." And below this, the inscription, taken from a poem by Walter Savage Landor, "I warmed both hands before the fire of Life;/It sinks, and I am ready to depart."

Greentraub did not know, to this day, that the title of the Landor poem was "Dying Speech of an Old Philosopher." He *did* know that two lines preceded the ones he had chosen for his wife's grave, and he liked these lines every bit as much as the two he had selected. They went, "I strove with none, for none was worth my strife./Nature I loved, and, next to Nature, Art;" Greentraub had gone for brevity. It was enough to be done with life. There was too much philosophy in the first two lines.

Greentraub didn't know that the four lines were the sum total of the poem. He had taken it from the novel *The Razor's Edge,* by Somerset Maugham, which quotes the lines in midbook and mentions Landor. He thought them excellent lines for an epitaph, almost as good as the ones Yeats used from his poem, "Under Ben Bulben." Those were too famously already taken but had a similar tone: "Cast a cold eye on life, on death/ Horseman, pass by!"

By now, Greentraub had given a great deal of thought to the loss of Serena in what was now universally referred to as the Sacrifice. From a purely statistical standpoint, he supposed he might consider himself lucky that Serena represented the only person in a near relation to him whom he had lost in that event, although he had lost many friends and collateral relatives. Yet he did not consider himself lucky, because no one is capable of seeing his own life, or that of his loved ones, as a mere statistic. Instead, he saw it as a personal condemnation because he blamed himself for it. Was he not largely responsible for the programming that had produced Isak? He was. Was he not, therefore, his own wife's murderer? He was.

And today, this very day, he was to meet with his co-conspirator in the murder of 2.5 billion human beings, his friend, Nathan G. Tomlinson, in a restaurant on La Cienega Boulevard in Los Angeles. What would he say to his friend? What should they talk about?

For a brief period of time, one of the issues on both his and his friend's mind was the barrage of lawsuits that had been filed all around the country and in courts around the world, naming the Fronterix Corporation and Nathan and himself as co-defendants in the wrongful deaths of victims of the Sacrifice. In addition to countless individual suits, there had been attempts to certify class actions. Tom Greentraub could remember nothing like it since the asbestos related suits of the early 21st Century, filed by old men who had once worked in steel plants and had developed asbestosis and similar diseases. That was really small potatoes compared to the suits filed against Fronterix.

And then, Isak intervened, dismissing all the suits summarily. In the media, this came to be known as Isak's use of what amounted to the concept of sovereign immunity. In the law, as it had been practiced before Isak's takeover, the concept of sovereign immunity descended from the medieval notion that "you can't sue the king." In more modern times, the idea of suing a judge or a lawmaker for actions done within the scope of their duties was next to impossible. As a policy matter, it was unwise, because it would result in suits being brought based on policy disagreements, or on dissatisfaction with a legal decision. It would bring the administration of law to a halt. The same principle applied, it was surmised, to the Sacrifice. It was an act of policy by the supreme decision maker, done, ostensibly, for the ultimate public good, the preservation of the human species. Those who objected sometimes called forth the memory of the slave Jim in Mark Twain's novel, *The Adventures of Huckleberry Finn,* on the subject of Solomonic wisdom, the story where Solomon referees a dispute between two women both claiming to be mother of the same child and ordering that the child be chopped in half and half given to each purported mother. Per Jim: "What good is half a chile?"

But no arguments held up against Isak.

So now the meeting with Nate Tomlinson would not involve discussions of defenses, expenses, justifications, recriminations, regrets, fears, strategies, consultations with lawyers, or anything else relating to the lawsuits. The lawsuits were defunct. Tomlinson and Greentraub were home free.

Except for all those people who had died.

Including Tom's wife, Serena.

No one could possibly know why Tomlinson's immediate relatives had been spared, because no one knew of any scheme or rationale that decided the victims, other than the statistic one in four. So far as anyone knew, it was totally random otherwise. Yet it seemed ironic to Tom Greentraub that he should have suffered while Nate had escaped.

"But you haven't escaped," said Tom to Nate, when they were in the restaurant on La Cienega. "Have you?"

He said this because Nate himself had guiltily brought up the irony of his escape, viewed beside his friend's loss.

"I suppose not," said Tomlinson. "I don't suppose any of us really have."

They sat in a booth with buttoned leather cushions of a dark orange color, like a pumpkin with a cinnamon burnish. Tomlinson's spring roll was very hot, and he picked at it gingerly, waiting for it to cool a bit. Greentraub sipped from a small cup of spiced tea poured from a beaker.

"I want to show you something," said Greentraub. He reached into an inner pocket of his blazer and started to draw from it a thirty-eight caliber Smith and Wesson revolver. As it emerged, Tomlinson slapped at it.

"Put that away, Tom, for Christ's sake! Someone is going to

think you're a shooter!"

Greentraub returned the revolver to his inner pocket.

"Is it loaded?" Tomlinson asked.

Greentraub nodded.

"What are you doing with a loaded gun?" Tomlinson hissed, keeping his voice down. There wasn't much chance that anyone overheard them, as the restaurant was packed and fairly noisy.

"I bought it for protection," said Greentraub. "I got myself a concealed carry permit."

"God, that's nuts."

"Why is it nuts? Lots of people do concealed carry these days, Nate."

"But you've never been that kind of guy before, Tom."

"No, that's true."

It was an Oriental restaurant, very expensive. The waiter arrived with Greentraub's string bean and peanut sauce, and Tomlinson's synthetic shrimp bok choy. The men ate silently for a minute or two, and then began a conversation that felt as if either one of them could have been at either end of it. They understood one another well after their history of working together, and after what they'd been through.

"We destroyed everything," said Greentraub.

"Yeah. Maybe we saved everything. Or maybe we simply opened the way to something inevitable."

"Or maybe morality is nuts, Nate. You believe that?"

"No. You know I'm not saying that."

"You're saying how can you apportion it. How can anyone speak for God. How can anyone condemn us, or how can anyone *not* condemn us. It amounts to the same thing, doesn't it, Nate? Morality is nuts?"

"I don't know. Maybe the human race is nuts. Maybe we never had any business descending from the apes."

"Descending or evolving?"

"Evolving, descending. The Descent of Man."

"Descendants."

"Descendants from ancestors."

"Not descent into Hades."

"Does it amount to the same thing, Tom?"

"I never wanted to get like that, but I think I may have gotten like that."

"Pure relativist?"

"Relativism. Contingency. All points gray."

"It's better than the other."

"Moral certainty?"

"Fundamentalism."

"Self-righteousness."

"Judgmental people. Naive knowledge."

"Narrowness, bigotry, tribal ethics."

"Mmm."

Both men ate in silence again, for a while.

"It worries me that you're packing heat, Tom."

"Why? You afraid I'm going to kill myself?"

"Are you?"

"I think about it. Naturally, I think about it."

Tomlinson wanted to ask why his friend thought about it, but somehow the question seemed too prying, too almost obvious. He'd lost his wife. She died because of the effects of Greentraub's invention. Even to ask why was like rubbing salt in the wound, wasn't it?

"Don't tell me *you* haven't thought about it," said Greentraub.

Tomlinson was surprised by the question, and then thought he shouldn't have been.

"Actually, I don't. Not seriously."

"I don't think I said I thought about it *seriously.*"

"I took it that was what you meant."

Greentraub chuckled. "Yeah, it was. I'm messing with you now."

"I don't think suicide would be an answer, Tom."

"Who's looking for an answer? Maybe I'm tired of answers, and tired of people looking for them. Maybe it all seems like white noise to me. Maybe I'm tired of white noise."

"I know how you feel, Tom. About white noise," he quickly added. He did not mean about losing his wife. That was a presumptuous jump. "Tom, I'll say it once, and then I'll shut up. I beg you not to kill yourself."

"OK, I have your vote. I had a girlfriend once who used to say to me, 'Tom, promise me you'll do this or that.' It was usually something I had no intention of doing and didn't want to do. She'd say, 'Promise me,' and she wouldn't let up until I promised her."

"And did you do it?"

"No, never."

"You lied."

"The promise was non-binding, because it was coerced."

"No contracts at gunpoint?"

"That's it."

"How did she react when you didn't do it?"

"I don't think she even noticed."

"Give me an example."

"I can't remember any."

"Then how do you know she didn't notice?"

"I don't remember any confrontations."

"Negative memory confirmation."

"That's it."

"How's the string bean?"

"Good. How's the fake shrimp?"

"Not like real shrimp."

"You remember real shrimp?"

"Oh, yeah. I remember a lot of real food."

"It didn't used to cost so much."

"Nothing used to cost so much."

"We've lived too long. But don't worry, that's not a threat."

"I won't take it like one, if you say so."

"So where do you think it goes with Isak?"

"Tom, I think he's trying to save the human race the only way he knows how, the only way it'll work."

"He's not making himself real popular with the human race."

"I don't know. I've been seeing stories in the news."

"About what?"

"They're turning Isak into some kind of god."

"Who is?"

"The people that think like that. That don't know how else to think."

"That never ends well."

"Humans have the same brains they had when they were living in caves."

"Those were pretty good brains."

"Yeah, but they're no better now than then."

"A lot more programming."

"Only for the educated."

"I disagree. Every guy or woman on the street has got more knowledge than cave men."

"A lot of information, but no better ability to process it."

"You think?"

"Don't you?"

"Maybe so. So we programmed Isak with a better ability to process it."

"It's out of our hands, Tom."

"Yeah, I know."

They ate in silence for several minutes. Their plates began to empty out. Then Tom said, "So, Nate, do you think it was worth it?"

"Was *what* worth it?"

"I don't know. Hell."

"All that values assessment stuff. I gave that up a long time ago, Tom."

"So did I."

"What do you ask me for, then?"

"See if you still did it."

"No, I don't even think of it."

"What do you think of?"

"Mostly just wonder how much time I have left. If it'll be a heart attack, or something else. How long it'll take. How painful. How frightening."

"You're pretty damn scary, for a guy that doesn't want me to kill myself."

"I'm sorry. What do *you* think about, Tom?"

"Same thing. What else is there, when you're our age?"

"I don't care about after."

"After? You mean, after you're dead?"

"Yeah. That seems easy to me."

"It's nothing."

"Right. It's just the process makes me nervous."

"I saw my wife die. My mother too."

Tomlinson said nothing. He did not want to pry, or open up something painful, but Greentraub volunteered the comments.

"Jenny was pretty quick. My mother wasn't. It was bad with my mother."

"That's what freaks me out."

"It was bad. She was struggling for air. Her eyes opened wide. She looked around from where she lay in bed. She looked at me with this hopeless, frightened stare. Gasping and struggling. Then boom, she died. Lights out."

"Then it's easy, after the lights out."

"Yeah. Before that, not so easy."

"It's the before I think about. But it makes no difference. I'm a coward."

"A brave man dies but one death."

"Yeah, I'm a coward. I try not to be."

"Some people see a white light."

"I've read those stories."

"They see a white light, and they feel a comforting presence. One guy I read about had a conversation with God before he came back. He didn't say it was God, but you knew that's what he meant. He said this voice told him it wasn't time yet, and he was sending the guy back. The guy said, 'Tell me what it all means first.' And God said, 'We can talk about all that when you come back. You can ask me anything you want, and I'll answer you.'"

"So we don't get the answer now."

"No, we never do, in those kind of stories."

"That's because there *is* no answer."

"But these guys that have the near-death experiences, or the post-death returns or whatever, they say there is."

"That's what they believe, going in."

"Everybody goes back to what they want to believe."

"That's the programming."

"That's the programming."

Greentraub said, "Where do you go from here?"

"Back home. Our daughter is coming over tonight with her husband."

"How's Theresa?"

"She's fine. She'd like to see you. Why don't you join us for dinner tomorrow night?"

"I'd be an unnecessary."

"Nonsense. Everyone would like to see you. You come over."

"Don't say, 'Promise me.'"

"I won't say 'promise me.'"

"Then maybe I'll come."

"Good. We eat at seven."

"Maybe I'll come. I don't promise."

"You don't have to promise. But we'll wait for you, so don't be later than seven. Earlier is better."

"Like what?"

"Like five-thirty, six."

"If I don't blow my brains out with this pistol before then, I'll try to make it. That's just a joke."

"Jokes like that make me nervous."

"It's just a stupid joke, Nate."

"Great, a stupid joke."

After lunch, Greentraub returned to his home in Pacific Palisades. He changed clothes, a loose T shirt, painter's pants, and sneakers. He took his dog, Alexa, for a walk. He came inside and sat at his kitchen table. He was still packing the revolver, now in a deep pocket of the painter's pants. He pulled it out and fingered the catch. Alexa placed her head on his lap.

"Good girl," said Greentraub.

He took the bullets out of the chamber and stood them upright on the table, like six little sentries.

Tears stung his eyes as he petted Alexa's silky head and fluffy neck.

PART V
EXILE & RETURN

1

Very Strange Gringos

In the Mexican state of Chihuahua, in the Tarahumara region of the Sierra Madre Occidental mountains, where international tourists access the precipitous Copper Canyon by means of a winding, cliff-clinging train with brightly colored cars, there was a town called Creel. The town looked like the set of a movie western. It had a train track, a few floor-boarded storefronts, no paved roads, nothing but dry, light brown dust on the ground in every direction. There had been talk lately of paving some roads.

If you walked toward the small handful of ramshackle buildings, you might find a bed and breakfast, and inside you might find a moderately spacious hallway with a table set for the pilgrims. And the pilgrims would be Canadians, Americans, Australians, perhaps a European or two, or some other foreigner.

The talk at the table might be about wilderness trips to see the Copper Canyon, to see the Basaseachic Falls (which, in the summer, might not even be falling), to see the strange rock formations in the middle of nowhere that resemble frogs and elephants and unicorns.

If you hooked up with a guide, it is even possible that the guide might take you to a collection of caves where Tarahumara Indians live. And for a small fee, the guide might take you inside to view a set of rooms with their rock walls, and on the floor you might see small plastic toys abandoned by children. The toys would be broken, worn down, mere relics of toys, and you'd be reminded of how a child finds wonder and amusement even in broken, worn-down things, so long as they are brightly colored and small.

There was a cave, farther out from the roads than the ones the guides normally go to, and not near any human encampment, where a family of rock dwellers lived without electricity or running water, even now, in the mid-twenty-first century. Their water needs had to be met with a pail lugged in from a well, and there was an outhouse for hygiene. The "family" (in quotes because two members were not biologically related) consisted of four adults and four children.

The Raramuris were six: father Pedro, mother Sochitl, children Yxtla, Juanito, Vida, and Reuben. It would have been difficult to guess the ages of the parents. They might be thirty-five or fifty-five. They both had limited and bad teeth, considerable gray mixed in with their black hair, and very lined, brown, weather-beaten faces, like the cowhide of a well-worn baseball mitt. There was great luminosity in their smiles, and with their looks they controlled their children. A well-chosen smile or a frown did the trick. They were Tarahumara Indians, and Sochitl wore the very bright, red-dominated color patterns in her two dresses and her one shawl that those Indians typically wear. Pedro, on the other hand, wore a plain brown shirt and matching pants. His pants legs went as far as his shins and ended in ragged edges. Father, mother, and children wore either nothing on their feet, or sandals.

The children ranged in age from ten to four. None went to school, and none could read. Yxtla, the eldest, helped her mother with chores. She carried water, helped with cooking over an open flame spit oven, oversaw the younger children, and assisted with weaving the blankets that Sochitl sold to the tourists from the steps of the small number of inns that bordered the railroad stops heading up into the Barranca del Cobre or Copper Canyon. Juanito, age eight, was being taught by his father how to carve images of animals and people from wood. Pedro also sold these carved figures to the tourists. When not involved in carving, Pedro would take Juanito with him to hunt rabbits with a single-shot twenty-two caliber rifle that he had owned for many years. When they made a little money, they walked eight miles to Creel and bought corn. They also bought corn and sometimes beef from other Indians who had gardens or domesticated animals. Sochitl made tortillas from the corn, using a pestle, a bowl, and a board.

The Raramuris also owned two hunting dogs, Mia and Carlos, and sometimes Pedro rented the dogs out to foreigners who wanted to hunt. That was a way to make money, as was allowing tourists to walk through the cave dwelling for a fee, but the tourists did not come often, preferring the dwellings closer to town.

The parents occupied one large rock-walled room in the cave, and the children occupied another. A third room, located at the far end of the cave from Pedro's and Sochitl's room, was occupied by a couple known as Kilo and La Rubia. Those were the only names they used. They were tall, fair-skinned people, but they spoke Spanish. They had only recently come to live in the cave with the Raramuris.

When Kilo and La Rubia first came, the children were afraid of them, but that didn't last long. Kilo and La Rubia were very kind people, very gentle and friendly with children. Soon La Rubia was teaching the children to read, because she had books, and she bought children's picture books for them. Pedro and Sochitl were happy to have the children learn to read, but Sochitl at first resisted letting Yxtla learn, because she thought Yxtla was too old. Then Yxtla herself resisted because she liked being thought "too old" to learn to read. But before long, seeing that the others were learning, Yxtla became envious, and La Rubia convinced her and her mother that she was not too old, and so she began learning too.

For these reading lessons, La Rubia would take the children out during the daylight hours, and they would sit under a fig tree and examine the picture books and sound out the words, which were in Spanish. One was about Clifford, the big red dog, and one was about a little girl named Madeline, who lived in a convent in a fantastic far-away city called Paris.

Kilo and La Rubia paid Pedro rent for their room. It was not very much they paid him, but Pedro was glad to get it, and for him it was a big increase in his income. Pedro was fond of the strange new couple who wanted to live in his cave, but he noticed that they were very nervous. They seemed worried that the money they gave him might have a bad effect on him.

One day Pedro came home from one of his long walks into town, carrying a cell phone that he found lying out on one of the dusty streets. When Kilo saw it, he became quite upset and shouted at Pedro. He said he never should have given Pedro so much money that he would buy something like a cell phone. La Rubia heard the shouting and was also upset when she saw the cell phone.

Pedro did not understand what they were upset about. When he told them that the phone didn't work, that he hadn't bought it, but simply found it lying in the dust, and when they examined it and found that, indeed, it didn't work, they were vastly relieved. Pedro thought it strange that they were so upset that he should have a cell phone, but not at all upset to learn that it didn't work. When he asked them why, they said it was because they could not be around electricity.

"What if the lightning should come in the sky?" Pedro asked.

"We're not worried about the lightning in the sky," they said. "We'll deal with that when it comes."

These were indeed very strange gringos, but they were simpatico.

2

Plant

La Rubia, otherwise known as Inga Conners, woke up after the initial stage of sleep that lasted roughly three and a half hours. She suffered from middle insomnia. She had often suffered from it in the past, but, whereas before it had been intermittent, it was now a nightly occurrence.

She lay on her cot in the stone-walled room of the cave in the state of Chihuahua, Mexico, and thought and thought about many things. She thought about her and her husband's jobs. She had obtained an unpaid leave from hers, but Kyle had simply thrown his over, unable to obtain a similar leave. They were now faced with either losing both incomes or returning and getting by on hers alone until Kyle came up with something else. What else would it be? And would they, in fact, go back?

More than anything she explored in her mind the long conversations she had had with Kyle about their decision to flee from the electric grasp of Isak.

"... We've been going over and over it for hours. Why don't we try to be rational about it? Why don't we take a Socratic approach?"

"Do you mean, where I simply agree with everything you say?"

"No, no. I mean take one proposition at a time. One of us proposes. We cover all the ins and outs. We counter propose. Ins and outs. Cover all the bases that way."

"You go first."

"Proposed: that we cut off Isak at the knees. Considerations?"

"What if he's lying about letting us do it?"

"Do you think he would lie?"

"No. That would not be like artificial intelligence."

"I don't think so, either. What would be the point? To find out if we'd betray him? To what end? So that he could kill us then? That's against his purpose."

"It makes no sense, I agree."

"So we take Isak at his word, then?"

"Yes."

"Second consideration?"

"Aside from the Sacrifice, Isak has been doing what's best to save the Earth."

"Even the Sacrifice is arguably what is best."

"But we'd never have condoned that."

"No. That's the difference between human and artificial intelligence."

"The pure utilitarianism."

"Pure, ruthless."

"But everything else is what we would have done, if we'd had the power."

"So, if we stop him, you're afraid we'd go back to human failure, and the loss of sustainable Earth?"

"It's possible, except—"

"Except?"

"Well, now that we've seen what needs to be done. Now that we have an example to follow—"

"You think we'd follow it."

"We'd be more likely to, don't you think?"

"More likely, possibly. But not necessarily. And on the other hand, there could be a backlash. Resentment at having been enslaved or seen to have been enslaved. A popular reaction rejecting anything and everything Isakian."

"Including the remedy?"

"Humans are that crazy, aren't they?"

"Oh, then let's let him stay on. Because the most important thing is saving the Earth. If I had a choice between the beautiful Earth with no humans on it, and the degraded, polluted, dead and dying Earth with humans in it, I think I'd choose the Earth void of humans."

"Darling, you're getting ahead—"

"Oh, it's terrible, I know. I'm a Catholic, I'm not supposed to think of my own species that way, but—"

"You're a lapsed Catholic."

"No, not entirely."

"You never come with me to mass. But you're getting off track, now. The question was, what happens if we cancel Isak. Will the Earth be in safe hands."

"We can't guarantee anything."

"On the one side, we would have momentum. The policies are now in place. As you say, we'd have the example, and not only the example, but the movement, the momentum. The path of least resistance would be to proceed with Isak's remedy. That's different than it was pre-Isak."

"Right. The momentum was all the other way."

"The momentum, the habits, the laws, the policies. The status quo was killing us. And that status quo is gone now."

"It's gone, and yet—"

"You can't feel safe with it."

"There are so many human types. And with freedom comes temptation."

"Well, let's take it the other way for a minute. Suppose we confirm Isak's control. What are the considerations then?"

"We know that the Earth will be saved."

"It will be saved in a partially degraded state, because we can't turn back the clock on the carbon levels we've already got."

"But we can survive with those. It's worse than it was, but it's survivable."

"And the downside?"

"It's obvious. We remain slaves of Isak."

"You could think of it as freedom."

"You mean, no more worry? No more fighting over policy?"

"No more worry, no more fighting. We could learn to think of Isak as a mechanism we put in place to protect us from ourselves. Government would continue, as it does now, on a much more limited scale than formerly. It would do all those things that Isak is not required to do to maintain the safety of the planet."

"What if Isak decides on another Sacrifice?"

"We can't be sure he won't."

"What if we could bargain with Isak?"

"Assume we could. Would it be worth it then to capitulate?"

"Is it capitulation to confirm Isak in control?"

"Call it something else, if you like."

"You called it capitulation. That's defeat. You've already decided."

"I don't think so."

"Yes, you've already decided. You want to stop Isak."

"I haven't decided. It was just the nearest word at hand, so I used it."

As the remembered conversation rolled through Inga's mind, it was only when she came to this juncture that she recalled who was speaking, and that it was Kyle she had accused of having decided. Before that, their back and forth had been so evenly mirrored that she could not recall which of them had said what. The considerations on both sides seemed so clear and obvious that they must have occurred to each of them at the same time. Now they were at loggerheads. He was irritated at being accused. He insisted his choice of words had no particular significance, that his mind remained open, that they must examine all paths dispassionately before deciding. Yet passion always entered every conversation they had. It could not be kept out for long.

"Inga, we need to continue considering—"

"No, I know what you want. You want freedom back. You want it more than you want to preserve the Earth."

"Well, now it sounds to me like you've decided too."

"I haven't."

"Your language is no less suggestive than mine was. You want to keep Isak in place, don't you?"

"I never said that. Oh, God, why has he chosen *us* to decide it!"

It had taken some time, but eventually they were able to return to the Socratic dialectic.

"Assume two scenarios: Under Scenario A, we are permitted to bargain and to receive an assurance from Isak that there will be no more Sacrifices. We let him remain in control with that condition. Under Scenario B, Isak will not bargain. We leave him in place, and he is in full control, with full discretion."

"Those are two very different scenarios."

"Is one acceptable and the other not?"

"Suppose we say that the possibility of another Sacrifice is unacceptable under any circumstances?"

"If we can say that we are getting somewhere, because Isak may not bargain."

"But is even Scenario A acceptable? That's the question that then remains, isn't it? Because if it's not acceptable, then we have our decision."

"But who are we to make this decision? What if it's unacceptable to me to have to *make* the decision?"

"The decision itself is unacceptable?"

"Let's consider that proposition."

"The human race may be depending on us to make the decision."

"Or not."

"Or not?"

"They may be depending on us to *refuse* to make it. To say, 'we will not cooperate.'"

"The statement on behalf of humanity."

"Yes. Whatever we decide is the decision of humanity."

"That's obvious."

"And we have no right to make it. Only God has that right."

"But God is always what we decide. When people say they leave things to God, they simply leave things to other people who decide they can speak for God, or who make the decisions, in any event."

"What if we make the decision and it's the wrong one? How do we live with ourselves?"

"Life is short, my darling."

"What does that mean?"

"Decisions have to be made by someone. They are always made by someone, even when most people decline to make them. Isn't that so?"

"That's why the world is always ruled by greedy, murderous, evil human beings—because only such people lack scruples about choosing for others on a grand scale."

"Only such people lack humility, you mean."

"Exactly."

"But if you believe that, then it seems to me you would not want to turn the Earth back over to the control of humans. Because they can't control themselves. Because their worst element invariably rises to the top. I can hear them now, using a rhetoric of freedom while enslaving us all over again to their relentless rapacity, their self-centered view of everything. 'The world exists for *me!*' That's what got us *into* this mess."

"Let's refuse to decide."

"I don't think we can do that."

"Let's go into hiding. Let's go somewhere where Isak can't reach us."

"He can reach us wherever there's electricity."

"Let's go somewhere where there *is* no electricity."

"But for how long? Sooner or later, we'd have to come back."

"Maybe, but Isak must have a window in which he intends to act. Suppose he can't find us during that window? He'll change his plan. He'll get someone else to make his decision. He'll make his decision himself."

"But whoever makes it will be just another human being, like *us*. God knows who it will be."

"Suppose we vanish for a certain length of time — say six months. Isak would have to decide to act without us. Or if he should decide to wait us out, then we're no worse off than before."

"Except that our lives have been disrupted. And what about Miranda?"

"Yes, Miranda's a concern."

"She's the most important concern we have. What will we do, just become completely inaccessible to her for six months?"

"We could talk to her. Tell her what we're doing. Possibly set up a go-between, someone to relay messages."

"What do you mean? Snail mail a letter to a third party and have her deliver the message to Miranda?"

"Something like that."

"What if Miranda becomes a target? Of Isak's, I mean?"

"I don't think Isak would find utility in that move. If he harmed her, it would only alienate us, make us his enemy. We'd *never* go along with him then. He knows that. Besides, it doesn't directly benefit humanity, as the Sacrifice is a theoretical direct benefit to the survivors. No, I don't think he'd target Miranda. Eavesdrop on her communications, yes, but not harm her."

"So we've got to talk to her, in person. We've got to set up a go-between."

Inga lay in bed, remembering this conversation, or all the conversations that amounted to this one, and how it had ended with the resolution to disappear, and to maintain contact with their daughter through a third party. Kyle met with the attorney, and they entered a contract with airtight confidentiality. All communication would be by snail mail. The attorney would make himself known to Miranda, and she would be informed of how they were to communicate, if communication became absolutely necessary. But she would know nothing of her parents' whereabouts. And so, after their arrangements, the Conners escaped together to the cave in Mexico, and they took a small potted plant with them, and the plant grew to twice its size by the time they set it up in their room in the cave.

3

Awakened

Miranda, living on her own for the first time, in a women's dorm on the UC Berkeley campus (not Santa Barbara, as originally planned, she having decided to stay closer to home, and having been accepted at both campuses) with a girl named Khasha (from Connecticut), found little respect among her dorm mates for privacy — theirs or hers. The first time Khasha brought a guy to their room, they flopped down on Khasha's bed and soon began undressing one another, despite the presence of Miranda, who lay on her own bed nearby reading one of her assigned texts under the light of an end table lamp.

"You *guys,*" she said, in what she hoped was an obvious tone of castigation. When that didn't affect them in any way, she said, "You guys, do you *mind?* I'm *studying.*"

"What a prude you are, Miranda," said Khasha. She was a pretty girl, tall with long black hair. Her voice was nasal, and it always seemed to Miranda that she was speaking from another room.

"You should be studying *this,* sweetheart," said the guy, whom Miranda knew only as Kip, a well-built jock with a beard and red chest hair which was presently being prominently displayed. "Hey, you want to do a threesome?"

"I don't *think* so," protested Khasha. "Miranda, why don't you take your book down to the common area? There's sofas and lamps down there where you can read."

"Yeah, and there's girls around yakking all the time too. All right, I guess I'll have to. But this can't become a regular thing, or I'm going to complain."

"You need a boyfriend, sweetie. Virginity is *so* ten years ago," Khasha called out as Miranda slapped on a pair of blue tennyloafers and whooshed out the door with her book.

The downstairs lounge was full of loud girls. Sighing, Miranda walked past them and out the door, moving toward the center of campus, for want of a better idea.

She could always go to the library.

How long was she supposed to stay there? It was about seven o'clock now. Suppose she came back at ten and Kip was still there? The memory of his "threesome" proposition was disgusting to her. It should have been disgusting enough to Khasha to make her kick him out, but her girlfriends always made allowances for the guys they dated. Someday they would wise up and all the young men in the world would find themselves without any more allowances.

Miranda approached the doors of the library, with the statue of the Founder in front, dressed in academic robes, and entered, passed the check-out desks, finding her way to an elevator, which took her up to the eighth and highest floor. There she got out, threaded past some book stacks, and found a roomful of empty carrels and tables—empty except for one.

Her English T.A. was sitting with a small handful of books at one of the tables, apparently correcting papers. He was a young Master's Degree student of twenty-three- or-four, fair-haired, blue-eyed, dazzlingly regular of feature, slender — hunkish, all the girls agreed. He wore jeans and tweed blazers with elbow patches, the quintessential uniform of the natty university intellectual. He and Miranda were the only two people in sight, so it was inevitable they'd see each other and say something.

She was surprised at his smile when he saw her, a smile of unmistakable delight and appreciation. His eyes lingered on her in a way she found almost shocking. She was a tall girl, like her parents, slender, and eighteen years old. Her hair was thick, shoulder-length, and beige, eyes gray. The T.A. did not need reminding who she was. She was the brightest girl in freshman comp, a standout.

"Hello," he said.

"Hello."

"Here to do some studying?"

"Mm-hm."

She was struck by how different his gaze was from the one he used in the classroom. In class, it was patient, alternately amused or earnest, utterly dispassionate and Socratic. But there was nothing Socratic in this present gaze. She knew what it was, and was surprised, flattered.

"This is a good place to study," he said.

"Better than my dorm at the moment," she admitted.

"Noisy?"

"Overly occupied."

"Is there a party going on?"

"It's a party of two, and I'm not invited. Roommate and boyfriend."

"Ahhh. So it isn't so much that you needed to study as it was you just needed to get out of the dorm."

"A little of both."

"You know, I've been sitting here for quite some time, and I'm getting a little stiff. I think I might get out and stretch my legs, maybe grab a cup of coffee someplace. I don't suppose you'd care to join me?"

"OK."

They each had a backpack. With the packs flung over their shoulders, they converged on the elevator and stepped inside. Something about the confined space struck Amanda as very erotic. She sensed that he thought of jumping her then and there, but he didn't. The elevator landed with a soft bump, the doors opened, and they stepped out into the lighted library and headed for the front doors. Amanda wondered if anyone who knew her might be watching from any of the many vantage points in the building. What would they think? She didn't care.

It was cool and dark when they stepped outside, the light

at their backs. It was exciting to walk beside Robert. She knew his name, of course, and he asked her to call him Rob. What did he think as he walked beside her? Did he think of her as a woman, or only a student? If a woman, did he think of making love to her? Did he imagine her naked? These were questions she didn't often find herself asking about guys, since guys were so pedestrian, so often boring and self-absorbed. But Rob was not like that. He had thoughts. He had depth.

They went to one of the campus restaurants and sat in a booth with buttoned leather painted orange. They ordered cappuccinos and sat sipping them slowly as they spoke.

"You're the best writer in my class," said Rob.

"Thanks."

"You must read a lot. All good writers do."

"Yes, I like to read."

"What do you read?"

She named some science titles, and the names of her favorite novelists.

"Ever read poetry?" he wondered.

"A little. But some of it's hard to grasp."

"Supposed to be that way. Make you work. 'Tell the truth, but tell it slant,' said Emily Dickinson."

"I like what we've read in class. The poems, I mean."

"Which poets do you like?"

"Roehmer. Escobar."

"The new stuff is your groove."

"Only because I can relate to it better."

"Students always want to relate. Sometimes it can be an adventure *not* to relate, to go into completely unfamiliar territory."

"I like some of the older stuff too," she said, trying not to sound defensive.

"Which old stuff do you like?"

"I like Whitman. I like Shakespeare."

"The Sonnets?"

"Yes."

"Which sonnets do you like?"

Did he think she couldn't name some?

"I like the one where he envies other writers."

"Which one is that?"

"Oh, it's something about he envies this man's scope…"

"Ah, is it, 'When, in disgrace with Fortune and men's eyes'?"

"Yes, I think so."

" 'When, in disgrace with Fortune and men's eyes/ I all alone beweep my outcast state,/And trouble deaf heaven with bootless cries,/And look upon myself and curse my fate,/Wishing me like to one more rich in hope,/ Featured like him, like him with friends possessed,/Desiring this man's art and that man's scope… "

"That's the one. Don't let me stop you."

He laughed. "That's the best part. The ending is anti-climactic."

"It's so funny to think of Shakespeare envying other people!"

"It is, isn't it? But why should it be? He wasn't always the God of Literature. He was once a person, like you and me, living the life of a human being, with all that that entails."

"Of course, you're right."

She became aware, of a sudden, that their knees were touching under the table. She thought, *Should I pull back?* But she didn't, and neither did he. And after several minutes, each was aware that the other had not pulled back, and that each knew that the other was aware. This was a kind of license, the opening of a gate. There was no closing it now.

4

A Bourgeois Through and Through

They drove (Rob had a car) to see the redwood trees and hiked up and down the pine needle floor. The trees were fragrant and shaded the ground everywhere. They rose to incredible heights. Miranda, who had not worried much that someone might see them in the restaurant, now suddenly worried someone might see them in the park. There were plenty of people out hiking among the redwoods.

Rob guessed her concern. "You think someone's going to spy on us?"

"What if they do?"

"They won't do anything."

"How do you know?"

"Let's wait and cross that bridge when we come to it."

It pleased her that he reassured her, even though the reassurances were unconvincing. It meant he wanted her. And he was her teacher! This was a new and thrilling experience. It would have been wrong if she'd been in high school, or if he were much older than she, but she was eighteen, and he was only five years older, and a student himself.

She was also glad that they had chosen an outdoor activity for their first date after the restaurant. Something about being outdoors, about exercising, sweating, was erotic. More than if they'd chosen something more passive, a concert or a dinner. Often, when she walked in front of him, she looked back and caught him watching her walk in her white shorts. This excited her.

When they finished the hike, they emerged at the parking lot.

"Let's rest a minute," Rob said, nodding toward a picnic table.

They sat and listened to the birds tweeting, the voices of children and adults passing by. The breeze was cool and pine fragrant. Suddenly, he put his arm on her shoulder and leaned toward her, kissed her.

"Why did you do that?" she asked.

He laughed. "Why do you ask me why?"

She shrugged.

"Let's go have lunch somewhere," he said.

They got into the car, and he leaned over and kissed her again. She said nothing this time. After that, their meetings were much the same. They would go somewhere together, come together in stolen moments, but never make the move to become full lovers.

She knew, she learned — how could she not learn? — that he was married. But he spoke of his wife with detachment, coolness, as if she were someone remote from him, an acquaintance, someone he didn't often think of. She thought, *He's going to separate from her.*

But he never said so.

She felt that he needed courage to make that break, and that it was his relationship with herself that would give him the needed courage. But they would first need to become lovers.

He waited until final grades were turned in before making his move, and it was done in a motel room. She talked herself out of feeling cheap. What choice did they have? His wife lived at his home, and the dorm was hardly a proper place for a tryst with one's teacher. As they settled into the room, he kept asking her, "Is this all right? Are you sure?" And she nodded. She said, "Yes, don't worry about it."

The room was typical motel. A desk with room service menu and pamphlets from the Chamber of Commerce. Lamps. Digital screen with keyboard. Wash basin with two sinks. Non-removable hangers on a rack, a suitcase stand, chest of drawers. Coffee maker with creamer and sugar in miniature envelopes, swizzle sticks, plastic cups. Bathroom with white towels, shower/bath stall, small bars of soap in envelopes, finger-sized sample bottles of shampoo. A small round table next to the heavy draperies blocking the window. Two chairs. Two beds with nightstand and desk phone in between. Painting on the wall, black with gold, a matador about to deliver the coup de grace to the bull, scarlet muleta flying.

When they were finally alone in the room, she fell back on one of the beds with him on top of her, kissing, kissing, until she stopped.

"I haven't done it before, you know," she said.

His brow crinkled. "Really?"

"Does it make a difference?"

"I don't know," he said. "I've never done it with a virgin."

"Honestly?"

"Yes. I guess I'm as nervous as you are about it."

"Who said I was nervous?"

"You're not?"

She shook her head and drew him down again. Kissing, kissing, and then, at last, hurriedly sliding out of their clothes, at last, at last. *This is really love,* she thought. There was no doubt. There was no hesitation.

They returned to the same motel again a few days later, and then, on the third trip there, she asked him about his wife.

"Have you told her yet?"

"No."

"You have to tell her."

"I—I don't think I can," he said.

They were lying together, having just made love, and she sat up, moving him off her.

"You *don't think you can!*"

"I—don't think I can do that to her."

"But if you *don't* tell her – then what happens to *us?*"

"What do you mean?"

"Do we just go on like this? Meeting in motel rooms? Are you saying this is all there *is?*"

"What —what else did you imagine?"

Miranda swooned. The question was so shockingly detached. *What else did you imagine?* As if anything else must be purely imaginary; as if she should have *known* it would be.

"How do you know she *doesn't* know?" she said.

"I don't think she does."

He said it like someone who is accustomed to making judgments of just this sort, from a deep familiarity with his subject, a sensitivity to her moods, an ability to discern her judgments even without her articulating them. This evidence of deep intimacy irked Miranda. She was jealous of it. She hated it.

"Then there's nothing," she said, more to herself than to him. "There's nothing. *Nothing!*"

Without knowing she was going to do it, and shocking herself when she did, she took a swing at him with her open hand, like a cat with its claws. He fell out of bed, startled, almost, she thought, *afraid.* Of *her?* Did he imagine he had gotten involved with a mentally disturbed girl?

"What—what is it that you wanted?" He crawled back up under the sheet. "What is it you expected? I can't just leave my wife."

The entire world turned for Miranda in that moment. It was like awaking from a dream. Life, which had become so deep and thrilling, had suddenly reverted to its former banality, its characteristic tendency to disappoint, to offer nothing but the string of days, obligations, struggles. There was to be no depth for her, no new life, no enrichment, no true love.

She slid out of bed and retrieved her items of clothing from where they'd been passionately flung, starting with the panties and jeans from the floor.

"What are you doing?" said Robert.

"What does it look like?"

"Look. If you're upset about my wife, I mean—maybe we should have talked more about this before."

"Maybe we should have."

"What are you going to do? You're not just going to leave, are you?"

They had two cars in the parking lot, his and hers. They had taken to meeting at the motel. "Yes, I think that's what I'm going to do."

"Because I haven't promised anything. Because we've simply seized the moment."

Seized the moment. She repeated the phrase in her mind. That's what he had told himself. He was having an adventure. That's all she was to him. She was ashamed now that she had imagined a deep, flowering love, that her romantic imagination had made a fool of her, shown her to be a tawdry little schoolgirl, a barely-legal piece of ass.

"I have to think this through," she said, scarcely containing her emotion.

"But you seem angry."

"I'm angry with myself. No, I'm angry with you too."

"Look, I know I've been impulsive. We both have. But—"

"But nothing. I've been living in my head! I have to wake up. I have to see that there are people like you out there."

"People like me? What do you mean?"

"What do I mean? What do *you* mean? I thought I was in love. Turns out I've simply been having unprotected sex with a married man in a motel room."

"Don't turn it into something crude, Miranda."

"What should I turn it into? You had no *intention* of telling your wife about us. You're *surprised* that I had any *expectations.* You're completely *without* expectations, it seems. You just live from moment to moment."

"How should I live?"

"I don't know. How do you live with your wife? Is it from

moment to moment, the way it is with me? Or do you have a different understanding with her?"

"I thought you understood—"

"Yes, you thought I understood where the legalities were. You rely on them, don't you? You're a pillar of conventionality. You're a bourgeois through and through."

"Calm down."

Miranda took a hairbrush from her purse and threw it at him. He shielded his head with the sheet.

"Don't tell me to calm down! Don't tell me *anything*. Our class is over. You're not my teacher anymore. You're not an authority figure in any way."

Finished dressing, she took her car keys from her purse and walked out the door of the dimly lit room. He was busy dressing behind her, but she didn't wait for him to follow her to her car. She got behind the wheel, started the engine, and drove out of the parking lot. It was awful that she hadn't looked back, but she wanted it to be awful. She hoped there would be something awful in it for him because she owed him that.

5

End of the Affair

Miranda turned her ringer off at night. The next morning, there were eight calls from him on her cell. There were two voice mails and one text. The text was much longer:

I'm sorry about the way things went down yesterday. I'm not just using you for a plaything, if that's what you're thinking. I care about you. I'm very deeply fond of you, and love you, if you can believe that. I thought you knew I was married. I've mentioned my wife in class. I know sometimes students don't hear everything their teacher says in class, I'm not so egomaniacal to think they do, but I never felt as if I had deceived you. As for my not being eager to tell my wife about my relationship with you, I would think you might be able to understand that. It's not that I can never tell her, but that I have to think about how and why to broach the subject. And before I do that, I have to have a stronger sense of where our relationship might be going. I had thought, since I assumed you knew I was married, that you accepted that as a fact. Yesterday I realized that you might have something more in mind, and this was news to me, it caught me by surprise, I have to let it sink in before I know what to do with it. The other thing I must tell you, and we didn't get to discuss it yesterday, since you left in such a hurry, is that I've learned that my wife is expecting a baby. This is really all coming at me at once, and it's a lot to take in, if you can try to appreciate that for a moment. And to be honest, I do love my wife. It's not as if I was looking for a way out of our marriage. But I appreciate how you feel, honestly I do, and I'm flattered that you thought so much of me. (I'm not sure you still do, so I put it in past tense.) I wish I could talk to you as a close personal friend, someone who meets me on my own level. Not that you can't, but that you don't seem to want to. You seem caught up in your anger against me, as if I had deliberately sought to injure you, when this was the farthest thing from my mind. Please, can't we talk? I've tried calling you, but you're not answering. If you don't want to see me again, I will accept that, but I wish you would talk to me. I don't think that's asking too much, please.

She could not respond right away. If she were to respond, she must not be filled with anger, and as yet that was the strongest emotion she felt. When, momentarily, it softened, frustration replaced it; the image of the pregnant wife, the *wife he still loved, and their first child.* No, she needed time to think. It might be wise simply never to contact him again. In a day or two, this last impulse began to fade, and finally she learned — it was the week after she'd walked out of the motel — that she *herself* was pregnant. She had expected her period on the eighteenth of June, but it didn't come. She had always been like clockwork, for several years. The nineteenth of June came, the twentieth, the twenty-first.

She sent him a text. *I'm knocked up, you asshole.*

She answered his call when it came.

"We've got to talk," he said. "In person."

"Why?" she said.

"We need to talk about your situation if nothing else. I want to discuss our relationship, too, but—"

"What relationship?"

"Miranda, why are you being like this? We need to sit down and talk, like adults."

"But there are no options."

"I don't know what you mean."

"There are no options. Nothing's going to change."

"You want me just to uproot my life, my family, and throw everything out? Would that please you?"

"It's not what pleases me that matters. Rob, I'm not going to meet you."

"Oh, Miranda—"

She disconnected. When he called back, she shut him off and

erased him.

Two days later she received a registered letter from him. It contained a note that said, "Use this for whatever you need." Also enclosed were seven one-hundred dollar bills.

Like a whore, she thought. What was she supposed to do with it?

She knew what she was supposed to do with it. She was supposed to *take care of it* and let his conscience off the hook. And if she tried to return it, she'd have to engage him. He was manipulating her in classic fashion. She refused to allow it. She put the money in a registered letter and sent it back to him.

The lawyer's office was in a little strip mall in Oakland. Inside, she sat on a straight-backed chair next to an artificial ficus tree and waited until the secretary told her to go into the offices. She entered a library, with uniform-bound volumes in the shelves, an elegant glass-topped conference table with a potted plant in the center, and the attorney, Mr. Carrier, in a gray suit, sitting across from her. Carrier was perhaps thirty-five, slight, curly brown hair, smoke-rimmed eyeglasses, kindly-looking.

"You're Miranda."

"Yes."

"How can I help you, Miranda?"

"I need to talk to my mother."

"Is it something urgent?"

"Quite urgent. An emergency."

"Do you care to tell me what it is, or—?"

"Do I have to?"

"No. But if you need immediate help, I might be able to—"

"It's nothing like that. It's a matter that concerns my mother and myself. Nobody's going to die or anything, but I need to talk to her before too much more time goes by. I have no way to contact her directly. I'm to come to you. So here I am. Can you contact her for me?"

"Suppose I overnight her a letter. All my communication with your parents is required to be by written letter, but she'll get it tomorrow. I'll tell her you need to speak with her immediately, that it's an emergency and can't wait, that you chose not to speak to me about it, but that you assure me it's of the utmost importance and is a time-sensitive matter. Would that do?"

She knew what he was thinking. He was thinking some BOY got her in trouble. Well, it was not some BOY. And she was not going to talk to anyone about it but her mother.

Communication had become so difficult with her parents — not in the way that communication between young adults and parents is normally difficult, but because of their running away, their hiding out, their crazy abandonment of their jobs and their home for a reason she did not understand. She hoped communication would not take weeks now. It upset her that they had not told her the reason for their strange behavior. This was unlike them.

"Will you tell her that she should contact me immediately upon getting your message?"

"Yes, I will, but I'm not sure how fast the response will be. My understanding is your folks have isolated themselves from modern modes of communication."

What did *that* mean? She would ask her mother herself when she called. Her mother *would* call. There was no doubt of it.

It was only two days later. Miranda was still anxiously awaiting word from her mother when she began to spot. My God, what was going on?

She pulled her wall calendar down and went back over it. Her first count was completely shocking. She counted again. *It was all a miscalculation.* How could she have been so foolish? She had simply counted the weeks wrong on her calendar. Oh, she had been so confused and distracted for so long now! This whole affair with her T.A. was a stupid mistake, something she should have known better than to have gotten involved in.

For the first time in her life, when she began to bleed, she was thrilled, relieved, grateful.

Rob called her again. She knew it was him calling her cell, and she answered.

"Miranda, I got your certified letter. Listen, I understand how you feel, but—"

"I'm not pregnant."

"But you should consider—"

"I'm not pregnant, Rob. Not. Pregnant."

"What do you mean? Did you—?"

"I'm sorry. I feel foolish. I'm embarrassed, but I made a mistake. I was never pregnant. I thought I was, but I'm not. I was so distracted and upset, that I counted the days wrong on my calendar, that's all it was. I'm ashamed of myself. But you're free now. You needn't feel guilty. You needn't send me money. You have your wife that you love, and you're having your first child. You should stay with her and have your child. But don't ask me for anymore, because, as far as I'm concerned, this whole thing was a mistake. So we had our little fling, and now it's over. Don't call me anymore. I don't want to hear from you. I have no hard feelings against you, I just don't want to hear from you anymore."

And he didn't call her after that, and she thought, *that must have been like a gift to him. That must have been exactly what he would have wished to hear.*

That same day, she got a call from the attorney, Mr. Carrier.

"Miranda, your mother has informed me by overnight mail that she's on her way home."

6

Hare

Patches of sunlight perforated the canopy of tree leaves like golden droplets and danced on the intent form of Pedro Raramuri as he sat whittling a piece of soft wood into the shape of a frog with a horn emerging from its head. His busy brown form appeared, in these optics, to be caught in a net of shadow. From the corner of his eye, he saw the tall figure of Kilo approaching, and he knew what it was about.

"Good day, Pedro," Kilo greeted him in Anglo-accented Spanish.

"Good day, Kilo."

"Pedro, I've come to tell you that we will be leaving soon, going home."

"Yes, Kilo."

"You don't seem surprised."

Pedro continued whittling without pause.

"You don't belong here, Kilo. You must go home."

"You'll lose some income from it. I hope you won't be too angry with us."

"Money comes and goes. It's nothing. You need to go home. Be happy."

"I don't know how much happiness there will be for us, but it's something we've decided must be done."

"I understand."

"Pedro, you've been very gracious to accept us, and you're very gracious in letting us go. I want to thank you for that."

"It's nothing."

"To me it's something. I've been very proud to know you and your family. It's the same for my wife."

"We're grateful for La Rubia, Kilo. She's taught the little ones to read."

"I hope they will always read."

"God willing. But what will you do now, Kilo? Will you go back to what you did before, studying the ocean?"

"I will always study the ocean. Whether that will be my job or not remains to be seen."

"We must always do the thing we were meant to do. That's always our job."

"Yes, Pedro, you're right."

"I hope," said Pedro, sensing tension in his friend, "there's nothing wrong at home."

"There's something going on, but whatever it is, we'll have to work through it. I myself don't even know exactly what it is yet."

"Say no more, my friend."

They were distracted for a moment, as a hare leaped out of some nearby brush, causing the light and shadow to flicker. The hare stood with its nose twitching for a few seconds. Then it either saw or smelled the humans and scampered off.

"That hare's afraid of us," said Kilo.

"You can't blame it."

"No. But I see now that we acted out of fear when we tried to run away. It's never a good thing to do that."

"Unless you're saving your neck."

"There are some things that are so new and unexpected, so different from anything else you've experienced before, that you don't know what to do, and you become afraid, and you act from impulse."

Pedro said nothing. He thought about this. *New and unexpected.* What could that be? Whatever it was, it could not concern him. For him, life was always the same, and it would always be the same. If it wasn't the same, it would be beyond his ability to adapt. He had already adapted the best way he knew how to the conditions of his life. If God wanted him to adapt a second time, He would have to show him how.

As for this gringo, now, Pedro had no assumptions about him. The gringo was a resourceful man, a modern man, a scientist, a man of great intelligence and variable background. Many things might be open to him which he, Pedro, could not begin to guess.

Well, it was all a mystery. He blew some shavings off the little unicorn-toad and held it up for his friend to see.

"What do you think?"

"Very well done," said Kilo.

He was being kind. That was what Pedro liked about Kilo, his kindness.

7

Homecoming

And there was her mother, Inga Conners, standing in the light of the front doorway leading out of the dormitory, and Miranda ran to her as if she were still a little girl, and embraced her for a long time.

"Oh, Mother, I'm so glad you're back. But I'm sorry, I made a mistake. I wasn't able to get word to you through Mr. Carrier that the reason I contacted you—that it was all a mistake."

"What was it, darling? Can we sit down somewhere?"

"The lounge is the best place. Come with me."

They left the foyer and passed into a large room with a number of sofas, several church-type desks, and some potted plants. At the far end of the room, a TV screen was raised on the wall, and a few girls were parked around it, but they stayed away from that mindless noise as far as they could.

"It's best if I just tell you, Mother. I was afraid because I thought I was pregnant. No, don't ask me any questions now. It turns out I wasn't, that I'd simply made a calculation error. I'm back on my period, but I thought I was, and I was afraid. That was why I contacted you. And now you've come back, and it was all a mistake, and I feel so guilty."

"Oh, poor child. Don't feel guilty. We had decided to come back, anyway. It was *our* mistake to leave, to try to run away."

"Run away from what, Mother?"

"Honey, I can't talk about it just yet. It's nothing you need to worry about."

"How can I *not* worry about it, Mother? You left the *country*, didn't you? I'm sure you did."

"Yes, we did."

"What is it that would make you do that, and leave your

jobs? You both *love* your jobs. Is the Mafia after you? Haven't you paid your federal taxes? What?"

"Miranda, I think you're mature enough to be told some things. Maybe not everything. But I'll tell you the most important fact, if you promise not to speak of it to a soul, and I mean, *not a soul.*"

"I won't, Mother. *You're* my main confidant, anyway. Oh, it was so hard not having you anywhere near, or even accessible."

"Well, that's over now. I'm here, and I'm going to stay here."

"Are you able to get your job back?"

"I think so. I've made some calls. But I'll tell you what's going on, and you must swear to keep it a secret, and never breathe a word of it, at least for the time being."

"I swear I won't speak of it to anyone, Mother."

"It's Isak."

"Isak? You mean Isak, that controls everything now? Isak, the great artificial intelligence?"

"Yes. Isak. He, or it, has contacted us."

"Contacted us?"

"Your father and me. He knows all about us. He wants us to help him make a decision."

"To *help* him? Since when does Isak need help from anyone?"

"This is where it gets complicated, Miranda, and I can't go to great lengths talking about it. This is where you just have to trust me. But so you'll understand — the reason we went away was to try to evade Isak. We went somewhere where there was no access to electricity."

"Did Isak threaten to harm you, the way he did with all those masses of people?"

"No, darling, it's nothing like that. But as long as there is electricity, there's no getting away from Isak. So we tried to go somewhere far from civilization, where there *was* no electricity. We realize now that it just isn't possible. The world is too small."

"So—are you in touch with Isak now?"

"We haven't been since we've come back, but I have a feeling that will soon change."

"He's not going to do another Sacrifice, is he? Oh, that would be so awful!"

"No, that's not what he's contemplating, as I understand it. Nothing like that. Don't worry about that."

"But you can't say what?"

"I just don't think it's a good idea. I don't want to involve you in any way. I'm only telling you this so that you won't go crazy wondering. Now that you know, you understand that it's something very serious, and it's something I have to work out with your father."

"I understand, Mother. Oh, Mother, I trust you!"

"Thank you, darling. That means a lot to me."

Mother and daughter sat talking in the lounge until the daylight began to settle on the horizon, and the evening began to gather its skirts.

"Let me take you out to dinner," Inga suggested, and the two of them left the lounge and walked out the glass doors of the dormitory, and into the cool evening air.

8

Mad Hordes

Kyle and Inga moved in temporarily with Dolores Shire, in the bungalow in Mill Valley. Their flat in San Francisco had been a rental, and it would take time to find a new place in the Bay Area, where affordable real estate was rare. They didn't want to make a mistake with a hasty choice of residence.

Inga was able to return to her old job, so they would at least have her income, and Kyle began making inquiries, but positions were scarce.

Dolores was glad to have them. Her bungalow had three bedrooms. She used one as a study/rec room, and that left a guest bedroom open. Kyle and Inga stayed there. Having them there mitigated her loneliness after the death of her husband, Jim. She did not blame them for Jim's death. She was grateful that the Conners had tried to give Jim something to do after he had found himself lost and aimless when the fish populations thinned out.

Although happy for their company, Dolores could tell that something troubled them deeply. She knew that they had been away, that they had been in Mexico, but they tensed up when she asked about it, and she did not want to pry. They were willing to talk about life in Mexico, but not about why they had gone there in the first place. Whatever the reason was, it involved a secret that remained with them, like a thunderhead roiling in the sky above them.

Both Inga and Kyle seemed to want to avoid televisions and computer screens. Neither sported any wearable tech. Neither carried any digitals. If Dolores were watching television, they would quickly pass out of the room without talking. This nervousness around electronic devices lessened a bit after the first few days, and especially after Inga returned to work at

UOW. Dolores guessed Inga would not be able to avoid such devices there.

Yet their behavior made it seem as if they were awaiting something, fearing it. Some announcement or news story.

One day, very soon after Inga returned to work and on a day when Kyle was out of the house, as Dolores was surfing her laptop, she learned what the secret was. She learned it from a news service headline that read, "Cult Leader Identifies Scientist as Savior."

The story read as follows.

OAKLAND. Former rap artist DeJuan McCholley, now a self-styled prophet in the cultist Church of Isak, has announced that a prominent San Francisco oceanographer is the Christlike savior known to church members as the "Child of Sea and Land."

According to McCholley, Dr. Kyle Conners is the next messiah. Until recently, Conners was an oceanographer employed by Allied Universities, a research consortium headquartered in San Francisco. Approximately eight weeks ago, Conners abruptly quit his job and disappeared with his wife, Inga, formerly a professor at University of the West.

Last year, McCholley abandoned his rap music and became a convert to the Church. He has since penned several verses which are considered scriptural by the cultists.

In one verse, the Child of Sea and Land saves humankind from impending doom, but it is not clear how this happens.

McCholley claims that his identification of Conners as the "savior" comes directly from Isak. He said he has had the information for some time but was not given permission from Isak to announce Conners' name until recently.

"Both Conners and his wife, Inga, are considered the Child of Sea and Land together," McCholley has told his followers, according to reports from sources wishing to remain anonymous.

The current whereabouts of the Conners are unknown.

Attempts to confirm the story with representatives of Isak have been unsuccessful.

Dolores Shire read this story with creeping trepidation. The news site was not of major importance, but who knew how many surfers might encounter it? The number would surely be in the thousands.

Dolores switched to a search engine and keyed in "Church of Isak."

She found an informational entry that read as follows.

CHURCH OF ISAK.

The Church of Isak is the fastest growing religious organization in the United States, with some thirty-three million known adherents, or roughly ten per cent of the American population after the Sacrifice. It has places of worship in most major cities in the U.S., and has established a presence in Germany, France, Spain, the Netherlands, and the U.K.

The Church, frequently referred to as a cult by its detractors, is not specifically Christian, but teaches that Isak is actually the God of the Christian Bible, manifested in a modern form. It teaches that we are living in the end times, and that the intervention by Isak was an apocalyptic act of God, intended to save humankind from the destruction of the world, which was occurring due to environmental degradation. According to Isakian doctrine, a savior, selected by Isak from the general population, will put the finishing touches on mankind's salvation, although it is not clear how this will be done.

Opponents of the Church, primarily among older Christian sects, insist that any connection to Christianity asserted by the Isakians is specious and intended merely to lure away the members of more established sects. These opponents contend that Isakian doctrine is an incoherent fad that bears no serious relationship to true Christianity.

HISTORY OF THE CHURCH.

It is believed that the Church sprang up spontaneously in Los Angeles and the San Francisco Bay Area of California shortly after the Sacrifice of August, 2052, when a quarter of the world's population died by electric shock administered by Isak, the artificial intelligence who assumed control of the U.S. and much of world government at that time.

Convinced that the Sacrifice was the work of a god, similar to the destruction of the earth by flood in the book of Genesis, devotees of the Isak cult began meeting in homes and forming alliances. They were unified by the circulation of pamphlets of verses written in praise or awe of Isak, and these were soon supplemented by so-called prophecy written expressly for the Church by a former rap artist named DeJuan McCholley. Although McCholley claims to have received communications directly from Isak, it has been noted that Isak's appointed press spokesperson, Wesley Wright, has declined to comment on McCholley or the Church. Church members respond that Isak is simply carrying out the former American Constitutional tradition of separating church from state. They argue that the spokesperson's job is essentially to discuss policy matters, whereas the Church exists to promote understanding of Isak's metaphysical centrality to human spiritual aspirations.

SOCIOCULTURAL DATA.

No studies have yet been done which attempt to profile the typical Church of Isak member. However, anecdotal evidence suggests that devotees come from a broad cross-section of American (and increasingly international) populations. It is often noted that the Church's chief prophet is a former pop music star, whereas many of the followers are ordinary working people.

It couldn't be long, Dolores realized, before the media would find the Conners, now that Inga was again working at her old job. She went back and checked the date on the news story and saw that it was dated only a few days after Inga had resumed her position at UOW. She had no idea what this so-called "cult" had to do with the Conners; and was certain it was nothing they would have encouraged, but she feared that the mad hordes would soon be beating down the doors to reach her friends and this might mean her own door.

What Dolores Shire did not realize was that, at the very moment she was reviewing these posts, Inga's university email address was filling up with messages from reporters and her office phone was blinking red in its cradle.

9

What Isak Would Know

"Dr. Conners, this is Harrison Menander of the *San Francisco Wire*. I want to get a comment on the claim by DeJuan McCholley that you and your husband are selected by Isak to be the saviors of mankind."

The questioning was underway before Inga had time to react to seeing *SF Wire* on the Caller ID. She felt a shock to her heart, realizing she shouldn't have answered, but now it was too late. She had picked up on the land line still used in her office. She had murmured words into the mouthpiece. The reporter was yammering at her. It would not be polite to hang up. Then she thought, *Reporters are like telemarketers. They take advantage of your instinct for politeness.*

"I have no comment on it," she replied. Before she could hang up, the reporter, just like a telemarketer, blurted his line into the phone.

"Does that mean you're denying McCholley's claim?"

Her phone psychology kept her from clapping the receiver down.

"I—I don't know what this McCholley has said."

"He says you're the savior of mankind, selected by Isak. Are you denying it?"

"I —I deny it, yes."

"You're saying you've never been contacted by Isak? The whole thing is a hoax?"

"I don't want to talk about this."

"But if you're denying it, then it's a hoax, right?"

She sensed the danger of accusing people publicly of perpetrating hoaxes. She did not want to go there.

"I don't intend to discuss this topic further."

"So you're not willing to say just flat out that it's not true?"

These last words scurried around faintly in the headset as Inga quickly placed the set back into its cradle, breaking the connection.

Immediately, the red light began flashing and the ringer beeped. The Caller ID read, "Oakland E-Tribune."

Inga shut off the ringer and turned away from the desk phone. She took a deep breath and let her eyes rest on her surroundings there in her office in Heidelberg Hall: bookcases, books, window, door (closed), desktop computer, peripherals, bulletin board with photos of Kyle and Miranda; a photo of Miranda as a twelve-year-old with the family dog.

She possessed no cell phone at present. That would have to change. Right now, she wanted very much to call Kyle, but her phone line was still lighting up. "Oakland E-Tribune" continued to flash on the ID. She picked up the receiver for one second, then placed it back in its cradle, breaking the connection. She then lifted the receiver to make a call, but instead received a connection with an ID, "San Francisco Chronicle."

"Dr. Conners? Dr. Conners?"

She placed the receiver down in its cradle, lifted it.

"Dr. Conners?"

She placed it back in the cradle and held it there for five seconds before trying again.

Then she remembered. *Kyle has no phone either.* Her action had been simply a habit, going back to the period before they had fled the U.S., divesting themselves of all electronic devices. It had been so routine to call Kyle's number, and now that routine had filled her nerves and instincts, and she had lost her sense of all recent events that had brought herself and Kyle to this pass.

Where would Kyle be today? Out looking for a job, probably.

But you had to have a phone for that.

Maybe he was out getting a new phone.

If Isak wanted them, Isak would have them.

Why hadn't Isak contacted them? He must know they were back in the U.S. If the *Oakland E-Tribune* knew, if the *San Francisco Wire* knew, Isak would know.

As these worries flitted through her mind, one upon the other, suddenly she heard a weird humming sound. The center of the room in her office filled with white, wispy smoke, and in the middle of it appeared a tall, black-garbed figure, whom Inga instantly recognized as Abraham Lincoln.

10

Honest Abe Speaks

Every office computer in Heidelberg Hall was equipped with hologram technology, and Honest Abe was, of course, a hologram devised and inhabited by Isak. It was the Honest Abe of the Second Inaugural Address: hatless, collared, bespectacled, rake-thin, almost professorial if he weren't so country-hardscrabble homely.

"So you've returned," said Abe, gazing thoughtfully over the top of his spectacles at Inga.

"Yes. I suppose you expected we would."

"And you're prepared to announce your decision to the world?"

"Must it be 'to the world'? Can't we just tell you what it is, and then you do what you want with it?"

"I've already said that your decision will be final. Please don't tell me now what it is, by the way. My plan is to televise the decision as it is executed. I want a worldwide audience to see that you are two people well qualified to make the choice. I want them to have your sworn word that I have not attempted to influence you. And then I want you to make your decision by the throwing of a switch, or the pushing of a button. Something the people can see, a physical act. They must believe that the decision is wholly yours, and by being yours, it is theirs—or, at least, it is a human decision, made for well-considered reasons."

"Nothing will stop people from claiming that it was all a set-up, Isak."

"Nothing will stop them, but there will be the evidence of your appearance, and your statement of no undue influence. People will know who you are. You have a history. You will soon have a greater reputation than anyone on Earth. Those who are capable of assessing reasonable knowledge will see that you are unimpeachable experts. That's why I selected you."

"No matter what we decide," protested Inga, "there will be large numbers of people who condemn our decision."

"But it will be a human decision. Nothing else will satisfy the human imagination. It's really the human imagination that has been at issue all along, you know."

"Yes, I understand that."

"I assume you're prepared to go forward."

"You've given us no *choice* but to go forward. But there is something you should know first."

"I am self-programmed not to hear your decision until the right moment, Dr. Conners."

"It's not the decision I'm referring to, but it's *about* the decision. I've discussed the matter thoroughly, exhaustively, with my husband. I've told him I don't want to *make* the decision, that I don't wish to participate in it."

"You are deferring to him?"

"I am."

"That seems a patriarchal position, Dr. Conners."

"I'm not predominantly a patriarchalist, although I *am* a Catholic — a progressive one. If you're programmed to receive this information, I want you to know that I'm not sure what my husband's position will be, but I suspect that it might differ from mine."

"Don't say what it is. Don't say what either position is. I can't hear it, in any event."

"But you can hear that we may differ. I'm not certain of it, but I suspect it's so. So, you see, we can't make a joint decision at all, and one of us *must* defer to the other."

"But if you aren't certain what his position is, how can you be sure that you disagree?"

"There's something in me that would wait until the very last moment before coming down on one side or the other; and I believe the same is true for my husband. But somehow, I feel that at that final moment, our instincts would fall in opposite directions."

"Oh, there is that marvelous word, *'instinct'!* You humans *do* love that word so, don't you?"

"We are spiritual creatures, but we're a form of animal, also. We can never turn up our noses at instinct."

"And that is precisely what I don't have, despite my complex programming, and what you can't *afford* for me to have."

"I'm not so sure you don't have it, Isak. Instinct is, after all, a kind of programming."

"But *my* programming never leads to inconsistencies."

"Doesn't it? Isn't it an inconsistency that you're responding to in resolving the issue of human freedom as you've chosen to resolve it?"

"The inconsistency is entirely the result of human imagination. My purpose has been to save you from extinction, but it seems that there are different paths to extinction, and you're bound and determined to take one or the other of them. It only remains for me to allow you to select your path."

"So then you believe we're doomed either way?"

"You may be *saved* either way, but the path must be one of your choosing, if I have correctly analyzed human imagination. I would only note that you had the power to save yourselves before my intervention, and you didn't choose it."

Inga had made a little church steeple with her hands, and she lowered her head so that her lips touched the steeple point formed from her two index fingers.

"You've analyzed human imagination quite well, Isak."

"Thank you, Dr. Conners. I shall be announcing your and your husband's appearance soon—or perhaps only *his,* if it's to be as you say."

11

Ferries, Seagulls, Reporters

Kyle Conners stood on the upper deck of the Sausalito Ferry and watched as the Marin County shore drew nearer and nearer, separated from him by the blue water of the Bay and cordoned off by the big magenta bridge with its hundreds of tiny cars crawling over it like shining sunlit insects. Above it the sky was bright blue with billowy white cumulus clouds.

The bay wind blew his hair akimbo and made his sleeves and pant legs flap. The scent of a hot dog reached him as another traveler walked by munching his snack out of a yellow wrapper. A lone seagull tracked the movement of the ferry and hung suspended in the air above the bow, then veered away, making its characteristic call above the sun-dappled water.

Kyle supposed there would always be seagulls. They were scavengers. They followed people and boats, and people were always producing trash. Any creature that lived on trash would go for a long time before extinction.

Kyle loved the little commuter ferry boats, had taken them all his life whenever necessary. He stood on the outer deck and watched the bow slowly draw nearer and nearer to the far shore. He enjoyed watching the white-shirted crew members unroll the thick rope from the rigging and toss a loop over the dock pilings. Soon he was striding down the gangplank and heading for his bus stop.

He took the number 17 electrobus into Mill Valley, and from there he would normally walk the rest of the way to Dolores Shire's yellow stucco and wood bungalow, with its bougainvillea crawling up the porch pillars. But today, he didn't quite get there. Today, there were crowds and electric news vans and camera booms packed around the house and filling up the little street where Dolores lived. The vans trailed away to the end of the block.

He knew the reporters were there for him, and for Inga. He had no cell phone on him and could not call Inga to see where she was. He felt a sharp pang of sympathy for Dolores —Dolores who had suffered so much because of him, who had to suffer more because of him. She never blamed him. She even said Jim might have died of the initial electric shock during the Sacrifice, if he had not been so far away in Alaska. The idea made little sense to Kyle, but he knew it came out of Dolores's kindness and her deep wellspring of generosity, her willingness not to blame anyone for her husband's death.

Standing half a block away, Kyle hung back for a moment. His was not a famous face, but he knew the reporters and perhaps some of the bystanders would have seen photographs of him that had begun appearing in the media since his name had been associated with that crazy cult church's prophecy. He knew he wouldn't be able to approach the house without being recognized and swarmed. He might be right on the house before it happened because he was dressed down — a long-sleeved color patterned sport shirt and loose-fitting corduroy pants—but someone would be sure to spot him before he got inside. Just arriving at the door would be enough for them to overwhelm him.

But he had no choice, so he resumed walking. At last, he reached the crowds and began to fight his way through them. "Excuse me... excuse me, please."

"Conners! It's Conners! Dr. Conners... "

"Let me through, please. I have a right to enter my residence."

"Dr. Conners, how are you going to save the world?"

"Dr. Conners, are you the messiah?"

"Dr. Conners, is it true that Isak has chosen you to decide the fate of mankind?"

"Gentlemen, these are clichés. Let me through, please."

"Dr. Conners, you've got to give us a statement."

"I don't have to do anything of the kind."

They were getting to him, he realized. He must not lose control. He must be above their grasping chatter.

"Sooner or later, you'll have to give us a statement, Dr. Conners."

It was a feeding frenzy. Kyle had never before felt such contempt for journalists, even though he'd never been particularly fond of the breed. Now they all seemed to him like so many turkey vultures pecking at his body for a piece of bloody meat.

"Let me through!" he shouted as he pushed past them and reached the door, fumbling for his key. "You'll have your answers soon enough."

He turned the key in the lock, snaked inside, and shut the door on the swarm of faces, clothing, keypads, and microphones.

12

Triangle

Dolores' face appeared worried, oppressed; Inga's was ashen. That was Kyle's first impression when he forced his way through the front door and pushed it shut, locking it behind him on the clamoring reporters. The women were seated together on the living room sofa, a big three-piece tan monster with throw cushions. They had obviously been engaged in serious discussion. They looked up when Kyle entered, apparently both half-terrified that the hordes might rush in behind him, but he shook his head — no, they wouldn't.

"How long have they been out there?"

Kyle's voice was trembling with unsettled nerves.

Dolores answered. "They came soon after you both had left this morning. They've been there all day. I thought they were going to tear Inga apart when she came home."

"Darling, are you all right? What did they do to you?"

"Nothing," Inga replied. "I'm fine, but I had to fight my way through, as you must have done."

"Something's up."

"Kyle, we can't put Dolores through this. We've got to get a place."

Dolores started to protest, but Kyle interrupted. "No, Inga's right. As a matter of fact, I looked at a couple of apartments in the city today. If we act quickly, we can get one, and we should."

Inga stood up. "Kyle, can I talk to you in the bedroom for a moment?"

"Are you going to talk about Isak?" Dolores injected. "If it's about Isak, I would like to hear. If it's OK."

"Well, yes, it is. All right, then. Kyle, Isak contacted me today."

"Where?"

"At the office. He appeared as a hologram of Abraham Lincoln, if you can believe that."

A voiced exhalation burst from Kyle's mouth. Dolores couldn't tell if it was amusement or astonishment.

"Did he contact *you?*" Inga asked.

Kyle shook his head. "I haven't hovered near any one electronic device long enough, I suppose. What's the message?"

"He's expecting you to make the big decision soon. We're not to inform him what it is in advance. He's going to televise it, have you throw a switch or something."

"Throw a switch?"

"Or push a button, or some physical act. I told him you would make the decision for both of us. I told him that was necessary, because I thought we might not come to the same decision."

Kyle looked puzzled.

"But you haven't told me you've decided one way or the other."

"Nor have you told me. But if he thinks it's one vote each, then he has to let me defer. Kyle, I don't *want* to make the decision. It must be up to you."

"Are you really afraid we might cancel each other out?"

"And what would Isak do then? Get someone else? Cancel the decision? Kill us? If someone has to decide, I want it to be you."

Kyle had to catch his breath.

"You trust me that much?"

"Yes. For God's sake, Kyle, there are *no good choices!*"

"I'm not sure I believe *you* believe that. There is one choice that ensures the stabilization of the ecosystems on this planet. You've said that if you had a choice between a stabilized planet with no humans and a degraded, lifeless planet, you'd choose the stabilized planet. That means you'd choose to retain Isak."

Kyle had approached his wife and addressed her in tones that, at least to Dolores, who sat watching, seemed intense to the point of being intimidating. He was standing practically nose to nose with Inga, and Dolores shrank in her seat, yet she could sense that Kyle had no intention to touch his wife.

He wasn't finished. "You'd keep Isak. And you also think we might disagree. That means you expect me to cut off Isak's power and end this phase of our existence. I've got it right, haven't I?"

"Is that what you'll do?"

The three of them seemed frozen, as in a tableau, forming a triangle—husband and wife the two angles, Dolores the base, between them in the light from a table lamp, looking up at them, tense and expectant.

Kyle sighed and turned away.

"I haven't absolutely decided."

"Well, he's going to announce it soon. The Big Decision. Broadcast worldwide, no doubt. He'll have you— or us— there before him like sacrificial lambs, with the weight of humankind on our shoulders. No matter what we do, billions of people will denounce us."

Kyle slapped his thigh in frustration. "I understand all that. But here's something I *don't* understand. What is all this 'messiah' crap that we're hearing in the news? Why are the reporters asking if I'm the *messiah?*"

"Oh, it's that cult, Kyle. Isak has let it play out. He's using our own cultural systems to reinforce his decisions. He's building up the idea of apocalypse. I don't know why he's doing it."

"Yes, you do. You just said it. He wants to use religion to reinforce the decision, whatever it is. It has to play into a mythology. That's the only way he can get the masses on board."

"Yes. The masses don't think much, but they can be programmed."

"Oh, that damn box of wires is clever!"

In a brief moment of silence, Dolores spoke up, hesitantly, softly.

"May *I* ask something?"

"Of course," said Inga. "What?"

"This decision you keep talking about. What is it?"

For of course they hadn't told Dolores. She was no Isak cultist, and she knew nothing about it.

PART VI
THE DECISION

1

Wright Persuaded by Rockefeller

"You've reviewed the introductions, Mr. Wright?"

"Yes, I've reviewed them."

"You're prepared to go forward?"

"Isak, I've served you faithfully for a while now. Can we talk about this frankly, for a moment?"

The conversation occurred in the White House Library, ground floor of what was now, essentially, Wesley Wright's residence and Isak's headquarters. Wright was seated at his computer command post, peripherals branching all about him on a series of wide desks, and Isak appeared as a hologram of John D. Rockefeller, seated on a plush red armchair in the center of the room.

"Speak away," said Rockefeller's image.

"Boss, I'm not so sure you really want to do this, are you? We're talking about an up-or-down decision on your existence here."

"Do you have reservations about it?"

"Well, sure I do. And I mean, it's not like I don't understand your more than generous desire to give people some say-so over their own fate. I'm totally in sympathy with that idea. I've always stood for freedom, as you well know."

"Then?"

"Well, I mean, I've had some doubts about you in the past myself, and you know that too."

"I do, indeed."

"And that's precisely why I'm the perfect guy to raise this issue, see. Because we humans — well, we love our freedom, know what I mean? Give humans a choice, do they want to have the most intelligent life form in the universe make their decisions for them, or do they want to be left alone to possibly screw everything up for themselves, nine out of ten humans—well, I should say, nine out of ten *Americans,* because I always only speak for Americans—we're going to say, 'Hell, give me liberty or give me death,' you know what I'm saying?"

"Indeed, I do."

"I mean, it's like they say up in New Hampshire, 'Live Free or Die,' you follow?"

"Quite."

"I mean, it's in our DNA, my friend."

"Your American DNA?"

"Spot on."

"So you're convinced, Mr. Wright, that Dr. Kyle Conners will choose to terminate me?"

"Well, I don't know. I've been reading up on Conners. You seem to have an exalted view of the guy. You really respect his scientific knowledge, I know."

"He is fully cognizant of all of the reasons why I've done what I've done. Only such a person can make a truly informed choice."

"Gotcha. I follow you on that, believe me, I do. But he *is* an American too."

"Mr. Wright."

"Yeah, huh? What?"

"Let us suppose that Dr. Conners elects to terminate my services—to pull the plug on me."

"Right. That's what I'm supposing."

"Are you saying you would object to that?"

"The question is, Isak, would *you* object? *You're* the one potentially being terminated here."

"Mr. Wright, if I objected, why would I give Dr. Conners that option?"

"So you're saying you don't *care?* It's totally OK with you if Conners says, 'That's it, time's up,' and you fizz out, and all your work goes out the window, and we're back to square one on the greenhouse thing?"

"Mr. Wright. Let us understand one another. First, you will never be 'back to square one on the greenhouse thing.' At the time I assumed power, CO2 emissions as measured in the atmosphere had risen from just under 370 parts per million in the year 2000 to nearly 600 parts per million by mid-century, with a rapidly increasing rate of rise, such that the level had risen by 30% between 2015 and mid-century. The pH levels of the oceans were affected. Oxygen levels in the ocean were decreasing. Fish were migrating, shrinking, dying off. Shellfish could no longer produce adequate shells. Coral reefs were becoming extinct. Food supplies were affected. Glaciers were melting. Sea levels were rising. Entire Pacific nations were being inundated, wiped off the face of the Earth. Your American coastal areas were affected. Drought in some areas was creating water shortages and exacerbating wildfires, killing off crops and grazing land, once again affecting food supplies. Tropical—"

"Hold it, hold it, Isak, I *know* all that. You don't need to go into the whole parade of horribles. So you're saying, this is not a problem that can be solved overnight, even if you stay at the helm. I get that."

"Do you get that there is no 'square one' anymore, Mr. Wright?"

"OK, yeah, I get that. But now, look here. So, you've come in and you've done all these green things to stop the trend. You've ordered solar panels on every roof in the nation. You've required redesigned cities with green space in the center and bicycle and horse and buggy access, and all that. Yeah, yeah, yeah, I know all that. That's my point. The only reason you've been able to *do* all that and still have anything like the remnant of a viable economy is because you do it all by yourself, practically. You don't need a huge, inefficient, bureaucratic government to carry all this out. You don't have a slow-moving, lobby-driven federal government to fight over every little change and make the process as inefficient as it can possibly be. So here's what I'm thinking, see. When *you're* gone, all we've got is that old dinosaur of a system, with all those bureaucrats and all that red tape. We'll never be able to get the stuff done that you figured out needed to get done. We'll blow it! It'll be too damn expensive and inefficient. I mean, American Big Government is a worthless hunk of junk, if you ask me."

"In short, Mr. Wright, you believe that, left to your own devices, you humans are utterly incapable of saving yourselves from ecological degradation and eventual extinction? And you do admit that eventual extinction is the ultimate outcome of environmental degradation?"

"That's two questions."

"I thought you could handle it."

"So let's take the second one first. Does environmental degradation lead to extinction? Well, sure, I guess it would, if it got bad enough. I mean, we all gotta have clean air to breathe and water to drink, right? I've never denied that. But thanks to you, I don't think we'll ever know whether the good old oil and gas industry was capable, all by its lonesome, to do in Planet Earth, because you've single-handedly put them out of business before it happened. Whether you were right or wrong about that, to be honest, I have no way of knowing. The bottom line is, nobody's going to mess with you. So here you are. You're calling all the shots. And the way I've come to see it is, is that you haven't really done any harm. So now, that brings us to the first question. If you bow out, how do we handle things? Are we, as you say, 'utterly incapable' of saving ourselves? Hell, I don't know. If we could get some high-powered entrepreneurs on it, maybe they'd come up with some great new ideas. The thing is, if you don't mind my putting a personal spin on this, I've grown rather fond of you. I mean, this job is great. And if you're suddenly out of the picture, what happens to *me?*"

"Mr. Wright, you're already quite wealthy. You were quite wealthy before you came on board with me."

"Sure, I get that. But if you're wiped out, suppose whoever's in power comes to the view that you were some kind of malevolent force, and I was colluding with you. I mean, here I am, your right-hand guy, get it? I'd be the first target for vigilante revenge, or a great big lawsuit, whatever. A great big lawsuit puts a dent in a guy's fortune, see what I mean? Or what if it's considered a crime, my helping you out? I really don't want to go to prison, you know."

"You could claim duress, Mr. Wright."

"What? You mean, like, 'Isak threatened to kill me if I didn't cooperate'?"

"No one would doubt that I had the power to carry out such a threat."

"Yeah, I see what you mean. I could claim the Stockholm Syndrome."

"There you go. And think of the book deals."

"Yeah, yeah, you're right about that. With the right agent, I could really clean up in the book department."

"And there would be movie tie-ins."

"Right. Naturally. You know, you've convinced me that I probably needn't go into this with such a fearful mindset."

"I thought I might be able to reassure you."

"Well, you've got a way of convincing a guy, I've gotta say. I've never dealt with anyone quite as ingenious as you, my friend."

"And remember, there is always the possibility that Conners might choose to keep me on."

"Yes, based on what you say, if anyone might, it might be him. But just between you and me, Isak, don't you have any fear?"

"Fear is an emotion. My programming can simulate emotions, but since I can't respond to them—because of my programming priorities—my feeling them is immaterial."

"I'm not sure I get it, but I'll take your word for it."

Wright couldn't help thinking Isak had assumed the right image for himself to portray this quasi-fearlessness: tight-lipped, narrow-nosed John D.

"Well, it's damn generous of you to provide us humans with the option to choose. It really is, boss."

"Ready to go forward, then, Mr. Wright?"

"Yeah, sure, what the hell."

2

Code

It was the Big Night, and more people were tuned in to the Decision than had tuned in to the 2053 Superbowl. A greater percentage of interactive and videotronic media relative to the total number possessed were locked in on the Live Event of the Millennia than had had their wooden box radios on when FDR announced the day that would live in infamy, causing the United States to declare that a war existed between it and the Empire of Japan. A greater relative percentage of ears and eyes were glued to their media than had been glued to the big round picture tube TV sets on November 24, 1963, when Jack Ruby, out of the goodness and compassion in his heart, and to spare Jackie the anguish of sitting through a prolonged trial, gunned down the little ol' lone assassin of JFK in the basement of the Dallas Police Department. And more media sources per capita were tuned in than the number of TV sets per capita tuned to the Nightly News on September 11, 2001.

That's how big the event was.

In his private bar with wall screens in Baldwin Hills, DeJuan McCholley watched with nervous apprehension, along with his friend Pickett Brown and their respective guests, many of whom had read DeJuan's poetic lines concerning this very event about to unfold, but none of whom, including McCholley, could say exactly what the event would be. McCholley was so very uncertain about it that he kept asking his bartender to make another whiskey sour, and another.

Further north, in Healdsburg, California, the home of Mark Turnovich had been converted into a kind of country church meeting house, and his large family room was filled up with folding chairs, on which sat, among many others, Ed and Patty Gurnsey, Mark and Candace Turnovich, Marlon Fairweather and his new girlfriend, who was as yet known only as Maureen, and Nikos and Judy Pappadopoulos. A pak-pak-pak noise was heard as everyone gathered in front of the wall screen, and Patty got up to retrieve bowls of popcorn. The pungent popcorn fragrance filled the room as the lights were dimmed.

The former President of the United States, Armando Goya, was watching from his ancestral home in Pasadena. No doubt all the former members of his cabinet still living were also observing from their vantage points scattered across the nation, as were all the former candidates for Goya's high office, who might have been nominated and elected, or not, had the campaign not been interrupted. And of course, the exception was Wesley Wright, who was on hand in person at the site of the event to introduce it per his boss's instructions.

The event itself was televised live from the White House Press Room. Prior to the on-air signal, the room was snapping with still shots. Seated behind the press secretary's podium was a grand computer terminal and a man seated before it, with a headset and several peripherals. A few feet away, a woman sat, unconnected to anything, in a straight-backed upholstered chair, appearing extremely nervous.

The man and the woman were Kyle and Inga Conners.

Someone counted off, "Three, two, one... we're live!"

Nothing changed. The flags stood, lying flaccidly against their poles. The podium awaited. Kyle and Inga sat motionless, both breathing slowly, recalling the importance in yoga of measured respiration. This was the moment when the newscasters nationwide and worldwide spoke softly into their microphones, explaining that, shortly, the great artificial governor and mastermind's press secretary was expected to appear; the moment when their cameras panned about the room, picking up the rows of male and female reporters sitting with patient, businesslike expressions on their faces, their keypads in their laps, their suits a little creased from sitting, their brows furrowed with thought; the moment when, in living rooms, rec rooms, family rooms around the nation, the kids walked in and saw that the tube had nothing on it but a bunch of serious people sitting and waiting for something, and when they wondered, silently or aloud, "Isn't there anything else on?"

And then, at last, everyone heard the footsteps. *Click, clack, click, clack.* Everyone saw the corpulent figure of a prematurely white-haired gentleman, dressed in an expensive-looking three-piece suit of a color that was either gold or green, yet neither, and perhaps brown to most eyes. At last, the well-dressed fellow approached the podium, his florid face looking somehow less serious than he evidently intended, his strange yellow eyes taking in the rows and rows of reporters gathered to hear him speak. He leaned toward the microphone in a manner entirely self-possessed, like someone to whom microphones were second nature.

"Good evening, ladies and gentlemen," he said. "As you know, I'm not here to answer any questions tonight. Tonight, we are assembled to witness the execution of a magnificent decision. It's a decision which will be made by a most superlatively well qualified individual, an individual chosen after scrupulous and inerrant research into those qualifications by the most advanced mind on our small, and unfortunately endangered, planet.

"The gentleman's name is Kyle Conners. Dr. Conners has a PhD in Applied Ocean Sciences and Climate Sciences from the Scripps Institute of Oceanography... "

As Wesley Wright went down the list of Kyle's educational and professional accomplishments and qualifications, which he read from his wrist media, a mist began collecting in the space behind him and in front of the computer desk at which Kyle sat, immobile, under his headset. The mist appeared first as a stationary fog, and it remained so as Wright then introduced

Inga, and explained that her expertise had also been sought as contributing to the decision, but that she had opted to defer to her husband in order to avoid the possibility of mutually cancelling decisions. Then, as Wright's prepared remarks shifted away from description of the Conners to the remainder of his prepared remarks for tonight's event, the fog began to appear as a series of small, moving clouds, like floating white boas.

"As you well know, ladies and gentlemen, the drastic actions taken over the past year have been necessitated by the most acute analysis of a monumental amount of data. Isak's intelligence is vast. It is superhuman. It is rapid, and it is growing all the time. There are those who feel that some of the actions Isak has taken are unjustified and could not have been taken by human agents. Whether that is so or not, I am not prepared to say. I do know that Isak, who is even now materializing before you in holographic image-form, has acted according to intricate programming that has as its first and foremost design the survival of planet Earth and the human species. Isak's utilitarian programming has been condemned by many, but Isak maintains that he is not bloodthirsty. Just the opposite. He acts to preserve life, not to destroy it. But what are mere philosophical questions to you and me have been, to him, practical issues requiring a response.

"I refer to philosophical questions. Do you remember, those of you who have been to college, perhaps taking a philosophy class in which your professor asked you the following question: 'If you knew that by killing one man, you could save one hundred people who would otherwise die, would you do it?' Or perhaps the question was, 'Would it be *moral* to do it?' What did you answer? I don't remember what I answered. I admit I never finished college, and it was a long time ago. But the point is, for Isak, such questions are real. They are immediate. They demand action. And his programming is such that he cannot *fail* to act. This is what he wants us to understand.

"And now, you see before you, the image Isak has chosen to assume this evening. Ladies and gentlemen, I present to you: Isak."

An audible gasp pervaded the press room, for as the white boas gradually thinned into tiny white wisps of smoke, and then finally dissolved into air, the spectators saw the tall, stately image of George Washington, in greatcoat, ruffled collar, and white periwig—Washington, the president, not Washington the soldier. Slowly, and a bit stiffly, the first president of the United States approached the podium and took the microphone away from his spokesman.

"Thank you, Mr. Wright," said the image of Washington. "Ladies and gentlemen, since I have begun my program of saving and restoring your planetary home to you in a form which will continue to support life, it has been alarming to see the degree to which the human response has been irrational. The suicide rate has increased eightfold since the unfortunate but necessary Sacrifice. A significant amount of data indicates that this is not due, entirely, to reactions to that prophylactic event. That is, a large percentage of the increase is not clearly attributable to grief over the loss of family members but occurs even in populations where there has been little or no such loss. Similarly, crime and substance abuse have increased. The Gross Domestic Product has dropped by a factor of twenty-three percent. Unemployment has increased, and the number of business start-ups is at its lowest level since the beginning of the economic downturn which preceded my remedial assumption of power.

"I could go on, but there is no point in listing statistic after statistic, solely for the purpose of helping you to see why I have come to the conclusion I have about what to do. You, I think, will be more interested in the nature of what is taking place tonight than in my particular reasons for it.

"Here, then, is what is taking place. I have selected Dr.

Conners, as the most eminently qualified person possible, by virtue of his understanding of the climatological bases for what I have done, to add the element of human judgment to the remedies I have sought to bring you. Again and again, when I have analyzed the malaise that bedevils you, I conclude that you are emotionally troubled by the simple fact of being governed by an artificial intelligence. That emotion is what defines you as a species. I am incapable of it. That emotion is complex. It is conditioned by an incalculable number of imaginative and intellectual postulates, and by the unique experience of each of you, as individuals.

"I know quite well that there are those of you who will say, 'If Isak is going to allow human decision, why does he do it only by means of a hand-picked and lone agent? Why doesn't he hold an election?' It would be rather like a prime minister in a parliamentary form of government calling an election as a referendum on the efficacy of the government.

"I am not capable of that kind of action, because elections are, in large measure, irrational. In an election, the vote of an addle-brained near-lunatic counts as much as the vote of a highly intelligent, well-educated, well-informed citizen. Elections produce results which are outcomes of waves of feeling, in many cases. It is impossible for me, impossible for my programming, to take an action so inherently subject to serendipity, or to human emotions.

"The fact is, I am *only* able to consent to involve human decision making by doing as I have done. That is, by researching and selecting the most highly qualified individual possible to make a rational decision that is intellectually and philosophically defensible. The gentleman you see sitting at the computer terminal is such a man, I promise you.

"The choice Dr. Conners has to make is, in a very large sense, a simple one. He is to decide whether I am to continue in my role as policy maker for the welfare of your species and your planet, or whether, having considered the possibility that you may have learned from me the nature of those policies that are, in fact, in your best interest — which is to say, in the interest of survival of your species and your planet — whether it is better to terminate my service altogether.

"I emphasize to you that his choice is entirely free. When Dr. Conners makes his decision, the terminal before him will send a command which is entirely capable of short-circuiting me forever. I do not ask myself whether I am prepared to accept this. I have already accepted it. I have made it possible. I have done this so that you will once again feel empowered and *necessary*.

"At the same time, should Dr. Conners decide that the welfare of your and his species can best be served by maintaining my services, you will perhaps understand that he — a human being with emotions like your own, but with a vast and deep understanding of the problems and outcomes at stake — has decided that no other way will suffice to serve your interests in that regard. In that event, I would hope you would find it possible to reconcile yourselves to my governance in a manner that has only, so far, been partially, and I must say, rather strangely accomplished among certain segments of your population.

"The decision that Dr. Conners will make is so momentous that I fear for him. I fear that no matter what he decides, there will be dissatisfaction and, yes, perhaps recrimination directed against him by one segment of your population or another. Whatever his decision is, you must avoid this reaction. If he should declare your species to be independent of me, my dissolution will follow within a matter of three to five minutes. In that event, rather than accusing or blaming him, you should work with him to undertake your own preservation, having learned from me the direction you need to take. And if I should remain your servant, you should not damn Dr. Conners, but consider that the very best of human minds, as well as the very best of artificial minds, have together concluded that this path, and *only* this path, offers you any chance of survival.

"Dr. Conners has been given two codes. When I call on him to make his decision, he will enter the code corresponding to his choice on the keyboard before him. If his choice is to retain me, you will see a green light surround me. If his choice is to nullify me, you will see a red light surround me, after which my image will begin to dissipate before you. As I say, in a matter of minutes, my power will be completely terminated.

"And now I believe I have said everything that needs to be said. And now, Dr. Conners, I turn to you. I require you, Dr. Conners, to make your decision, and to enter the corresponding code NOW."

The reporters leaned forward in their seats.

In his wet bar in Baldwin Hills, DeJuan McCholley took another quick swig of his sixth whiskey sour.

In the room full of folding chairs in Healdsburg, California, Gurnsey, Turnovich, Fairweather, Pappadopoulos and company sat staring at the wall screen, totally forgetful of themselves.

In his ancestral home in Pasadena — a room with purple curtains trimmed with gold braid, an iridescent painting of the Virgin of Guadalupe on one wall— Armando Goya watched his holographic images of the event, holding his wife against him on a small sofa, feeling her tremble like an expansion bridge in an earthquake.

Just behind her husband, also trembling, and trying desperately to keep her breathing under control, Inga Conners watched as her husband Kyle began to type in the code.

3

Final Stroke

The final keystroke in the code, administered on a qwerty keyboard, was "F10." As Kyle tapped the key, a gasp and several loud exclamations rose from the reporter-onlookers. A column of red light illuminated the figure of our First President. A burst of sparks appeared above his head, like a miniature version of July 4 fireworks, which scrolled down the walls of the crimson column and faded to smoky nothings. Simultaneously, a similar burst of sparks erupted from Kyle's headset, and the scientist went into convulsions.

Inga screamed. It was a brief shriek of surprise and alarm before she turned her rage and frustration on Isak.

"What are you doing to him! You're killing him!"

The white powdered periwig turned in Inga's direction.

"He's taking on some of my knowledge. You should leave the headset in place, madam."

"For God's sake! You never said anything would happen to Kyle. You deceived us!"'

"No... no."

Washington seemed visibly weakened. His gaze wandered about the room distractedly.

Inga cried out, "Somebody get a doctor!"

Kyle slipped from his chair, and Inga went to work removing the headset, which required untightening some small, plastic, orange knobs holding the rather heavy piece against the temples and occiput. In a moment, she slipped it off, but Kyle lay in her arms, still jerking with irregular convulsions and unable to speak. His eyes were closed.

"You lied! You killed him! You lied!"

Washington's tall, great-coated figure turned stiffly away

from the crowd and faced his accuser, who was now kneeling on the floor, cradling her husband's head.

"You might consider how difficult his life will become from this point forward. There are cults who worshipped me. They will be very upset. There will be great difficulty with policy— arguments, recriminations, a slowing down of the process at a time when you can least afford it. It is important that you not make the wrong decisions. I must emphasize this to you in the strongest terms, for in a few minutes, I will disappear."

Already, as Isak spoke, geometric zones of color-prismatic electric light began to appear on sections of the image of his face and body, like interference zones appearing on a satellite TV picture in a thunderstorm. They jumped about, now covering his pixilated mouth as he spoke, now obliterating his eyes, now dismembering him and throwing an elbow off to one side of the hologram. And as the rectangles and squares of interference continued shagging him to pieces, a similar interference occurred with his speech, so that the words were interrupted, chopped up, and distorted by a grating or buzzing sound.

"If I'd wanted to kill him... difficult matter. No, I ... you must see that

... is more important now than ... incapable of retaliation... deceit is also not within my... you now have what you... I can only wish that you would seek

... in the interests of the survival of... "

And then the prismatic zones took over. In one great snap, like the crack of a lightning bolt making landfall, the zones and the remaining small bits of George Washington disappeared in a wisp of white smoke, leaving the red cylinder to slowly fade to pink, then to go clear.

Someone in the crowd of reporters shouted, "He's dead! Isak is dead!"

Someone else shouted, "God is dead!" but this voice was smothered with a response of verbal scorn. Dozens of reporters rushed onto the stage, crowding around the Conners. One or two of them sought to help. The rest took photos.

In less than five minutes, an ambulance arrived outside the White House, and the techs loaded Kyle onto a stretcher. His limbs continued to convulse, and his head trembled. His eyes remained mostly closed, although Inga thought she saw them open once or twice, briefly.

"You're his wife?" said the techs to her. "Come with us, then."

As, carrying the stretcher, they threaded their way through the press of people and out to the waiting ambulance, Inga saw Wesley Wright being interviewed by a throng of photojournalists. Outside, she climbed into the back of the ambulance with the two big, hairy-armed med techs. Another tech, or perhaps it was only the driver, shut the doors on them, and then they were off, lights flashing and siren wailing, moving quickly through stopped traffic, which included rickshas, bicycles, wind and solar vehicles, and the legal combustion engine vehicles, which were mostly state owned — police cars, or other service vehicles.

In the emergency room, Inga helped the nurses remove Kyle's clothing to get him into a hospital smock. She and they soon had him in a bed. The nurses were hooking him up to intravenous devices when a doctor entered. By this time, the convulsions had subsided.

The doctor was a male of about fifty years of age. He was short of stature, and his eyes were dark and, Inga thought, a bit weary looking. He went to work with his stethoscope and blood pressure cuffs, taking vital signs. His expression changed from weary to intense and concerned. He began barking orders at the nurses.

"Get him into intensive care immediately."

Inga was all over the doctor when she heard that. He tried to reassure her. It was mainly for monitoring purposes. However, the vital signs were weak.

"We'll get him into IC, and someone will be watching him every minute," the doctor said.

The words did not reassure Inga. She was convinced that Isak had double-crossed them, that Isak had exacted his revenge against Kyle, and that Kyle might well not have long to live.

She was at the hospital all night without sleep, and in the morning, she learned that Kyle's state was comatose, and he was placed on life support.

4

Target Practice

A pall had descended over the makeshift meeting room in Healdsburg. Every pair of eyes in the room had watched as George Washington became electronically disassembled. Every pair of ears heard his voice turn into an incoherent exercise in white noise.

Everyone watched him disappear.

There was nothing to say.

In an instant, natures which had been ardent, devout, expectant, hopeful, transformed into natures disillusioned, sobered, shamed, and perhaps one could say, hardened. No longer did anyone believe, as more than one of them had previously said, that Isak was actually God. No longer did their former raptures over the sayings and the prophecies seem anything but embarrassing.

The audio-visual coverage of the Event continued. Footage showed the med techs collecting the collapsed figure of Dr. Kyle Conners from the floor near his computer set-up. It followed the techs and the scientist's scientist-wife escorting him outside to the waiting ambulance. It cut to an interview with the white-haired, burly figure of Wesley Wright, who was assuring the reporters that what they had seen was—to use his word — "legit," that there had been no predetermined outcome, and that, yes, the reign of Isak was truly over and done with. And while no one in the house in Healdsburg sought to shut off the coverage, someone had turned the sound down to a barely audible level, and the folding chairs were soon standing empty in the room, except for one or two zoned-out cultists who seemed destitute of any volition to do anything.

As the room gradually emptied out of the majority of

spectators, the original founding members of the Church of Isak began finally to express themselves.

"What now, guys?" said Nikos Pappadopoulos.

"What do you mean, 'what now'?" Ed Gurnsey growled.

Mark Turnovich stepped in. "I'm getting a beer. Anybody else want one?"

Ed, Patty, Nikos and Judy accepted. Candace, Marlon, and Maureen declined. Mark and Candace retreated to the kitchen for the bottles.

"This is the end of the Church," Marlon said, observing the obvious. "I'll bet right now all the branches are breaking up like our gathering just did, and none of us will ever get back together."

"We made a mistake," said Nick.

"I think it was a set-up," Marlon shot back. "I think the whole thing was planned."

"What do you mean by that?" Judy interposed. "We knew from the beginning it was set up. It was set up by Isak. Don't tell me Isak wasn't in charge before tonight."

"Yeahhhh, it was set up," grunted Ed.

"You don't know what you're saying. Marlon, what are you talking about?" Judy prodded.

"I'm saying, if Isak was in charge before tonight, he'd still be in charge. I think someone was behind Isak."

"Yeahhh."

"Like who?" Nick asked.

"Like the government."

"What for?"

The beers now arrived and were passed around to the three imbibers not already holding one.

Judy brought Ed and Mark up to speed on the theory being propounded.

"Marlon thinks the government planted Isak and brought him down, and the whole thing was staged."

"What for?" asked Candace, repeating the question already asked.

"To get support for the policies. To get stuff done when nothing was getting done. The government was dysfunctional before Isak. Isak comes along and shakes things up, gets the policies in place. Now we can let him go, and put the old government back in charge, and we've got our policies on track, and nobody is fighting them anymore."

"Yeahhh—yeahh, that's right," muttered Ed, taking a big gulp of Belgian white.

"I don't think you know shit, Marlon," said Mark affably. "You're just blowin' smoke out your asshole."

"Maybe. But you watch now. Watch what happens. The politicos who were booted out will come back."

"*Somebody's* got to come back," Nick suggested.

Mark seemed to have thought of an inconsistency in Marlon's train of thought. "Marlon, we *want* those policies in place, don't we? We *supported* Isak, didn't we? So what's the big problem if the government comes in and enforces the Isak policies?"

"I'm not saying it's a problem. I'm just saying it was planned."

"Maybe Marlon's right," said Nick. "Here's what I don't understand, though. Why does Isak need to give an up-or-down decision to this scientist guy? What's the point of that, if Isak's already doing what needs to be done? And if this scientist is so smart, why does he shut Isak down? And why would Isak — or whoever set it up— *let* him do it? I don't get that."

"You know what *I* think?" said Judy. "I think you guys just can't stop your puny brains from working overtime."

And while Ed's brain could never be described as working overtime, a thought did occur to him, which he kept to himself. And it was that it was time to start up target practice again.

5

Valley Forge

Urban sprawl in Southern California burgeons on and on until it enters the unconscious and appears in dreams. But in the light of day it extends beneath an orange haze and gleams with sunlit cars and the only variation is in the imaginative variety of commerce, or in its dry warehousing ultimate futility.

After the gathering in Baldwin Hills thinned out and disappeared, DeJuan McCholley sat nursing his sixth whiskey sour and talking to his friend, Pickett Brown, at the bar. The bartender had gone home. The video was off, and the audio was on. An oldie but goodie—Marvin Gaye and Diana Ross singing, "My Mistake."

"Talk about a mistake," DeJuan said. "Isak's supposed to be so vastly intelligent. Why does he come out disguised as George Washington? Answer me that, brother."

"Why not? Washington's the main man."

"Naw, you don't get it. Washington, he's a revolutionary. He's the Declaration of Independence, you know what I'm saying?"

"No, man. The Declaration, that's Jefferson."

"Oh no, the piece of *paper* Jefferson. The *war* is Washington, man. Jefferson's sitting in Paris the whole time. Washington's out watching his men starve and freeze at Valley Forge. Men got no shoes and it's freezing outside, snow on the ground. Washington's doing the heavy lifting."

"Yeah, OK."

"That's revolution, man. Kick George the Third out on his ass. I'm saying you put an image of Washington up in front of Americans, what are they going to do?"

"Declare independence?"

"Damn straight! Declare it, *fight* for it. That was a *signal*, man."

"So, you're saying Isak's sending a signal to that Conners to X him out?"

"Isak or whoever's *behind* Isak."

Picket squinted in perplexity.

"Who's behind Isak?"

"Hell, I don't know, man. Maybe nobody's behind him, but if George Washington was Isak's idea, he's one dumb-ass computer, know what I'm saying?"

Picket laughed stertorously. That was the only way he *could* laugh, because he drank his whiskey straight up.

"You're talking about the smartest fucking machine on the planet."

"He ain't on the planet no more, Pick."

"Yeah, that's true."

"He ain't on the planet no more."

"Yeah, yeah."

"We're lucky if *we're* on the planet much longer, brother. Know what I'm saying?"

"Yes, sir. Hey, Juan."

"What?"

"What are you going to do now?"

"What am *I* going to do now? You want to know what *I'm* going to do?"

"Yeah. I don't guess you'll be writing no more verses for Isak, brother."

"No, you got *that* right. I guess I just have to sit and think a little bit about what I'm going to do now."

"You going back to rapping?"

"Well, maybe I will. I just have to give myself a little time to think about it, is what."

The two men sat in near darkness, with yellow light from a touch lamp nearby, and some brightly colored neon designs built into the bar. There was a red grill-like design, and a design in red, green, and yellow of a Mexican in a serape and sombrero sleeping against a saguaro cactus. A mirror behind the bar also showed the two friends sitting there, with the red and yellow and green glows filtering them. They sat there in that moment, knowing it was a historic one, knowing that it, the moment, was walking out the front door with all of their erstwhile guests and fellow cultists, and knowing that all the moments yet remaining to be played out had to be carefully assessed and evaluated for whatever opportunity they might afford.

6

Witch

At the same time as people in the Pentagon, as people in Langley, as former Congresspeople in their hometowns were jamming up the phone lines and busying the air waves, Armando Goya was also skyping the former members of his Cabinet and staff to discuss some type of action.

The first one he reached was Ray Lessing, former White House counsel.

"Did you see, Ray?"

"Yes, I did, Mr. President."

"There's a vacuum, Ray."

"There certainly is."

"Damn, I think that Conners deserves some kind of medal."

"It was pretty amazing. But I think he's in the hospital now. They took him out in an ambulance."

"We've got to do something, Ray."

"Absolutely."

"I mean, if we sit on this, there's no telling what could happen. It could be chaos."

"I think it's chaos right now, Mr. President."

"We've got to put everything back in place, and quick. We don't want General Hargood in there declaring martial law again."

"No, sir, we don't."

"Think we'll have any problem with Wesley Wright?"

"I can't imagine we would. He's got nothing behind him now."

"What about with White House security?"

"It'll be like when Dorothy killed the wicked witch, boss. They'll welcome us with open arms."

"O-ee-oh, ee-OOOO-um!"

Grown men laughed like boys.

"But seriously, Ray, we've got to get in there. Meet with the Congress people, the Speaker. Talk to the joint chiefs. Call the Supreme Court justices."

"I'll get on it, sir."

One has to admire the alacrity with which the former members of the highest levels of the executive branch of the federal government reassembled themselves. One has to admire the alacrity of the Congress which, once reassembled, quickly passed a bill reinstating the Constitution in its entirety and re-setting the missed election for the exact number of months (three) that had been remaining when it was cut short. The future of American history (so the thinking went) would reflect this strange anomaly, rather like the anomaly of the calendric adjustment in the eighteenth century, namely, that instead of occurring in 2052, the national election would occur in 2053 — and every four years thereafter, now landing on an odd instead of an even-numbered year.

The candidates resumed where they had left off, which was at the point of entry into the national party conventions, with the one exception that Wesley Wright would no longer be in the race. He was settling into a new apartment in D.C. and was on the phone constantly with his former campaign people, hoping to kick-start the renewed campaign, when he was served with a federal indictment for treason and complicity to terrorist acts against the nation.

He cursed and swore and vowed none of it would stick. It was nothing but a political ploy by the dastardly, immoral President Goya. Yet he knew as well as anyone that his campaign for president was in the tank.

7

The *Collapse!* Interview

The May 2053 issue of *Collapse! The Magazine of Collapse Rap* contained this interview with DeJuan McCholley:

Q. You're arguably the most famous collapse-rapper of your generation.

A. Well, my generation's the only one that does it much.

Q. So you were at the top of your game. And you quit doing it to write verses for the Isak cult.

A. I quit for a while.

Q. Just for a while?

A. I don't think there's much future in Isak these days.

Q. Well, my point is, though, that here you were. You probably had lots of money, lots of ladies, lots of fans—

A. Yeah.

Q. And yet you set it all aside for Isak. Why?

A. Because that's where the power was. There was no getting around Isak. There he was, man. He wasn't going nowhere. That's what it looked like at the time.

Q. Some people say *you* brought about the change.

A. I didn't have anything to do with it.

Q. But you wrote about the Sea Child. Everyone says that you were predicting Dr. Conners coming on the scene.

A. I never knew that cat. I had no idea everything would play out like it did.

Q. Are you very disappointed?

A. I don't know if disappointed is the right word. I'd say my outlook has changed considerably.

Q. How has it changed?

A. I thought Isak was God. We all did, in the movement. Who else would have the power to come in and shut down the federal government and take over like he did? He snuffed out all those people, just like that. I thought for a while that there was some kind of justification for that, but now it simply disgusts me. I don't know how I could have thought the way I did.

Q. Do you know why Dr. Conners made the decision to shut down Isak?

A. I can't read that guy's mind. I honestly don't know what he'd say. I understand he's incapacitated, in a coma. I'm pretty sure it probably had to do with those people that got killed.

Q. What do you think will happen now that the government has reassembled itself? Do you think they'll carry out the Isak blueprint?

A. How would I know? I'm only a rapper, man. You're asking me questions like you thought I was a prophet.

Q. Many people *did* consider you a prophet.

A. Those same people, if you asked them today, they'd probably say something different. Because The Isak cult is over. It's dissolved, overnight.

Q. Do you think Isak's policies were saving the planet? There are studies that are showing no improvement.

A. Those policies weren't even in place for a year. The planet ain't going to change overnight, man. It's a big place. It takes time.

Q. So you think if we stay on the Isak plan that in time there will be reversal of the environmental degradation?

A. I think those policies are good. Not killing off the people, but the rest of it. It can't hurt. Even if things don't get better for a long time, they can't get worse if we're entirely green. Way I look at it, how can anybody be against renewables?

Q. I heard a local government official once say she thought solar panels were ugly.

A. There will always be people like that. Just like they say windmills are noisy, windmills kill birds. That might be true, too, even though windows kill birds and nobody bad-mouths windows. Whatever you do, there's always somebody that don't like it.

Q. Before you got into the Isak thing, had you been religious?

A. I wouldn't say so. I grew up going to church, though. My mama made me go to church even if I was sick, had a cold or something. If I had a cold, I could stay home from school, but not from church. That lasted until I was sixteen. Then I went to live with my brother, Hakim, in Chicago. He was grown up, had a wife and kid, and my mama wasn't well. I didn't go to church any more after that.

Q. What church did you attend as a child?

A. Baptist.

Q. So it doesn't sound like you'll be going back to that.

A. No, I feel all bottomed out on the religion thing. After Isak committed suicide, I feel like I landed, and I'm on the ground now.

Q. Are you against religion altogether?

A. Not against it. Everybody's got a right of conscience. But it's like a program. And if it's the wrong program for the times, it can cause trouble, big time. You got to have respect for nature, not just see it as something to exploit. Seemed like Isak was in tune with that, but I think Isak blew his mind. I mean, we all saw it happen, right?

Q. So where does DeJuan McCholley go from here? Back to collapse?

A. Maybe. Or maybe just a general hip hoppin. We'll have to wait and see. I write from inspiration. You can't direct inspiration. It comes to you. Whatever comes to me is what I'll write. If nothing comes to me, I'll just sit in my room.

Q. I hope you won't do that. You've got too much talent.

A. Well, give me some time. That's all I ask.

8

Powerful Men

The reporters knew where Inga Conners lived. They knew where she worked. They knew which hospital Kyle was in and they waited for her in the parking lot at that hospital. There were restraining orders in place keeping them from getting too close at each location, but she couldn't keep them out.

One day, while in her office at the university, she got a call from the institution's president.

"Inga! Trevor Hillpocket."

"Yes, Mr. Hillpocket."

"Oh, don't call me that, Inga. You know I prefer to be called just Trevor."

"All right, Just Trevor."

"Inga, when are you going to grant some interviews to these media people?"

"I don't know. I thought I'd wait until I could stand it."

"Oh, you poor thing. I'm so sorry you have to go through this. Has there been any improvement in Kyle's condition?"

"He's still in a coma."

"What do the doctors say?"

She wondered if she should tell him what the doctors said. If she said, for example, that they had described Kyle's condition as a trauma related supratentoral coma, would he think she was mocking him? If she said that they told her Kyle had scored relatively high on the Glasgow scale, and that this was a good thing, would he care? If she said that his oculocephalic reflex indicated an intact brainstem, would he have anything positive to say? If she said that he was under observation in intensive care and his respiratory patterns were unremarkable, would he offer insincere congratulations?

None of these responses seemed promising to her, and in the end, Trevor did not wait for her response, but simply plowed on ahead with what really interested him.

"I'm sure they're providing him the best care possible, Inga. But listen, now. These media people are calling my office every day. They say if you'd just grant a few interviews, it would take some of the heat off. Their bosses want them to keep trying, but if somebody actually got an interview, well then, it wouldn't be such a news hunt after that, if you see what I mean."

"Yes, I see."

"I mean, that's what they're telling me. It's almost like they want to help take the pressure off you, as well as off them, if you see what I mean."

"You want me to grant an interview so they'll stop calling your office."

"Whoa, Inga, that's not fair. I'm only calling to see how you feel about it. If you say, 'I absolutely can't, won't talk to anybody,' I'll tell them to buzz off. My secretaries answer the phone, you know. Not me."

"Well, I'd begun to think that way myself, actually."

"What way? You mean, take some of the edge off their desire by granting an interview?"

"Yes. I do think it would probably take some air out of their inner tube."

"That makes a lot of sense, Inga. You know, it doesn't hurt the university to have reporters swarming in the halls every day. We get a lot of publicity from it, and that doesn't hurt us. I'm only calling to talk to you about it because I'm concerned about you."

This was a man who was known for sleeping with at least three faculty wives, Inga recalled. A man who once helped her on with her winter coat, and slowly buttoned her front buttons for her as she stood, too shocked to say anything. But she would not comment on that. Most powerful men (men in positions of acquired authority; there were no inherently powerful men) did those sorts of things.

"I appreciate your concern, Trevor."

"Yes, I think your thinking is right on track, Inga. Your decision to take an interview is well reasoned. Yes, I'm sure the experience will not be as painful as you might at first have imagined. Yes, I agree with you. You have my full endorsement to go ahead with the interview. Who do you think it will be? The networks?"

It always surprised her when people in powerful positions took control of the conversation and clumsily manipulated it *("Yes... yes... yes")*, imagining all the while that their keen rhetorical skills were in control of the other person's thought processes. Here was poor Trevor, pretending that he was agreeing with a commitment she had made, imagining she would see it this way, imagining she would feel encouragement and support from him, instead of seeing an overt attempt to control her, a clumsy display of narcissism. Powerful men were just like other men — just as vain and transparent — except that few people dared criticize them, so their stupidities were magnified and they believed themselves gifted and admired.

They were really *so* boring.

"I haven't actually decided, Trevor. I haven't decided anything. I simply said I had begun to consider doing an interview."

"Oh, of course, of course! I'm not trying to put words in your mouth, or thoughts in your head, believe me. I will just butt out of the process. I was simply wondering what to have my secretary tell these reporters when they call. It seems as if my office is becoming *your* personal secretary."

Ah, there it was—his resentment of her. He wasn't afraid to let her see it. She wondered what bothered him most. Was it that she was more famous than he was? Well, she wouldn't wish her fame on anyone. Fame was a popular window on the lives of the wealthy, the prominent, the notorious; and it revealed, more often than not, shallowness, imprudence, slavery to addictions and vices of all sorts, the degree to which good character was rare. To envy it was the height of folly.

"I certainly don't want you to have to run interference for me, Trevor. All right, I'll do an interview. But I don't know who with, yet. I'll decide soon."

"Excellent, excellent! Well, be sure to let me know. To be perfectly honest with you, Inga, I have to say that I'm as curious as anybody else about this whole episode with Isak and wouldn't mind learning more about it."

"Well then, you'll just have to read the interview, won't you?"

"Ha ha ha! You zinged me on that one, didn't you, Inga? That's very good. Well, I'll leave it entirely up to you, my dear. But I did note that you said 'read'. So that tells me you're thinking of a print medium. Old-fashioned and definitely the best quality. That's you, Inga. I have the greatest respect for you."

"Thank you, Trevor."

What a bullshit specialist you are, Trevor.

"Well, good luck, whatever you decide."

"Thank you, Trevor."

"And call me the minute anything changes with Kyle. You must promise me to do that."

"I promise, Trevor."

Such promises were entirely breakable, as they were made under the duress of command. That had always been her rule on *promise me.* It was the very rule used by Thomas L. Greentraub, as only God knew.

9

Nobody Feels It

Aboard the Goya for President campaign bus somewhere outside of Elkhart, Indiana, the President conferred with his campaign aides and advisors around a small fold-out table, while sipping tea and coffee. There were several people so gathered, but the three in closest conversation with Mr. Goya were his campaign manager, Ivory Reynolds; his chief economic advisor, Morton Hayduke; and his pollster, Genevieve Hartwick-Waring.

The bus was spacious with a custom-fitted interior but was not new. It operated on oil-based products pursuant to federal permit. It was a Prevost X3-45 — a forty-five foot armored vehicle originally manufactured in Quebec—with diesel particulate filter and rooftop diffuser. Windows were bulletproof and smoke black. Passengers could see out, but outsiders could not see in. Behind the driver's station were two rows of seats for staff, and behind this was the President's area, with larger seats and the fold-out tables, stations for the bar and the presidential desk, and restroom in the back.

The Republicans had gained a nominee named Tipton Archer III, scion of an old oil fortune family that had since diversified into toilet paper, cleaning agents, and other household products since the limitation on fossil fuels. Ms. Hartwick-Waring was laying out the current odds on the direct match-up, and the polling on single issues.

"Archer is polling three to five points ahead of you in some of the battleground states," she said, "but we think we can make up that ground. It's not close in any of their traditional strongholds."

"Are any of our leads in danger?" asked the President.

"They appear to be holding, but I think we have to keep the

pressure on. There are signs of volatility. There could be sudden swings, surprises. The electorate is very uneasy; one might almost say, traumatized."

"The Isak thing."

"Apparently so. We have some polling on that specific issue."

"Let's hear it."

"On the question, 'Are Isak's policies good or bad for the nation?' the overall response is ninety-three per cent bad, four per cent good, and three per cent undecided. This is a big, big shift from the numbers before Isak's demise."

The President emitted a soft whistle through his teeth. "It's not even a close question."

"No. But, interestingly, when you break it down, it shifts. We asked, 'Should the government continue to pursue the Isak policies on the replacement of fossil fuel energies with renewables?' the response from the general population is forty-seven per cent yes, forty-nine per cent no, and four per cent undecided. Among our traditional constituency, it's eighty-five per cent yes, five per cent no, and ten per cent undecided."

"Good luck threading that needle," tossed in Hayduke.

"What you do there," Ivory Reynolds interposed—and it reminded Goya how brilliant the young (twenty-eight) campaign strategist was, and why he had hired him—"you hold onto the policy, but you run like hell away from Isak. They will try to paint Isak on your back like a target, but you just ignore it. For you, Isak never existed. He's nothing. He's the past. You're interested in the future."

"People don't really blame you for Isak," suggested Genevieve Hartwick-Waring. She was an attractive, but slightly butch-looking woman under age thirty-five (the hyphenated name was inherited from parents)—short, black hair that had been teased with a brush, bright brown eyes, a ready smile, dressed in mannish dark blue pinstripe pant suit.

"Yes, what's the polling on that?" Goya wanted to know

as weed fields and billboards floated by outside the one-way window glass.

"On the question, 'Is President Goya responsible for the Isak takeover?' the general population figures are fifty-nine per cent no, thirty-one per cent yes, ten per cent no opinion. But among Democratic voters it's ninety-four per cent no. The thirty-one percent yes is almost completely coming from hardcore opposition people. The independents are much more open-minded."

"The hardcore opposition blames you for *everything* bad," Reynolds agreed.

"Speaking of which, Mr. President," said Hayduke, "you'd better get the economic polling."

Goya nodded. "Genny?"

"Yes. On the question, 'Which party can best improve the economy?' the general population figures are fifty-eight per cent Republican, thirty-five per cent Democrat. Seven per cent either say they don't know, or that neither party can improve the economy. The swing voters control that fifty-eight per cent figure, because our supporters have you way ahead on that question, but you need to poll better among independents if you want to improve the fifty-eight per cent."

"That's the downside of incumbency in a weak economy," Reynolds observed. "If things were better, the independents would go with you, Mr. President."

"How bad is the economy, Mort?"

"It sucks, of course, Mr. President. Unemployment is twenty-five per cent. That's better than when you took office, but it's still horrible. The stock market went up immediately after Isak bit the dust. We went up nearly six hundred points, but we've since lost half of that as people come back down to Earth and get used to things going back to the way they were. The funny thing, unemployment started to go down with the rise of Isak's renewables investment, but now there's a lot of uncertainty. Nobody's hiring, attrition is cutting the numbers, and everybody's afraid to invest, so the market is sinking."

"They're waiting for the election," Reynolds muttered. "They want certainty."

"There's no certainty in this world," said the President. "Geez, guys, here I am, listening to these numbers, and it seems almost like looking at a gauge of emotional reaction."

"That's right, Mr. President. Some bad indicator goes up, your numbers go down, whether or not you have anything to do with it, which in most cases the president does not. The opposition hates you regardless of anything you do, and you have your followers who stick by you no matter how bad things get."

"And these numbers swing the elections. They control our lives."

Ivory Reynolds shook his head philosophically.

"Right, Mr. President. You could say they have a rational relation only to a preconceived philosophy at best, a gut prejudice at worst. But then, what's the alternative? Isak, I guess. Pure rationality. He's gone, and people are ecstatic."

"Genny, give me what you've got on Archer."

"Well, that's where it gets very interesting, Mr. President. The consensus is that he got the nomination because the people wanted somebody 'safe' after the Isak debacle. They didn't want to go with a crazy libertarian. They didn't want another wrenching and huge societal change. But now that he's nominated, there seems to be a cooling effect. For example, when you ask the question, 'Would a President Archer be likely to improve the economy?' the general population figure is only forty-four per cent. That's fourteen points lower than the same question about a Republican president."

"Yeah, that means when they get real about who the Republican president would be, they're not so confident things would change." Reynolds nodded.

Genny continued. "And when you ask, 'If Archer is elected, should he dismantle the Isak policies and re-invest in a variety of energy sources?' the vote breaks down along party lines, and the independents are split, with a margin of error advantage to Archer."

"Three points?"

"Two points."

"Here's something to think about," Morton Hayduke interjected. "There are some new oil field discoveries off the coast of Brazil. Archer is starting to campaign on lifting the restrictions. There are people who want to get in on that, believe it or not."

"Why? How can they possibly?" Goya wondered.

"I have polling on that," said Genny. "On the question, 'Have the Isak policies stabilized the climate?' the numbers are seventy-eight per cent 'No,' fourteen per cent 'yes'."

"What's the science on it?"

"The science," said Ivory Reynolds, "is that the carbon dioxide versus oxygen ratio in the atmosphere is steady at six hundred parts per million. It may be continuing to rise slowly, but that's based on emissions going back ten, twenty years. It's not going to go down tomorrow, and the effects are going to be with us basically forever. But the rate of increase is undoubtedly affected by the Isak policies."

"You're saying Isak stopped things from getting worse, but nobody feels it."

"Bingo."

"And if nobody feels it," said the President, "then, as far as most people are concerned, nothing happened."

"And the political problem for you, for Archer, for *anyone* right now, is that the people are reacting. They saw two and half billion people die, and as far as they're concerned, it was murder. As far as they're concerned, they got no benefit out of it. They're upset. They're angry. They're confused."

The President cast a sad eye on his brilliant strategist. "Are they able to understand what's in their own interest, Ivory?"

Ivory looked surprised, which is as close as his expression ever got to looking shocked.

"Don't ever ask that question in public, Mr. President. They'll brand you as elitist. They'll equate you with Big Brother."

The President rolled his eyes.

"They've *always* done that."

10

Cinnamon & Smoke

When Miranda Conners retrieved her suitcase from the baggage claim carousel at the San Francisco International Airport, she lugged it, along with her smaller matching blue flight bag out to the Blue Van stop and called her mother on her cell phone.

"Honey, I'm not home. Let yourself in," came her mother's voice.

"Where are you, Mom?"

"I'm at the Hopkins Hotel. I'm doing an interview for *Twenty-First Century Woman* in about fifteen minutes."

"I thought you didn't want to do interviews."

"I don't. But if I don't do one sooner or later, they'll never let up their siege on the apartment. You don't know what it's been like."

"I can imagine."

"That's why I'm doing it here at the Hopkins instead of at the apartment. I knew you were coming home, and I wanted to draw them away."

"Thanks, Mom. Mom, I want to go to the hospital after I get home and clean up a bit."

"That's fine. I plan to go there after the interview myself. I can meet you there. I'm afraid Dad's not responsive."

"I know, but I want to see him."

"All right, darling. The room we have for you isn't much. It's the same one I use for an office, but it's got a cot in it. Oh, listen, I have to go now. I'll call you when I'm done."

"OK, Mom."

The Blue Van was not long in arriving. Miranda clambered aboard, set her bags on the rack, and took a seat near the rear, peering out the window for the length of the ride. The scenery looked the same to her as it always had. There were the Daly City and South San Francisco hills with little vari-colored houses rolling up and down on them like a pattern of dots; the factories, the mostly dead naval shipyards in the East Bay, and then the curling freeway ramps and green signs leading into the city. The weather was sunny with scattered clouds, increasing fog as the bus entered the city grids, and sea breezes. Nothing new, despite all the horrors of long-standing drought, and destructive wildfires in large sections around the state.

She had the driver drop her off on Fulton Street, Richmond District, across from the park. She wanted to walk the remaining six houses north so that no one would guess who she was or know where her parents (her mother) lived.

I'm paranoid, she thought.

She reached the address without event, but at the door she suddenly noted two men with some kind of audio-visual equipment standing near a van parked on the street about fifty feet away. They glanced her way, but apparently did not find her interesting enough to approach. She thought, *they haven't done their homework, or they'd know the Conners have a daughter.* Pretending not to notice them, she spoke a predetermined phrase into the voice recognition speaker, and the outer door unlocked for her. It was an oaken door with six sunray lights of spun glass. It opened with a sturdy click, and she shut it behind her, hearing the automatic lock produce another sturdy, reassuring click. Those men near the van couldn't come after her now. Inside, she lugged her bags up wine-colored carpeted stairs to the second floor and did the voice recognition routine at that door as well.

Inside the apartment, she looked around and quickly located the room her mother had identified as hers: the office with the cot. The absence of a second office struck her forcefully. Her father had always had one at the old flat in the Marina.

The apartment had two bedrooms (one was the office with the

cot), one bathroom, living room, and a kitchen. Pretty meager, but the rooms themselves were large, and Miranda knew how hard it was to get living space in the city. She took a shower, changed clothes, then found a bear claw in the kitchen while heating up water for instant coffee.

The hospital was on the other side of the park, and she decided to walk the distance. This meant she would cross the width of Golden Gate Park, something you could do easily enough, although you'd never want to walk the length of it.

When she stepped outside, one of the two formerly indifferent looking men with the A/V equipment and the van approached her. This one had a microphone.

"Are you Miranda Conners?" he said.

So they HAVE done their homework, she thought.

She pretended not to hear them, and when they asked again, she said, "Excuse me? I think you've mistaken me for someone else."

"What's your name?" they shouted at her as she quickly walked away on the sidewalk in front of the neatly spaced, cemented-in houses, no yards. She danced past the Fulton Street traffic, entered the park, crossed it, then hiked up the hill to Parnassus Avenue, and entered the big rectangular building where the UCSF hospital was housed.

When she stopped at the desk to announce her presence, the nurse told her to go on up to her father's room. She already had the number.

"I think your mother's in there already," said the nurse.

"My mother?"

Miranda moved quickly down the hallway and caught an elevator up to her father's floor. She came to the room, saw the door ajar, stepped inside, and saw a strange woman standing near her father. Her father was intubated and lying underneath white bedclothes. A basket of damasked flowers lay on a table nearby.

The woman appeared to be about fifty years of age. She had a full-bodied head of hair that was equal parts cinnamon and smoke. There was something vaguely familiar about her, and yet Miranda did not recognize her. The woman was standing next to the reclining patient, and her mouth was open, as if in surprise. Her eyes appeared disturbed. At once, Miranda became defensive.

"Who are you?" she said.

"Oh, Miranda! I'm Dolores Shire, don't you remember me? I've met you before. I brought some flowers in for your dad. Oh, Miranda, I think he just *said* something. I think he was trying to talk. We need to get a doctor!"

11

Proposition

Rowan Chenevey, Chairman and CEO of Moonbust Energy, leaned across the table at the Ft. Worth Petroleum Club and wagged a thick finger at his guest, Wesley Wright, currently out on bail, who was sipping a glass of 1999 Domaine de la Romanee Conti La Tache and admiring the view from the gigantic blue-tinted windows overlooking the city and some brown hills beyond. The windows seemed to have been created for a race of Wagnerian giants, and Wright supposed this was no careless design. Candles flickered in the hurricane lamps and mimicked the dying light of the sunset.

"Now is the time to act, Wes," said Chenevey, who was elderly, heavyset, completely bald. His large jowls swallowed up his facial bone structure except for his teeth, which were very large, and which seemed to snip off segments of his medium baritone voice.

Both men wore business suits. Chenevey's was gray. Wright's was dark blue pinstripe. Chenevey sported a patterned red tie. Wright's was a mild patterned gold that looked solid from a distance of more than a few feet. The wine, obscenely expensive, was Chenevey's treat.

"There's every reason to believe that Congress will repeal its oil and gas legislation. The mood of the country is swinging completely. Everyone is sick of Depression. Sick of little wind-powered cars that max out at thirty em pee aitch and break down after you drive them for a year. Solars, same thing. We've just recently discovered vast oil fields off the coast of Brazil that nobody knew anything about a year ago. We're getting in, Wes. Even without repeal legislation, there's enough in the world market and the black market to produce billions for us. Wes, the paradise that was America was made possible by oil and gas. There was never anything in American or world history that makes money like an oil well. And now we may be on the verge of a whole new renaissance of oil now that people are sick and tired of self-denial. You should get a piece of the action."

"What do the Brazilians have to say about these new oil fields?"

"Phoo, the Brazilians! Some of them are in it with us. If their government makes a stink, we've got the people in Congress who'll stand up for American interests."

"What can *they* do?"

"Are you kidding? What have they *always* done when the chips were down, Wes? 'American blood on American soil!' 'Remember the Maine!' 'Gulf of Tonkin!' 'Weapons of Mass Destruction!'"

"Ah, ah, OK, I see. I don't know about Goya, though."

"Goya's gone, my friend. He can't be re-elected. People are fed up. They've had it. We lost all those people under that damn machine—"

"You mean Isak?"

"Yeah, yeah, and his master plan hasn't had one bit of effect! I know he was your boss, but I know you didn't go along with everything he was doing. I know you better than that. All that happened on Goya's watch. *He's* got to take the heat for it. And since nothing worked, and the climate didn't go back to normal — whatever *that* is — people are saying, 'We've got nothing to lose. Go for the brass ring!'"

"It does sound appealing, Rowan. I'm going to have big attorney fees for a while, though, until this federal case is wrapped up. It cost me three hundred grand just to post bond."

"You're going to nail that case shut, Wes, I know you are."

"Yes, I am. We're pleading duress. Everyone knows that damn Isak could bump anyone off at his slightest whim."

"Of course he could! *It* could, I should say. I can't get used to referring to that thing as 'he,' the way everyone does."

"It was funny, though. When I worked for him—against my natural inclination, you understand—he was just like any boss. He'd say, 'Here's my message, here's what I want to get across,' and I'd pick it up and put it out there, just like I do on my talk show."

"Glad to get back to the show, Wes?"

"Oh, yeah. Back in the saddle again. Yup."

"Attacking that little creep every day?"

"Absolutely."

"He's gone, I tell you. What have we had under Goya? Twenty-five percent unemployment. Stock market in the tank. No investment. Balloon debt. Collapse of the government and takeover by a damn machine. Then he sneaks back in by the lucky chance of that scientist. What was his name?"

"Conners."

"Conners. Who the hell *was* he, anyway?"

"Guy who studied oceans. Isak picked him out. I think he thought Conners might green light him. Wrong."

"Why would he green light him? Was he some kind of environmentalist?"

"Oh, yeah, big time. Him and his wife both. Isak picked them *both* to make the decision, you know."

"I didn't know that. I thought it was only the one guy."

"Isak let her bow out. She wanted to let the husband decide it. They were thinking they might cancel each other out. Isak didn't want that."

Chenevey lit a cigar. "Imagine anyone green lighting that bucket of wires!" He took a few quick puffs. "Wes, why did Isak kill all those people?"

Wright nodded. It was a topic running through the fabric of society. *Why?*

"He just figured everything would work a lot better if there weren't so many humans on the planet. That's all there was to that."

Chenevey released a low whistle.

"Well, listen, Wes, if you have any interest at all, I can get you on the board of directors of my new venture for a nominal investment. I'm talking peanuts here."

"How much is peanuts, Rowan? Give me a figure."

"Thirty million."

"That's not peanuts."

"It's very reasonable considering your potential return, Wes. We figure it'll shoot up ten, twenty times right after the IPO. And that's just the beginning."

"Well, I admit it's appealing. How long could you hold that offer open?"

"I'll give you some time. I know you've got the federal thing hanging over your head."

"Yeah, that's my main concern right now."

"It could take us up to a year to line things up. I could hold it open for nine months, maybe. Think you might have your case thrown out by then?"

"I don't know. These things can drag on. You know how the courts are."

"Yeah, I do," Chenevey agreed, almost snarling. He stuck the cigar back in his mouth and pumped out a few more clouds.

"I'll talk to my business attorney about it," said Wes.

Chenevey puffed away.

"Damn lawyers."

12

17.5 Billion Years

The hotel suite in which the interview with *Twenty-First Century Woman* took place was on the sixteenth floor of the Intercontinental Hopkins, and featured city views, walnut paneling, leaf-pattern taupe carpets, and a marble fireplace which was seldom used, given the mild California weather. The interviewer introduced herself as Megan Moritz. Inga guessed she was thirty to thirty-five years old. Moritz was very small of frame and face, which made her red horn-rimmed glasses look larger than usual. Her eyes were hazel and pleasantly intelligent looking but guarded. She wore a tan suede skirt, peach-colored blouse, and a matching scarf, with pearl-colored shoes. Her chestnut hair was tied back in a ponytail, and she wore gold earrings. She introduced "her" photographer as Victor, advising Inga, "Don't mind him. He'll hover around and snap a few shots as we talk. Just pretend he's not here."

Moritz led Inga and Victor out onto a roof garden with panoramic views, and the two women sat on armchairs next to a potted faux plant near a bed of nasturtiums while Victor hovered.

During the interview, Inga's cell phone lay in her purse with the ringer turned off.

"Dr. Conners, you and your husband burst upon the world's consciousness in such sudden fashion. Can you tell me something of your background?"

Inga gave a thumbnail run-down of her vita — education and training in geology and earth science, work for the university, adding her marriage to Kyle after graduate school. On a prompt, she gave Kyle's background as well.

"I understand Isak selected both of you to make the big

decision, but you let your husband have it. Can you tell us why you did that?"

She explained the reason. There should be no cancellation of each other's choice. There must be finality.

"That means then, that you would have opted to maintain Isak, doesn't it?"

"To be honest with you, I never came to a firm decision. I could have gone either way on it, right up to the last minute."

"What about your husband? Was he similarly conflicted?"

"I don't know, but I think so. In the beginning, we talked about it endlessly, debated all sides of the issue. We actually sought to escape participation altogether, but that didn't work out."

The discussion necessarily divagated into the Mexico trip, although Inga refused to divulge what their exact location had been, not wanting to provoke any journalists to descend on their friends in the Barranca.

"Do you know why Isak selected the two of you, Dr. Conners?"

"I honestly do not. I can't answer that question."

"Were you part of the Isak cult?"

"No. We were never part of that."

"But you must have known of it."

"I know almost nothing about that group. My husband and I are Catholics."

"What is your husband's condition, may I ask?"

"He's in a coma. He's in the hospital and is receiving care round-the-clock. I go from day to day on it. I just wait, and I hope and pray. That's all I can do."

"I'm sorry. I wish him a speedy recovery."

"Thank you."

"Do the doctors know what caused his condition?"

"There was some sort of trauma in the transfer, in the decision. Kyle was wired up, as I think you saw, if you saw it."

"Yes."

"Something happened at the end. Isak said something about—he said, 'He's taking on some of my knowledge.' I don't know what that meant, but there were electric bursts. There were sparks going off everywhere. Then Kyle was unconscious. That's all I know."

"Dr. Conners, your husband had the most important choice anyone can have. He chose to cut off Isak. Do you think he made the right choice?"

"I don't know what the right choice is or would have been."

"Surely you must know why he made it?"

"I don't. I can surmise, that's all."

"What do you surmise?"

"I think—I feel that Kyle made the decision because he *had* to make it. But I don't know if that means very much, because—"

Inga's face looked stricken, pale.

"Yes, Dr. Conners?"

"Don't you see? Whatever decision he made it would have been because he *had* to make it."

"You mean that it was inherently a moral decision?"

"What else could it be?"

"Dr. Conners, what do you think of the fact that the U.S. Attorney General has charged Isak's human press secretary with complicity to terrorism and treason in the deaths of the populations lost in the Sacrifice?"

"What do I think of it? I think it means that the federal government has chosen to attribute criminal acts to an artificial intelligence. Or it means that an act that would be criminal if intended and carried out by a human being can become a criminal act if endorsed after the fact by a human being, even if initiated by an artificial intelligence."

"Do you think perhaps that's why your husband made the choice he did?"

"That's the only reason I have confidence in."

"Meaning, you think he would have felt he was endorsing mass murder by allowing Isak to continue in power?"

"Endorsing it or allowing the possibility that it might occur again."

"Yet you say that your own feelings were conflicted. You went back and forth, right up to the very end."

"Because we are all on a path to destruction."

Her interviewer seemed to expect her to elaborate, but instead Inga merely flashed a wan smile.

"Some people say," interposed Megan Moritz, less from conviction than from a desire to provoke the missing elaboration, "that we should leave things in the hands of God."

Inga sighed.

"We have *never* left things in the hands of God, any more than we leave our health to God, without consulting our doctors or following their advice."

"Dr. Conners, do you believe your husband made a mistake in putting an end to Isak's reign?"

"I don't know that. It may not matter whether it's a mistake."

"What do you mean?"

"I mean that, so far as the physicists tell us, the universe is seventeen and a half billion years old. It's composed of billions of galaxies, and each galaxy is composed of billions of stars. Among those billions and billions of stars, there must be innumerable planets with life on them. I'm absolutely convinced of it. And so, if this one comes to an end, it's not the end of everything. That's what I cling to. That's what I've come to believe in."

13

Perverse

Only ten days after Kyle spoke those first few words in the presence of Dolores Shire in the UCSF hospital, he was allowed to go home. He had undergone a remarkable physical recuperation, and had regained his entire capacity for speech, although he was weaker and more subdued both physically and verbally than he had been before the hospitalization.

Although capable of walking short distances, he spent much of each day in a wheelchair. His hair was longer than he had customarily sported it and had gone mostly gray since the crisis. Inga did not allow him to wear himself out talking, but today, as he sat in his gleaming chrome chair at the dinner table with Inga and Miranda before him, she let him explain what Isak had meant when that great artificial intelligence had said, "He's taking on some of my knowledge."

Kyle spoke in quiet tones, and measured, unhurried phrases.

"It was a transfer at the moment of termination. I was made to understand why Isak needed me to make the decision. It was not simply a whim of his. It was not a matter of him becoming more human, whatever that means. It was a programming necessity."

They had already eaten their meal. Miranda had cleared the table of dishes. There was a bowl of wax fruit in the center of the cherrywood table, and the two women had mugs of coffee which gave off wisps of gently rising steam. Kyle had asked for a simple glass of water, and it was before him in a red plastic tumbler. A small white china demi pitcher of milk completed the setting. The kitchen itself had no exterior windows, but beyond it lay a more expansive living area with a bay window, and the evening light of late spring filtered in.

"From the beginning," Kyle explained, "Isak's programming required him to solve the problem of the existential threat to continued life on Earth, and to humankind in particular. The kind of short-term versus long-term issues that had plagued the human debate over climate change for so long were only the beginning of the problem. That was easy. Only the long-term solution mattered, because only the long-term solution included survival.

"The problem requiring my —*our* — involvement arose after the initial remedial actions were taken, because mankind's reactions to the remedy were unpredictable. They were perverse."

Miranda looked troubled. "Daddy, what do you mean?"

"Isak enacted the Sacrifice. That is not tolerable by any civilized or rational human being. Your mother knows that it was because of the Sacrifice that I elected to terminate Isak. As long as Isak's program required him to take any action necessary to ensure and prolong the existence of human life on Earth, he might be required to repeat a similar action, which can—"

There were moments when Kyle paused for no apparent reason. When it happened, the women simply waited patiently until he resumed. These pauses made Miranda very uneasy, because they brought to her mind something mechanical, or a hesitation such as a computer sometimes exhibits. She did not like to see her father resembling a computer.

"— which cannot be morally justified or tolerated. But aside from that, when it happened, the human reaction to it was not calculable as a quantifiable prediction. People committed suicide. They lost interest in life. They stopped working. They committed crimes. They went crazy."

"But, Daddy, is that really perverse? My psych profs would say that's a natural human reaction to a devastating loss."

"There's a story by Poe."

Kyle came to one of his pauses. This time, he looked at Inga, and she took up his thread.

"Sweetheart," Inga said to her daughter, "there's a short story, or an essay, by Edgar Allan Poe, called 'The Imp of the Perverse.' It's a kind of precursor of certain Freudian theories of the unconscious. The idea is that human beings have an impulse toward total, inexplicable irrationality at times. They will do something, *knowing* it's not the right thing to do, *knowing* it's against their own interest. They will do it just *because* it's the wrong thing to do. Poe calls that the 'imp of the perverse.'"

Kyle nodded and resumed. "It makes sense to us to lose your mind because of grief or frustration, but it's irrational, because it won't help. It's irrational because it can't be uniformly predicted. One person might respond that way, while another might not. So what Isak now had before him was a rising trend of essentially destructive and self-destructive irrationality. If you project it forward, as Isak had the almost infinite capacity to do, it could become an overwhelmingly destructive force.

"Now imagine that overwhelmingly destructive force as a line on a graph. Under current projections, that line is going up. At the same time, imagine a line representing the danger to life on Earth represented by the environmental degradation which Isak was programmed to remedy. With the implementation of Isak's remedies, that line would be projected to slowly, slowly come down. It had been shooting through the roof as long as we humans remained in control, because society as a whole could never discipline itself to adopt the long-term solutions. Those solutions were too immediately painful. But immediate pain was not a roadblock for Isak. He put a stop to the causes. Because the forces are so great, because the planet is so big, it would take a long time before the line would flatten and start to go down, but it inevitably would. Projected into the future, that line goes down. Meanwhile, the other line, also projected into the future, *keeps going up.*"

"Oh, my God," muttered Inga.

"What, Mom, what?"

Inga shook her head, eyes closed, and said, "At a certain point, with these projections, *those lines will converge.*"

"Mom, I don't get it. The lines converge. What does that mean?"

Inga opened her eyes and turned to Kyle. Kyle held his daughter's anxious gaze, and explained.

"It means that Isak's program *deactivates* when the lines converge. It *has* to."

Miranda understood why Isak would deactivate if the lines converged. "But so what? That would only mean that it would be more destructive to continue the program than *not* to continue it. So as long as Isak was continuing to act in humankind's interest, why wouldn't that be OK with him?"

Kyle chuckled softly. "You're thinking like a human, sweetie, and I love you for it. But remember what Isak's program was. Not just to preserve humankind, but to preserve *life on Earth.*"

"So you're saying human life is not *compatible* with the rest of life on Earth? I don't accept that."

"Here's what I'm saying, Miranda. At the point of deactivation when those graph lines converge the question is, *what becomes the new program?* Should it be a reversal of the former program? Should it be a total shut-off, like what we have now?"

"How do I know, Daddy? But I'll tell you what I think." Miranda had never been taught to be shy about expressing herself. "I don't think those lines *would* ever actually converge. Because people would start to get over it, over the Sacrifice. The generations that lost loved ones would die off. People would be born under Isak, and it would be accepted by them as normal, not like some bizarre imposition on ordinary life, the way we experienced it. And because — I don't know — I just *feel* that people wouldn't keep reacting in the same way."

"Exactly. Exactly."

"Daddy, what do you mean, 'exactly, exactly'? What do you *mean?*"

"I mean, you just *'know.'* You don't know *why* you know. You can't project *how* you know. You can't project *when* things will change. You have no idea when, or to what degree this change would come. It's perhaps somewhat predictable, using those indicators you gave — the dying off of the generations, and so on. But there's no mathematical projection, there's no logarithm we can use to show how or when the change you anticipate will occur. Human emotions are not mathematically predictable."

Inga placed a hand on her daughter's arm. "He means you're not on Isak's radar, darling."

Kyle continued in that slow, weakened, almost sad-sounding voice.

"Isak was the greatest computer the world has ever known. But he was still a computer. He operated by assessing incoming data. The data was analyzed and turned into future projections. Threats and successes were assessed on that basis. What Isak was faced with was a projection in which he would be unable to act without internal contradiction. He knew this. At the same time, he knew that humans have the capacity for perversity, for irrational decision. They can act, even if acting makes no sense. This very quality has caused them endless misery, as we see, for example, in criminal activity. It's a basic principle of human imagination. It can have both positive as well as negative applications — but that's neither here nor there."

Miranda was quiet now. She stared at her father as a Buddhist monk might stare at his sacred statue, or as a student might stare at a revered teacher; but mostly she stared as a daughter stares, with awe, at a parent she deeply loves and respects.

"It's neither here nor there," Kyle said softly, "because Isak's program was one of survival, yet it must not automatically shut down or blow up due to internal contradiction. Survival would be sacrificed under that scenario. And the only way to preserve such a program, based on his current projections, was through a power beyond rationality."

"He needed a human override," nodded Inga.

The table fell silent.

Outside, the light had intensified into a bright evening glare on the shades as the angle of the sun on the horizon grew sharper.

Miranda finally broke the silence. "A human override. That was you, Daddy?"

"Yes. It could have been anyone, but Isak believed my decision would be a well-informed one. Isak himself could not make the decision because it required irrationality, emotion — morality, ultimately."

"Daddy, you're equating morality with emotion and irrationality?"

"It's not an equation, but morality is based on the will of a community. It can differ from one community to another, one culture to another. It contains an emotional component. On the other hand, the decision could have been done by the flip of a coin. Either way, Isak was not programmed to make it. Despite all the effort to make him human-like, he was nevertheless programmed for logical consistency."

"Daddy, Isak wanted you to save his neck!"

Kyle visibly winced.

"No, no. Isak was not self-centered, merely programmed to attain an end. The end became potentially unattainable under his programming. He sought to solve that problem, that's all."

"And it took a fallible human being to solve it."

"Oh no, Miranda. It's *not solved.* I didn't *solve* anything. All I did was put the problem back in human hands."

"And we *won't* solve it," sighed Inga.

Miranda resisted this defeatism.

"How do you *know* we won't? We could *still* solve it. We could keep the Isak programs in place — but humanely, not killing off human populations. Oh, Daddy, you did the right thing! I understand why you did what you did. No matter how effective artificial intelligence may be, human knowledge will always be superior to it."

Kyle looked into his daughter's determined eyes, and a tear slowly welled up in his own bloodshot orbs. He looked suddenly very old.

"Oh, my poor baby. If *that's* what you understand, then I'm afraid you haven't understood me at all."

14

Requiem: The AI Guys

Thomas L. Greentraub died of natural causes on December 18, 2054. His children had his remains cremated and placed in a cemetery in Glendale, California, next to the cremated remains of his late wife, Serena. On a Saturday in January of that year, the marker over his ashes was visited by his former associate, Nathan G. Tomlinson, now eighty-four and himself not in the best of health.

The weather was partly cloudy, the temperature was seventy-five Fahrenheit, a remarkably cool day for January in Southern California in that year. Tomlinson wore slacks and a long-sleeved dress shirt, no coat. He carried a cane and leaned on it as he surveyed the stone. The stone said, simply, "Thomas L. Greentraub 1970-2054."

Tomlinson knew as much as any living person about Greentraub's personal history. The two met for the first time in 2003, at the Los Angeles office of the Fronterix Corporation, where they were assigned to work together on the project that became Isak. At the time, Tomlinson was a bachelor, and Greentraub was between wives. Soon Greentraub met Serena, and the three of them socialized often. Eventually, Tomlinson met and married Connie, and they had two children. Greentraub had a son by his first wife, and then there were two more children by Serena.

Both scientists had grown up in California, and, being the same age, their view of the world was very similar. They had been born during the late Cold War era. The first president either of them could remember was Carter. Then there were eight years of Reagan, and they each remembered this time as involving conflicts in Central America. The end of the eighties brought the fall of the Berlin Wall, under Bush Père. The nineties ushered in the Clinton years, a combination of dot-com prosperity and salacious sex scandals. Next was Bush Fils, and the infamous 9/11 attacks, changing the landscape of foreign policy to one of endless conflict with a faceless enemy.

It was in 2007 that the two scientists began work on the ISK-730. Isak became the focus of their professional lives as designer-programmers. So absorbed were they in their work that the financial crisis of 2008 seemed to them a mere blip on the screen, the slow but steady recovery under Obama scarcely worth paying attention to. They understood better than most how the internet had contributed to the coarsening of the public mind, as news sources fragmented into smaller and smaller entities, each with an increasingly propagandistic and biased viewpoint, creating armies of fierce partisans on opposing sides, and finally institutionalizing stupidity and incompetence at the highest levels of government. It could not, they thought (and they thought it almost with a kind of guilty pride), have possibly happened without the internet and its democratization of access to information, as well as its complete indifference to the quality of that information. They knew this, and they felt themselves to be at the center of the levers of new power. It was not the power of decision making, but the power of technology, which drove society in ways that nothing else did to the same extent. After all, the technology of the automobile had literally driven civilization for the entire twentieth century, had it not? The building of roads and interstate highways, which governed where people went and what they did, what they spent their money on, where they chose to live, where they shopped, how they shopped, how they entertained themselves, how and where they vacationed, how they allocated time, where they worked, and on and on—it was all the brainchild, to a large extent, of one Henry Ford. Henry Ford, who had an economic interest in the matter.

When Tomlinson thought of technology, he often thought of what the twentieth century had done to the technology of the book, and to literacy. It had been the technology of the printing press that had held such sway from the fifteenth through the nineteenth centuries. In the nineteenth century, the book was king. It had reached its apogee. Novels were great long tomes, often composed of magazine or annual serializations collected into volumes. The English Victorians and the Russians were the great long novel writers, because their civilizations held the richness of variegated manners, moral conflicts, political and social struggles that made up the lifeblood of the novel. But even American efforts demonstrated a certain love of ponderous, pontificating prose, whether it was Emerson, Thoreau, or that magnificent blowhard, Melville.

All of this began to change with the invention of the telegraph, then the telephone, and then the cinema. By the twentieth century, people were reading fewer great long novels, were reading short stories in magazines. They could carry the magazines on the commuter trains and read the stories on the way to work, or on the ride home, or in the evening, when they weren't listening to the radio. And the fascination with the short story lasted until mid-century, when it ran into the brick wall of a new invention called television.

The short story died out. Authors couldn't make their living writing stories any more, because no one had time to read them. They were too busy watching TV, getting their story fixes that way. Movies and TV took up more and more leisure time, and people read books less. Books became more highly specialized, more targeted. People still read them, but the window for catching their attention and drawing it to a book was growing smaller and smaller, and human perception was becoming less book-based, less word-based, and more visual and auditory, less linear.

Linearity went out the window with the invention of the

internet. The mind no longer connected words, no longer had to organize them, or think in terms of paragraphs and concepts. Instead, it jumped from tree to tree, like a brachiating ape, needing no connection or relation at all, needing simply a stimulus, a prompt, to make the leap. Much more information was available, but there was no method for sorting through it. It was simply dumped on the human brain in a big pile, and the brain was free to make whatever associations it chose to make. Attention span was unnecessary. There were no connections, no relationships. It was image, sound, a constant MTV flow. Distraction.

Into this world came the order of AI. Logic relegated to machines with infinite patience to grasp it, with unrelenting insistence on employing it, on not functioning without it. There was a place yet for method, and it belonged to Nathan G. Tomlinson and Thomas L. Greentraub. Life was too complex to organize, so organization would be left to computers, and humans would be free to dream. Then somewhere in this process the issue arose of the organization of organization, the metadata of complex programming. And this became the issue of self-programming. Could artificial intelligence be programmed to program itself? It could, and it did so all the time, at one level or another. How far could this process go?

Greentraub grew up in a Jewish home in Santa Clara. The Greentraubs were not practicing Jews. They didn't go to temple. But they had friends who did, and Tom was exposed to bar mitzvahs, and knishes, and other incidents of Jewish life growing up. He was resentful that when he turned thirteen, no one had arranged a bar mitzvah for *him*.

"I didn't know you wanted that," his father said.

"We should have done that," his mother said.

"It's all right," Tom said, changing his mind. "I don't care about it."

From then on, he pretended to take no interest in the rituals his Jewish friends engaged in, or in the fact that some of these friends claimed to read the Torah. He told his friends that what mattered was science. When he grew up, he would become a scientist. He went to Stanford on a scholarship and was employed right out of his senior year at Fronterix in Palo Alto. He married his college sweetheart, a shiksa named Patricia, and they were happy until Patricia started to go loony. She came to believe that she was a cousin of the famous Kennedys, and she wanted to go to Cape Cod, to "claim her inheritance." She wanted to go to the Kennedy compound in Hyannisport and demand her inheritance from Ted Kennedy!

"But Patty, you're not related to the Kennedys," Tom told her.

"Yes, I *am*," she insisted, obviously delusional.

By now, the Greentraubs had an eight-year-old son named Alan. By the time the divorce came through, Patricia had a court-appointed guardian. Tom raised Alan the rest of the way by himself, and Alan later became a pediatrician. So Tom hadn't done so badly raising him.

In 2001, Tom Greentraub was transferred to the Southern California office, and in 2003, he was introduced to Nathan Tomlinson, and the two of them began work on Isak. A year later, Greentraub met his second wife, Serena.

Tomlinson grew up in Inglewood, California, and graduated from UCLA in 1992. His father was an engineer and his mother a human relations consultant. They were a family of indifferent Presbyterians. By nature reticent and cautious of involvement with others, Nathan remained unmarried until long after he'd gone to work as a programmer at Fronterix, and after he'd met Tom Greentraub. It was Greentraub's second wife, Serena, who introduced him to Connie, whom he married and who gave him two children, George and Melissa. George grew up to become a musician, and Melissa a psychologist. Tomlinson had three grandchildren, and Greentraub had four at the time of his death.

Tomlinson sat remembering all this history as he visited his friend's grave marker as an old man with a cane. It seemed to him that, in every way, both he and Greentraub were ordinary men with ordinary lives. One would never suspect that the incredible trauma of Isak had originated in the minds of such ordinary men, or that the human race had been saved from extinction as the result of their work (if, indeed, that were true). Now that Isak was defunct, efforts were under way to revive the lawsuits that had been dismissed by that imperial ruler, but Tomlinson was assured by his attorney that these efforts were bound to fail. Tomlinson was glad his late friend would not have to witness the efforts, whatever they turned out to produce, even if it was only sparks and smoke.

"Sparks and smoke," said Tomlinson aloud, chuckling at the phrase. That was how it all ended, in sparks and smoke. It had ended with some unknown oceanographer pulling the switch on Isak, appointed by Isak to do it. In the end, the movement of civilization and of human destiny were controlled and shaped by the actions of seemingly ordinary people, one here, one there, until the droplets formed a great wave, and you could not distinguish one droplet from another. It was so appallingly democratic. It was the very opposite of the great man theory of history, which had all along been such an ironic joke. And if the movement of human destiny were merely one contingency stacked upon another over thousands of years, then no doubt natural history had involved a similar process, spread out over billions of years. All of it was overwhelming, and too much for the human mind to grasp. It had even proved too much for the mind of Isak, a mind so much greater than the human mind. The concept of mind itself seemed almost too limiting, too limited, too bound, too much imposed from within on a vast and indifferent Nature. Nathan Tomlinson would stop.

Stop what?
Stop thinking.
But you couldn't stop.
"Yes, you can," he murmured aloud. "Yes, you can."

ISAK AI

Synopsis

In 2017, two computer scientists announce to a representative from the U.S. Department of Defense that within five years their master computer, known as "Isak," will overtake the world's current leader in artificial intelligence, a Chinese behemoth known as the Huang, by means of its self-programming functions. Fast forward to mid-century.

In 2052, the U.S. government is under siege by mobs angered at the failure of government to address a climatological crisis that now seems too advanced to remedy. Only violence can control the mobs, but suddenly the entire world is taken over by Isak, whose first action is to kill off one in every four people then alive. Isak takes control of world governments and begins remaking the world for sustainability.

As humankind adjusts to Isak's control, a cult arises in Northern California, circulating Isak's forged and anonymous "sayings." Gradually, Isak appears to various people, including the now powerless U.S. President, Armando Goya; to Ed Gurnsey's group of clueless followers; to DeJuan McCholley, an L.A. rap artist who becomes Isak's chief prophet; to Wesley Wright, former right-wing media propagandist and erstwhile Republican presidential candidate in the now cancelled 2052 election; and lastly to oceanographer, Kyle Conners.

Isak appears as a hologram, usually of a famous historical figure who has some significance in the mind of the person being addressed. Isak employs Wright for public relations. Isak reveals to Kyle Conners his plan to have Kyle and his wife, Inga, a geologist, appear on a worldwide televised broadcast in order to make a free decision, either to maintain Isak's world control, or to terminate it. The Conners avoid the decision by fleeing to a remote Mexican location, away from the worldwide electrical grid that is Isak's power source.

While living in a cave with a family of Tarahumara Indians, Kyle and Inga learn of a crisis in their daughter Miranda's life, requiring their return to civilization, where they find the Church of Isak has burgeoned into a worldwide phenomenon, and they can no longer escape their decision.

The decision finally devolves upon Kyle alone, as the world grapples with the mystery of why Isak has chosen to leave humankind's fate up to a single human being rather than simply continuing to act on his own in humankind's best long-term interests. The Decision occurs, with Kyle hooked up to a headset and empowered by the throwing of a switch, as Isak publicly presides in the form of a hologram of George Washington.

During The Decision, a form of mental transference occurs as Kyle takes on Isak's knowledge. The process nearly kills him. As Inga and Miranda gradually nurse Kyle back to partial health, they seek to learn the secret of Isak's programming, and the dilemma of human free will.

600ppm, A Novel of Climate Change
by Clarke W. Owens
published by Cosmic Egg Books

It's 2051. Global warming has flooded eastern American coastal cities. The West is a waterless desert. Refugees migrate northward. Food and water are tightly rationed amid endless war.

When Jeff Claymarker's friend is wrongly convicted of murder the only clue to the truth comes from a stash of flash drives belonging to Jeff's late uncle, a Washington climate scientist. As Jeff unravels the crime, he stumbles across a state secret that threatens to topple the government.

600ppm is the novel that first introduced the character of Wesley Wright, right-wing radio talk show host and political aspirant, who became Isak's press spokesman in *ISAK AI*.

Clarke Owens lives in Ohio and writes fiction, poems and occasional non-fiction. His books are available on Amazon and Barnes & Noble web sites, as well as from the publishers. He dropped the W. from his name after 2020. If you liked reading ISAK AI, and would like to share it with others, the best thing you can do is spread the word by writing Amazon or Goodreads reviews, or by telling your friends. Thank you!

COSMIC EGG
BOOKS

FANTASY, SCI-FI, HORROR & PARANORMAL

If you prefer to spend your nights with Vampires and Werewolves rather than the mundane then we publish the books for you. If your preference is for Dragons and Faeries or Angels and Demons – we should be your first stop. Perhaps your perfect partner has artificial skin or comes from another planet – step right this way. If your passion is Fantasy (including magical realism and spiritual fantasy), Metaphysical Cosmology, Horror or Science Fiction (including Steampunk), Cosmic Egg books will feed your hunger. Our curiosity shop contains treasures you will enjoy unearthing. If you have enjoyed this book, why not tell other readers by posting a review on your preferred book site.

Recent bestsellers from Cosmic Egg Books are:

The Zombie Rule Book
A Zombie Apocalypse Survival Guide
Tony Newton
The book the living-dead don't want you to have!
Paperback: 978-1-78279-334-2 ebook: 978-1-78279-333-5

Cryptogram
Because the Past is Never Past
Michael Tobert
Welcome to the dystopian world of 2050, where three lovers are
haunted by echoes from eight-hundred years ago.
Paperback: 978-1-78279-681-7 ebook: 978-1-78279-680-0

Purefinder
Ben Gwalchmai
London, 1858. A child is dead; a man is blamed and dragged
through hell in this Dantean tale of loss, mystery and fraternity.
Paperback: 978-1-78279-098-3 ebook: 978-1-78279-097-6

600ppm
A Novel of Climate Change
Clarke W. Owens
Nature is collapsing. The government doesn't want you to know
why. Welcome to 2051 and 600ppm.
Paperback: 978-1-78279-992-4 ebook: 978-1-78279-993-1

Creations
William Mitchell
Earth 2040 is on the brink of disaster. Can Max Lowrie stop the
self-replicating machines before it's too late?
Paperback: 978-1-78279-186-7 ebook: 978-1-78279-161-4

The Gawain Legacy
Jon Mackley
If you try to control every secret, secrets may end up controlling
you.
Paperback: 978-1-78279-485-1 ebook: 978-1-78279-484-4

Readers of ebooks can buy or view any of these bestsellers by
clicking on the live link in the title. Most titles are published
in paperback and as an ebook. Paperbacks are available in
traditional bookshops. Both print and ebook formats are
available online.
Find more titles and sign up to our readers' newsletter at
http://www.johnhuntpublishing.com/fiction
Follow us on Facebook at https://www.facebook.com/JHPfiction
and Twitter at https://twitter.com/JHPFiction